Dear Reader,

Writing together as Jane Worth Abbott, my dear friend and wonderful writer Virginia Myers and I produced three books. *Faces of a Clown, Choices* and *Yes Is Forever* are each complete novels but share core characters.

In *Yes Is Forever* Donna McGrath, adopted daughter of Sara and Evan McGrath from *Choices,* and Bruce Fenton whom we first saw in Laura and Mark Fenton's story, *Faces of a Clown,* have an extraordinary whirl with love...and risk.

Bruce is twelve years Donna's senior. They first met when he was the kind man who took her about in San Francisco. Six years have passed and Donna is still only approaching twenty, but she is so in love with unsuspecting Bruce.

Visualize the scene when Donna decides she must tell him how she feels—and how she expects them to proceed:

> Bruce tried to sound amused, but his voice was strained as he went on. "And to think, while I was buying you popcorn and we were looking at polar bears..."
>
> Donna's lowered lashes hid her eyes. "It's just that I've always known I had to do something about the way I felt when I was with you...and the way I thought about you when we were apart."
>
> "And that's where you went wrong," Bruce said reasonably. "You followed some adolescent whim. But don't feel bad or embarrassed."
>
> "I don't expect us to march up the aisle this week," Donna continued, as if she hadn't heard him. "We've got a couple of months to get to know each other. Now for starters, why don't you kiss me?"

If you're feeling sorry for someone, don't let it be Donna, because Bruce is in for the most exciting, the most vexing and the biggest struggle of his life. The odds against him are formidable, and he is only a man.

I hope you cry a little and laugh a lot when you read *Yes Is Forever.*

Best wishes,

Stella Cameron

Books by Stella Cameron

Stella Cameron

Yes Is Forever

HQN™

ISBN 0-373-77002-2

YES IS FOREVER

Copyright © 1987 by Stella Cameron and Virginia Myers.

Originally published under the name Jane Worth Abbott.

www.HQNBooks.com

Printed in U.S.A.

For Claire Cameron
"...the greatest gift is love."

CHAPTER ONE

WHEN HAD SHE FALLEN in love with Bruce Fenton? Six years ago, here in San Francisco, when she'd been a spindly thirteen-year-old he took pity on for a day? Or had it happened more slowly, while she'd made phone call after phone call from her home in Vancouver, British Columbia? There had been so many of those calls, perhaps more than she should have made, but at first she'd needed a friend, and later…later she'd simply needed him.

Donna rested her elbows on the desk and blew into her steepled fingers. How could she not have fallen in love with Bruce? Twelve years her senior, already very much a man when they met, he must have laughed at the adolescent dramas she'd shared with him, yet he'd always been too kind to let her know.

Joy, pure clear happiness, made her smile while at the same time she blinked away tears. She was back in San Francisco, this time to stay, if she had her way. Her dream would come true, and soon. Bruce was the lonely one now. He needed her; he just hadn't admitted it yet.

She wondered what the rest of the office force in this wonderful, discreetly sumptuous suite would do if she suddenly started singing. Something loud and suited to this bursting sense of high excitement, or anticipation, this sense of shivery expectation.

Everything was turning out right for Donna McGrath—everything. She was doing this summer job very well with, say, a quarter of her mind. Working at Fenton and Hunt, Attorneys-at-Law, in a gofer capacity would do nothing to further her actual career plans, but right now the work was perfect. Her parents were happy that she was staying with their old friends, the Hunts. She was happy as well. Mark and Laura Hunt and their six-year-old son, E.J., were a lot easier to live with than she'd imagined they would be. And she'd already seen Bruce three times this first week!

Her cup wasn't just running over: it was bubbling wildly. And she had the whole summer ahead of her—the whole summer!

Donna glanced at the clock and shuffled a stack of memos into a tidy pile beneath a brass paperweight. In a few minutes, at noon, she was to meet Laura Hunt for lunch. Laura had promised they'd go to some posh place to celebrate Donna's first successful week in what everyone in San Francisco called "the City"—as if all the other cities in the world, including her own hometown in Canada, were inconsequential hamlets.

Today bustling Vancouver seemed very far away and small, even to Donna. Sara and Evan McGrath, her adoptive parents, and her little brother, Jim, were there, and she loved them, but today this was Donna's City, too. She grabbed her purse. Laura would be waiting on the ground floor of the building. She made a breathless dash for the bank of elevators and was lucky to get one right away.

"Well, that was prompt," Laura said as Donna left the elevator. "I thought you'd have to take time to make up or something."

"No, I don't use much," Donna said. "And my hair is so heavy it usually stays put most of the day after I comb it. But I did wash my hands."

Laura grinned. She was a beautiful woman, with soft dark hair, startlingly blue eyes and cameo features. And she always seemed so young that Donna had stopped calling her "Aunt" years ago.

"It's really beautiful hair, so thick and shiny." Laura touched Donna's black curtain of hair.

"And straight," said Donna with a laugh. "I'm afraid the Asian genes determined the hair. But once I get it bent at the bottom, it stays. Like florists' wire."

"Oh, come on!" Laura laughed, too. "It's soft and gorgeous, and you know it." She tucked her arm through Donna's and headed across the busy lobby. "One thing about Eurasians, they usually seem to get the best of both races. I'm glad your natural mother chose a Chinese man as your father."

Donna nodded at the green-liveried doorman, and led the way outside. "With all due respect to Prairie, wherever she may be today, I don't think she chose, Laura. I think I was just an accident. Poor little Prairie's life is a continuous series of happenstances." Prairie Crawford's image, her long, tow-colored hair, and her flapping clothes, came and went quickly. "I hope she's doing okay," Donna murmured, almost to herself.

"Have you seen her recently?" Laura asked.

"Two, maybe three years ago, she turned up in Vancouver for a couple of days. Mom and Dad are certainly great with her, I must say. If I had an adopted child, I don't know how laid-back I'd be if the birth mother came strolling in every once in a while."

"Evan and Sara are special people," Laura said thoughtfully, shading her eyes against the sun to look at Donna. "Prairie Crawford should see you now. You've become absolutely exotic."

"So Dad always says. To hear him, you'd think I was a raving beauty. Let's hurry. I'm starved."

"Yes, me, too, and I promised Bruce I'd get us a good

table. He called this morning, and I invited him to join us.
I like to keep tabs on that cousin of mine. He doesn't
always take very good care of himself these days. I hope
you don't mind if he comes,'' Laura said, quickening her
pace.

"No, Bruce is fun,'' Donna replied, without missing a
beat. She had already realized she'd better tell Laura how
she felt about Bruce, but not yet, not this instant. She'd
know the time when it came.

"He'll meet us at the restaurant. He even told me what
to order for him. He was gearing up for some report he
wanted to go over with Mark, and he expected to be a bit
late.'' Laura paused, then added, "I wish those two got
along better. Come on, we've got the green light.''

They went with the rest of the surging tide of people
going to lunch in the financial district. A blast of cool wind
plastered their clothing against their bodies. Buildings of
dark shining marble and sparkling glass soared around
them, creating man-made canyons beneath the clear blue
of San Francisco's summer skies.

Donna's mind held on to Laura's last comment about
Bruce, as it always held on to any idea about Bruce, until
they were seated in the restaurant. Bruce was the Fenton
part of the firm, the only remaining member of his family—at the moment. Bruce's father, George Fenton, and
Mark's father, William, had been the founding partners of
Fenton and Hunt. With both older men dead, their sons,
Mark being the senior partner, held the reins, administrat-
ing what had become a huge and celebrated corporate law
practice.

"I didn't know they didn't get along,'' Donna said tentatively, holding the menu open before her.

"Who?'' Laura asked. "Oh, Bruce and Mark? They
never have, really. I think they like each other a lot, but

their differences over the business get in the way. They try to keep the peace for my sake, because Bruce is my cousin, and we've…well, we've become very close. And I must say Mark has always bent over backward to be nice to Bruce—and about him.

"You're too young to know this, but Bruce was a pretty wild kid. He's a late bloomer. He was almost twenty-four before he even started law school. Mark has done his best to help him. Then, of course, since they both inherited a piece of the firm, they have to work together." Laura pursed her lips, looking over the menu. "The age-old question arises. What shall it be—fattening or non-fattening?"

"Well, something light for me. I guess you've already gathered I'm my family's health nut."

Laura put down the menu. "I can't say it's done you any harm," she said. "Since I quit work, I've had to really watch it. Running around after one small son doesn't seem to quite use up the calories I want to eat. I suppose you're going to have the pita-bread thing full of sprouts and chestnuts or something?"

"Sounds delicious," Donna agreed, then asked casually, "What don't they get along about, Mark and Bruce?"

"Just have a general difference in philosophy, I guess," Laura said. "Mark is a pretty solid citizen, a stick-to-business type, and Bruce, well, Mark says Bruce is really a social worker posing as a lawyer. He says if Bruce has a choice of a client worth a big fee or a small fee, Bruce will find a client for no fee. That's an exaggeration, of course. It's not that bad. But Bruce always wants to help the underdog, you know."

"Well," Donna said dreamily. "Somebody has to help them."

"But does he have to help them all?" Laura laughed. "Mark says it's because of a summer job he had a few years ago. He was helping those refugees from Hong Kong. You know, somebody has to teach them how to cope with the bus system, tell them which areas of the City to stay away from, how to shop in the supermarkets and all that. They don't have an easy time getting used to an alien culture.''

Donna spread her napkin on her lap. "He liked dealing with the Chinese, didn't he? He's mentioned it a few times.''

"He liked the work a lot. And he made a million friends. That's led to a lot of dealings with Immigration coming into the firm. Some of the cases Bruce simply waives his fee on. That's what bugs Mark sometimes. Donna…what is it? You're absolutely sparkling. Now what's up?" Laura leaned across the table. "Ever since you got here you've been popping with excitement of some kind. At first I thought it was all the health food you eat. Now I think you must be in love. Tell me—are you? And if you are, for heaven's sake what are you doing in San Francisco? How can you leave him alone and unprotected up in Vancouver all summer?''

"He isn't in Vancouver," Donna said, grinning. "He's here. In the 'City,' as we say in San Francisco.''

"You're kidding." Laura was entranced. "But you don't know anybody here. The only people you know here are Mark and me. And Bruce, of course. Oh, Donna! It can't be Bruce! It is Bruce," she concluded in surprise, the delight fading from her lovely face.

"Donna," she said soberly. "Bruce is…let's see…he's thirty-one, I think, and you're only—''

"Nineteen," Donna supplied firmly. "Twenty in August. And yes, I think I'll have the pita sandwich with sprouts and chestnuts. I'm in love with Bruce. I guess I have been since I was thirteen. I think I first fell in love with him because he was so kind.''

"Bruce is always kind,'' Laura said, her voice a little weak. "You know, Donna, Bruce has been married and divorced. His...er...track record with women is...er...a real track record. I mean, I'm not putting Bruce down or anything, but I don't think he's in a hurry to get serious about another woman.''

"I mean to make him want to get serious,'' Donna said, "and I have one summer to do it in.''

"You sound a bit grim. What else is up?''

"It's my parents. They are dead set on my going to university in the fall. Because I've won some trophies in gymnastics they have my future all mapped out for me. They envision me having a long and happy career as a physical education instructor, or coaching the girls' basketball team or something. Terrific vision.''

"You always had a bent in that direction.'' Laura's voice was gentle. "Evan's very athletic, and he's so proud of your ability. Sara, too. They just want you to be happy in something you're good at. But you see yourself doing something else?''

"Yes. I see myself...please don't laugh, Laura.''

"I would never laugh at you, Donna,'' Laura said, and Donna knew that she never would. There was a sweetness in Laura that she had always appreciated. She could trust Laura.

"Well, sure I want to go to school—one day. And I probably would choose to major in phys ed. Training young gymnasts interests me. But first, I see myself as a wife. More specifically, I see myself as Bruce's wife and eventually as the mother of Bruce's children.'' She swallowed. Dammit, why did she have to get emotional when she wanted to sound mature and determined? She began to turn over the pages of the menu again, looking at them blindly.

"This is pretty important to you, isn't it?" Laura asked finally.

"It is vital to me," Donna answered, her voice almost a whisper. When she felt more composed she added, "Look, Laura, all my favorite role models are who? They are Mom and Aunt Christine and you. What have you all got in common?"

"We're all…we all became homemaker types," Laura answered ruefully. "All of us opted for the wife-and-mother role."

"And you're all happy, fulfilled? Aren't you?" Donna demanded.

"Uh…yes. I suppose we are," Laura said. "And that's what you want?"

"Absolutely. I know that ninety-nine out of a hundred women seem to feel they need to start out with a career for fulfillment. I don't. I'm the one in a hundred." Donna had noticed the moment of hesitation before Laura's answer, but she'd brushed it aside.

Laura drank some water, watching Donna over the rim of her glass. "I don't disagree that becoming primarily a wife and mother is an acceptable goal," she said thoughtfully. "But remember, Sara and I had other careers first. Your mother had a high-powered job, and she loved it. She still says she would always have wondered what she'd missed if she hadn't been part of the business world. And she doesn't rule out going back one day." She leaned toward Donna, her eyes bright. "And the clown in me hasn't totally gone away. You may see me back on the old unicycle yet."

"I'd like to," Donna chuckled, remembering the picture Evan carried of himself and Laura during their days as part of her clown troupe in Seattle. "I've never seen you in that crazy wig Dad says you wore."

"I'll show you," Laura said quickly. "Maybe tonight we'll get out some of my old stuff and—"

"Laura," Donna broke in. "You're changing the subject. I want to marry Bruce, and I want him to agree before the end of the summer."

"Evan will—"

"I know what Dad's likely to say and do. That's why I thought if I could get everything sorted out sensibly with Bruce and everyone here, and be able to present Mom and Dad with the logical way we've arranged things they would—"

"You mean a logical way like, 'Look, Dad and Mom, old dears, I've decided I'm going to marry Bruce, even though he's twelve years older than me and already divorced once and a bit of a playboy, what do you think?'" Laura asked dryly.

"Well…not exactly, but something like that, I guess. And I've got the whole summer." Donna couldn't keep the exultant note out of her voice. She refused to be put off by anything. Her mother and father would understand and approve of her plan once they saw how much she and Bruce loved each other.

"May I be the voice of reason for a minute?" Laura protested. "I know Bruce and, Donna, love, he's had plenty of practice in not getting re-hooked. He's a good-looking guy with lots of money. A fantastic house. A boat some would kill for. Do you think the women don't try?"

"Of course they try," Donna said patiently. "But I've got a lot going for me."

"Like what?" Laura asked, but before Donna could answer, the waiter came for their order.

"I think I'll go along with your pita sandwich," Laura

said. "So that's two of those, and we'll be joined by another person in a few minutes. He'd like the scallops. His
name is Bruce Fenton—I told the maître d' he'd be
along."

When the waiter had gone, Donna resumed talking.
"Like what, you asked. Well, for one thing, the old friendship between our two families is an advantage. Dad, and
later Mom, have been friends with you and Mark and
Bruce since the beginning of time, I think. So Bruce is
used to having me in his life. I mean…his guard isn't up
against me. How could it be? I've been part of his scene
for years. We haven't spent that much actual time together,
only occasional visits, but when I was a kid I used to call
him all the time because he was the only one who really
listened, and lately…well, he's been making as many calls
as I have for a long time. He cares about me. And all I
have to do is help him realize how much."

"And if he doesn't realize? What then? It seems to me
you could find yourself nowhere."

"That's what I have to accomplish this summer,"
Donna said emphatically. "Make him look at his real feelings for me. As a woman, I mean."

Laura regarded her intently. "Don't underestimate
Bruce. He's very perceptive, and he's likely to catch on
quickly. And my educated guess is that as soon as he gets
an inkling of what's going on he'll turn and run. I think
maybe the old family feeling will be against your case,
rather than for it. The last woman he'd start something
with is the daughter of a friend of the family. Don't you
see that? I hope you aren't disappointed, but I'm afraid
that as soon as Bruce sees you—really sees you—you'll
be lucky to wave to him as he speeds past."

"Ah. But I've already thought that out. I intend to involve him." Donna laughed somewhat gleefully until she

saw the shock in Laura's eyes. "No," she said hastily. "Not that. Don't look so horrified. Nothing sexy. Not yet, anyhow. I mean to involve him in something interesting, something he won't want to give up."

"Well, he plays a fair game of tennis when he can't avoid it," Laura said uncertainly. "You're not thinking of trying to involve him in some sort of health program, are you? Jogging followed by a sunflower-seed omelet at six in the morning? I can tell you now. Don't waste your time."

Donna fell back in her chair and laughed. "No, no. I've worked it out very carefully. I'm counting on, A, his frustrated social-worker instincts, and B, his familiarity with the Chinese community and—oh, here he comes now."

She watched the maître d' escort Bruce to their table, loving every line of him, every motion that made up his careless, loose-limbed walk. The air seemed to thin as she took in the tall lean physique, the casually elegant suit, the fair hair, just a trifle too long, falling over his forehead and brushing the top of a crisp white collar. Loving a man was wonderful.

"What a great way to spend the lunch hour," he said, smiling, his mobile mouth turning down slightly in that fascinating way Donna remembered so often when they were apart. He sat and picked up his napkin. "This is my salad, I take it. You're both looking gorgeous. But I suppose you know that." He turned his attention to Donna, his blue, blue eyes glinting with humor. "Happy anniversary."

She stared back blankly.

"Your first week on the job." He patted her hand. "How's it going? Still like it?"

"Oh…oh, yes. Great. I love it," she stammered. "And

everybody seems satisfied with my work. That is," she amended, "nobody's complained, that I know of."

"Mark says she's doing fine," Laura said, her eyes looking from one to the other, a tight smile touching her lips. She seemed tense, and Donna wondered if Bruce would notice, but he appeared not to.

"Go ahead, start your lunch," Laura told him. "Donna and I have pita sandwiches coming, but you get a salad first."

"Okay, if you don't mind." He picked up his fork. "Discussing anything with Mark always gives me either a whale of an appetite, or it kills it completely. Today I kind of won, so I'm feeling like king of the mountain and I'm ravenous."

"Bruce, I wish you would grow up," Laura said mildly. Then she added, "What are you going to do for Donna's first-week anniversary?"

"I dunno. Any suggestions?" Bruce said, looking back at Donna again with open fondness.

"Well, Mark and I are tied up tonight—some people are coming to dinner. Maybe you could take her out somewhere."

Donna could feel her skin growing warm. Laura was being a little obvious, and she was tempted to give her a gentle kick beneath the table but was afraid she'd kick Bruce instead.

He speared a tomato wedge and paused with it halfway to his mouth. "That would be a good idea, only I've already got something on. Tomorrow night's no good, or Sunday...let me see..." The tomato remained in midair while he considered.

Donna risked a glance at Laura, who gave her a distinct I-told-you-so signal.

"Wednesday," Bruce said, oblivious to the charged

atmosphere around him. "I'm free Wednesday night. We could go out for dinner...some place with dancing and young people. Would you like that, Chickie? Or is there somewhere particular you'd enjoy?"

Donna didn't let her annoyance show. *Chickie.* She despised it when Bruce called her "Chickie." He'd done so when she was thirteen. And a place with young people? As if he were a hundred and ten!

"Well," she said slowly, trying to appear thoughtful. "I think maybe I'd like to go to Chinatown again. I haven't been there in a long time."

"Fine," Bruce agreed pleasantly, taking another forkful of salad. "That's it, then. Chinatown next Wednesday."

Donna took the opportunity to study him. His downswept lashes were blond at the tips, his cheekbones high and clearly defined. Laugh lines fanned out from his eyes and made creases beside his mouth. When he smiled, deep dimples formed in those creases. With an effort, she turned her attention to Laura. "You know you mentioned my natural mother, Prairie Crawford, a while ago, and it crossed my mind again that although I know her, I've never even met my biological father."

"Do you ever wonder about him?" Laura asked with quick interest. "Did you ever want to meet him?"

"Yes, I did." Donna turned her shoulder as the waiter placed her order in front of her. "Every once in a while I think of it. It's a...a loose end, you know? Something I don't feel quite right about."

Bruce's attention was on her again. "Do you know anything about him at all?" he asked.

"Not much, really. His name is Raymond Sung. And let me see. He was kind of a wild one along with my birth mother. They did drugs and got into any trouble they could. He and Prairie met here in San Francisco."

Laura was looking pensive. "There are probably hundreds of Sungs in San Francisco," she said. "Do you know anything else? I remember when your dad adopted you after his marriage to Sara he—"

"A few things," Donna cut in quickly. "Mom already found out a bit when she adopted me, before she and Dad met: my biological father's name, that his family were bankers or something like that. Then Dad found out from Prairie that Raymond Sung was an artist, or wanted to be one. Prairie told me that, too, the last time she came to visit." Donna placed one hand in her lap and crumpled her napkin. She felt slightly sick. This was very close to out-and-out deceit, which she hated, especially the bit about wanting to meet her real father.

"Wait a minute," Bruce said. "I thought you said once that Prairie named you after somebody named Don—he wasn't your father?"

Donna forced herself to laugh. She'd done as planned, she'd captured Bruce's whole attention, and she was supposed to feel good. "She did name me after him, but he wasn't my father. He was named Don Hatch or Hatcher. He was her man of the moment, I gathered, so that's why I was named after him. Prairie thought at the time she had a permanent arrangement with this Don person." This was beginning to feel like a bad idea. Even as she dealt lightly with the few known details of her early days, the pathetic truth wounded Donna afresh.

Laura shook her head in wonderment. "Poor little Prairie."

"No, not really," Donna said. "She's never unhappy, you know. That's just her way of life. I don't think she wants to be any way but the way she is." *At least I hope not*, she wanted to add.

"I suppose you're right," Laura agreed.

"What else do you know about Raymond Sung?" Bruce asked. "That is, besides his name and the fact that he wanted to be an artist. What was his citizenship status, do you know that? Was he from this area, or did he drift in from somewhere else?"

"He was a good swimmer," Donna answered and grinned, trying not to think about how her father and mother would react to this conversation. "Does that help?"

They all laughed.

"Oh, yes, and he had a motorcycle. That seemed to impress Prairie. At least, she remembered it vividly enough to mention it several times."

"Well, that really rounds out the picture," Bruce chuckled. "A Chinese-American male named Raymond Sung, from somewhere or other, who wanted to be an artist, swam and had a motorbike. With that complete a profile, he would be a cinch to locate."

Donna stared at her plate. Her hands were tightly knotted in her lap. "I may give it a try anyway," she said in a small, tentative voice.

"You're serious, aren't you?" Bruce asked, bending closer to her, his intense blue eyes holding sudden sympathy.

"Quite serious," Donna said softly. She was aware that Laura took a quick sip of water and raised her napkin to her lips.

"I'm sure he could be found," Bruce was saying.

"Think so?" Donna gave him total eye contact and prayed he wouldn't see into her thudding heart. She put a hand on his tanned wrist and willed her eyes to do no more than flicker from the impact of feeling his warm skin beneath hers. "It doesn't sound like a total waste of time to try?" she asked, almost hopefully.

He held her fingers in a firm grip. "I could certainly give it a try. I'm not without resources, you know."

Donna didn't move. Bruce's hand was broad, the fingers long. She wished she never had to move. This had to be dealt with carefully. There must never be any question of hurting anyone, least of all her family. "I can't trouble you with this, Bruce," she managed to say at last. She heard a little gulp from Laura, but refused to turn in her direction. "I was just going to go down the list of Sungs in the telephone book. I thought a few calls each day…" Her voice died away uncertainly.

Bruce grinned wryly. "Then, after you finish with the Sungs, you can start on the Soongs, I suppose. Don't forget Chinese names are rendered into English pretty much on a phonetic basis. You don't know how your father pronounced it, do you?"

"No. I just know how Prairie pronounced it, and I thought it would be S-U-N-G."

"But you've never seen it written down?"

"No," Donna admitted. "It's a hopeless job, isn't it? I'd better forget it." She began to wish she'd never thought up such a wild strategy for gaining and holding Bruce's attention.

"Of course it isn't hopeless," Bruce said quickly. "We'll give it a try anyhow. After all, we have the whole summer." His words were so close to what Donna herself had said that she almost spilled her tea.

When lunch was finished and Bruce had to hurry back to the office for an appointment, he mentioned the search again.

"Don't worry about Raymond Sung, Chickie. We'll find him, if he can be found. We'll talk about it at the office on Monday. And don't forget our date next Wednesday. Will seven be okay?"

"Yes, wonderful." She smiled radiantly at him.

Bruce stood and flung his arms wide. "Wear your dancing shoes, kid. I cut a mean figure on the dance floor."

As soon as he was gone, Laura tossed her napkin on the table; she looked scandalized. "Donna. What have you done? You dangled the appropriate carrot and Bruce galloped right after it."

Donna didn't need to be told she'd probably made a terrible mistake. "Oh, Laura. I've got a horrible feeling I'm going to regret this. All's fair in love and war, as they say, but I think I've already gone too far. I don't want war, not if Bruce is on one side and my folks are on the other."

"Let's not overreact." Laura braced one elbow on the table and cupped her chin. "I really think you do love Bruce. I could see it in your eyes every time you looked at him. When he notices, his reaction should be interesting. Maybe things will work out, but you're going to need more than luck, and I don't like this Raymond Sung thing you've started. Don't I remember both your father and mother trying to locate him? They never did, did they?"

"No. They did try—twice, in fact. For legal reasons, I think. You have to advertise for both natural parents before the courts will release a child for adoption. Mom did it first, because she was still single when she adopted me. Then, when she married Dad, he went through the process. So I'm what you might call double-adopted. And neither one of them was able to find Raymond Sung. He was a drifter, bless him. He drifted into Prairie's life and then drifted out again. Nobody knows where to. Nobody ever will."

"You set poor Bruce up." Laura shook her head. "Shame on you. Bruce is such a do-gooder. Now you've given him a little do-good thing to do, and he's going to work his tail off all summer trying to find a man who can't be found.''

''I know,'' Donna said weakly.

''What if he finds out?'' Laura persisted, frowning. ''What if he learns Evan and Sara already tried to locate your father and failed? Then what's he going to think?''

''Well…'' Donna felt panicky. ''I've already messed up, haven't I? I'm going to have to tell Bruce I'm not interested in finding Raymond Sung at all. He'll think I'm a childish idiot.''

Laura picked up her purse. ''You're probably right, Donna. You should tell him. But you'd better pick the right time. Say Wednesday, when the two of you are out? You'll both be laid-back, and you can make a joke out of it. Bruce is pretty even-tempered, but he can get riled if he thinks someone doesn't take him seriously. That's what gets between him and Mark sometimes.''

''Yes,'' Donna murmured, pushing back her chair. ''I'll tell him on Wednesday. I want Bruce to know that I take him very seriously.'' And, she decided, she could already have blown her chances with him for good. ''He can get riled,'' Laura had said. It occurred to Donna for the first time that she had never in her life seen Bruce angry.

BRUCE PARKED HIS Lamborghini at the curb in front of his Pacific Heights house and turned off the engine. The afternoon consultation had been a waste of time. It had been his own fault because he'd been preoccupied, and now he'd have to meet with the clients again before they went into court on Monday.

He didn't feel like going into his empty house tonight, any more than he felt like going to the party Sally Viorst had talked him into attending, later.

One more party. One more round of laughing faces, and

booze, and empty talk. He didn't miss Anne. Their marriage had been a disaster, and was best forgotten. But he did sometimes miss what he'd hoped a wife would bring to his life.

He sighed and reached behind the seat for his briefcase, climbed from the car and headed for the front steps.

The scent of roses filled the hall as he shut the door. Good old Violet. His housekeeper did a great job of trying to make his house a home. Too bad she couldn't infuse his brain with the right attitudes to complete the charming picture. His body lived here, but heaven knew where his heart was, if he still had one.

In his study, he poured a small amount of Scotch over a glassful of ice and settled at his desk to attack the mail.

He picked up the paper knife and set it down again, slowly. Something had happened to him today, something that had begun months ago, insidiously, and had grown bit by bit. Today, in that restaurant with Donna, he'd finally identified the little sensations he'd chosen to deny until today. He could no longer ignore what he felt. The girl... intrigued him. And by choosing to be honest with himself, he must also face that there wasn't a damn thing he could do about what he now acknowledged as fact. He must do nothing.

Donna had looked at him like...a woman? A woman interested in a man? "No, dammit, no," he said aloud and leaned back, holding his drink to the light, watching the amber liquor glow. He couldn't believe Donna felt more for him now than she ever had—trust and love, the love good friends could share if they were very lucky. Maybe he needed Sally Viorst and her party more than he'd realized. When he started fantasizing about a nineteen-year-old girl who trusted him, he must be spending too much time alone.

But Donna's face was unforgettable, her eyes—he'd seen the way men looked at her. Men at the office who were years older than she was. He might have to warn her about that; she was young and inexperienced. Yeah, he'd have a few words with Donna...

The phone rang and he snatched up the receiver. "Bruce," he said, then added, "Fenton," and felt like a fool.

"Sorry," a man's voice said. "I must have the wrong number."

Bruce put the receiver slowly back into its cradle. He'd actually expected, no, hoped to hear Donna's voice. He finished the drink in one swallow and went to look out the French doors at the ochre evening sun.

Who was he fooling? What he felt for Donna definitely no longer resembled the amused, brotherly instincts she'd aroused in him for years. Back-off-and-tread-lightly time had arrived.

CHAPTER TWO

"E.J.," DONNA SAID and smiled. "What are you doing in the kitchen? Get yourself back up to your room before anyone else sees you. Your mother told you not to come down till dinnertime—and that's pretty soon now," she added to soften her words. Her little brother, Jim, and E.J. seemed like ideal children—the kind she wanted for herself and Bruce one day.

"Nope." E.J. Hunt plunked his skinny, six-year-old body on a chair and scooted it close to the kitchen sink where he could watch Donna wash a crystal swan. "Mom's in her rotten old rose garden. Just like she is every Sunday. She's already forgot she told me that. She's already forgot me. See if she hasn't."

Donna sighed and shook water from her hands. She was making herself useful to Laura and enjoying every minute of it. This was the kind of home she would make some day. She peered through the window and caught a glimpse of Laura pottering among her prize blooms. "Your dad's in his office. He could decide to come out for coffee any time."

"He won't even notice I'm here. They don't ever notice me unless I do something bad."

"Well, you're doing it, so he's bound to notice then, isn't he?" Donna said, laughing as she dried her hands on a tea towel. "And you know and I know that swapping your mother's special clown shoes for a saw that your little buddy, Craig Lommer, swiped from his father wasn't the way to get the *right* kind of attention. It was dumb.''

''But Mom wouldn't let me use Dad's saw,'' E.J. said as if that fact explained it all. ''And I wanted to make something.''

''Don't you *want* to be good, E.J.?'' Donna sighed. ''Every time I turn around, you're in trouble.''

''I wanna do stuff, that's all.''

''Well…maybe you're doing the wrong stuff too much, and that's why your mom and dad don't give in more often.'' She stared into his tawny eyes, eyes so like his father's, trying to decide the right thing to say next. Mark and Laura were too protective of their son. Laura, particularly. E.J. was rarely allowed to play with other children in the neighborhood. He wasn't a Cub Scout, or on a sports team of any kind. Laura insisted he wasn't strong, but he was. Strong, and very bright. When she and Bruce had children, being overprotective was one mistake Donna wouldn't make. Meanwhile, she could give E.J. some extra time and attention while she was here. That would help. She'd go into a sporting-goods store tomorrow and see what she could get to interest him. A small tennis racket? A softball? Maybe a skateboard?… No, better not get him a skateboard yet. She smiled to herself.

''What's funny?'' E.J. demanded.

''I just had a great idea. I'll tell you what. Just because you're my dad's namesake, I'm going to get you a softball and we'll play catch out on the side lawn sometimes.''

''Really?'' He beamed.

''Really. And don't forget your mom and dad love you. Try shaping up and see if things don't improve.''

''Naw, they won't.'' He shrugged. ''I wish that baby hadn't gone and died. Maybe with him around, they'd have let up on me.''

Donna sobered. She hadn't realized E.J. knew about Laura and Mark losing their second child. She looked at the little boy speculatively. In his child-wisdom, he might have put his finger on the problem.

"How old were you when it happened?" she asked, reaching over and stroking his bowed head gently.

He shrugged again. "Four, maybe. I was just a little kid."

Two years ago. Donna leaned against the sink, the towel hanging limply from her hands. Surely Mark and Laura could have had another child by now, if they had wanted one. She wondered, frowning faintly, if they had changed their plans. Perhaps they intended not to have any more—to let E.J. grow up alone. Oh, she hoped not. Their plans hadn't started out that way. Laura, the product of a lonely childhood herself, had always wanted a big family.

"I hate it here," E.J. announced. "It's stuffy and dull."

"E.J.!"

"Well, it is. Not like Grandma Irma's apartment or Uncle Bruce's house. It's fun there. He lets me run around all over the place and he doesn't care what I eat or when I come in."

Donna smiled automatically, but admonished him, "you shouldn't say those things." Privately she agreed that Mark's mother's place was a casual delight and that Bruce's house was definitely more full of fun than the Hunts'. It was a charming old Victorian, a few blocks from where the Hunts lived, full of nooks and crannies any child would love. Much too big a house for a man living alone. He needed a family to share the place with. She smiled again. She'd be very glad to help him make the change.

Wednesday couldn't arrive quickly enough. Wednesday, and a whole evening alone with Bruce. She looked at her left hand and allowed herself a tiny fantasy. What kind of engagement ring would he get her? Probably a diamond. Under the surface, Bruce was a traditionalist. He might choose a ruby, though. He's always said red suited her.

The kitchen door opened and Mark Hunt came in, barefoot and dressed in faded denim shorts and a baggy T-shirt that was stretched and sagging at the neck. His blond hair was rumpled, as it usually was when he'd been working. "Boy, do I need a cup of coffee..." His voice trailed off as he caught sight of E.J. "What are you doing here? I heard your mother tell you to go to your room, you little crook."

Donna hid a smile. Mark invariably seemed to have trouble being harsh with the boy.

"I got hungry," E.J. muttered. "So I was getting a snack."

"No, you don't," Mark said firmly. "Lunch is long over, and the next meal around here is dinner, so hit those stairs before I think of something worse than time in your room."

The child left, head hanging, feet dragging. Donna's heart tugged. Tomorrow she'd make it up to him. What else could she get for E.J. beside a softball? From the corner of her eye she saw Mark hesitate, and she knew he was fighting the desire to follow his son and swing him onto his shoulders as she had seen him do so often.

She turned to pick up the swan again. "There's fresh coffee in the pot. Laura made it."

"Where is she?" Mark's expression took on the distant preoccupation Donna had noticed again and again since she first arrived.

"In the rose garden, see?" Donna said, pointing. What was wrong here? She felt tension between the Hunts, saw it in their faces whenever they spoke to each other.

Mark stood staring through the sliding door. He seemed

to forget Donna's presence. His lips parted, and a deep sigh lifted his broad chest. He looked older, strained, and his eyes darkened as he watched his wife.

Donna turned on the faucet to rinse the crystal. "You look as if fresh air would do you more good than coffee, Mark," she said, thinking that the worst he could do was tell her to mind her own business.

She heard the door slide open, and when she glanced around he was walking outside. In the garden, Laura lifted her head and wiped her brow with the back of her wrist as she waited for Mark to reach her. He picked his way over rough ground, hopping when a rock snagged a bare foot. He got to Laura and put an arm around her shoulders. She smiled up at him, and they stood leaning close together. Donna grinned, and deliberately moved away from the window. Every couple had differences sometimes, but with love, they worked them out.

The housekeeper didn't come on Sundays, family days, as Laura called them. She and Mark liked to unwind before the new week started. "We live casually," she insisted, although Mark usually disappeared into his walnut-paneled office while Laura spent much of the day gardening. Today Donna was to prepare dinner, a barbecue, Laura had decreed. Donna could choose the entrée and make whatever she decided should go with it.

Donna checked her watch, calculating the time. She'd better get started on the salads.

Minutes later, she was humming and tearing lettuce into a large wooden bowl, so immersed in her task that she didn't hear the kitchen door open again.

"Why don't you cut it? Wouldn't that be quicker?"

Bruce! At the sound of his voice, she swung around. "Hi. What are you doing here—did I hear you right? Did you say *cut* the lettuce? What a barbarian! You do not *cut* lettuce for a gourmet salad.'' She paused for effect. ''You *tear* it.''

''Is that a fact?'' He laughed. ''Now that's interesting. And I never knew.''

''Bruce, you're a fast-food freak. What do you do when you want hot cereal for breakfast? I'll bet instead of cooking up whole grain from scratch, you buy that stuff in little packets. The kind you pour hot water over.''

''I thought that was the only way they grew cereal. I thought they went out and harvested little packets from packet bushes. You mean they don't?''

Laughing, he came and placed his hands gently at her waist, leaned over and kissed her forehead. ''How is my very favorite girl?''

''Fine.'' She laughed, but the edge was off her pleasure. It was his old greeting—the one he'd been using since she was thirteen. ''If you want some of this gourmet salad, you're welcome to stay for dinner. That is, if you want to.'' Her mind pleaded silently for him to accept.

''Thanks, no. I wanted to talk to Mark for a minute. Where is he?''

Protectiveness toward Mark and Laura quickly overcame Donna's disappointment at Bruce's refusal. The Hunts needed to be alone for a while. ''They're busy. But they'll be in soon. You look tired.''

''I'll wait,'' Bruce said, praying he could pull off what he'd come to do. He sat by the table and propped his chin on his fist. Mark was the last person he felt like talking to today. He had the dull remnants of a hangover, and combat with his eager-beaver partner was low on his list of desirable pastimes. The real object of this visit was to talk with Donna. Evan and Sara were relying on him to find out what had made their daughter so desperate to spend this summer in San Francisco, and he'd already waited too long to start investigating.

"One too many last night, Bruce?" Black hair swung forward over Donna's face, obscuring all but those beautiful downcast eyes.

He sat straighter. "What do you mean 'one too many'? I thought you were the original Miss Health Nut. What do you know about overindulgence? Maybe I just did one too many push-ups this morning before my sunrise run."

He watched her head come up, stared thoughtfully at her wonderful face with its perfectly oval shape and small features. She was going to be a knockout. Going to be? She was a knockout now.

Donna studied him, too, a half smile curving her lips, and her obsidian eyes narrowed. "When did you last do a push-up, Bruce?"

He squared his shoulders. "What is this, an inquisition?" His body was in great shape, and he could find several witnesses to back up that claim any time he wanted to. The thought brought with it an instant wash of irritation.

"Just asking," Donna replied slowly. Her unwavering appraisal could make a man feel he hadn't quite finished dressing.

"Are you having a good time here?" Perhaps, Bruce reflected, he should have taken more care shaving. The jeans had seen better days, too. He probably ought to set a better example as an adult role model, for Donna's sake.

"Marvelous," she said.

She had a wonderful smile, Bruce reflected. "Good." He'd better get on with his project. Evan and Sara would be calling soon to find out what progress he'd made. "I expect you miss Vancouver, though, and your friends."

"No." Delicate but capable hands scooped some

chopped onions into a pile. She reached for a bowl of fresh peas and started to shell them.

The McGraths were right. There was something different about Donna lately. "You'll have plenty to talk about when you get back."

"I sure will," she said, quietly emphatic.

"Yes, well..." What the hell did she mean by that? Evan had told him that he and Sara had the feeling that Donna didn't want to go to college, that she might even fight returning to Vancouver at all. For months her only apparent interest had been making the official arrangements to work in the States. They were worried sick. "Have you talked to your mom and dad since you arrived?"

The peas beneath Donna's thumb sailed in a stream directly into his lap. "Sorry," she cried, and grabbed for several peas still rolling on the table.

She's jumpy, Bruce thought. "Why don't you open a can like everyone else?" He slid to the floor and gathered the rest of the runaways. "Or use frozen ones?" He tossed them into the sink.

"Because fresh things are better for you," Donna responded. "You really don't look very well. Can I fix you a drink?"

He certainly didn't feel very well. "Chickie, I'd love you forever. I will anyway," he added quickly. "Anything will do." A hair of the dog might be just the thing. But maybe he should watch what he ate and drank a bit more closely—just as an experiment. Donna certainly looked fantastic on whatever diet she followed.

"Relax then." She pushed the bowl of peas aside. "Would you like me to make you comfortable on the terrace? It's cool out there, and you can see the water."

Damn it all, he hadn't got to first base with his questioning. Some lawyer. Then her question hit home. "Make you comfortable." He wasn't exactly ready for the old folks' home yet. He got up and strode around the kitchen. "I'll stay here and keep you company."

"That's nice." She slipped back and forth between the counter and the refrigerator, gathering ingredients and ice.

"I don't see enough of you," he announced. She was absolutely lovely. Stunning. "What kind of things do you want to do this summer—apart from work?" Edginess tightened his jaw. She was charming, maybe too charming—and bright. "Have you made any friends, yet?" Could there be a boy—man—someone she'd met on a previous visit?

"Oh, a few. There are some nice people at the office."

"Who?" He faced her abruptly and waited.

She dropped ice cubes into the blender. "No one special...so far," she said with an airy wave of her hand. "Bruce, you're nervous. Sit down, now. And drink this." Her fingers on his elbow were cool. "No, better yet, I'll have one too, and we'll both sit on the terrace."

He opened his mouth to say she shouldn't be drinking, then changed his mind. The shapely little woman before him had definitely left childhood behind. He waited while she poured a second glass, then followed her broodingly through the library to Mark and Laura's flagstone terrace.

"I'll share the swing with you," Donna said, and he suddenly felt their positions had been reversed. She was caring for him.

They sat together on the white wrought-iron swing and rocked gently.

"Smell the roses?" he asked, inhaling deeply. Laura did have a way with flowers. "Well, that's healthful anyway."

"What do you mean?"

"Mental health. You're supposed to stop and smell the flowers, aren't you?"

"Right. This is our mental-health minute." She tilted her head back and stretched her bare legs. How beautifully shaped they were, he thought. Her skin, always slightly golden, glistened in the sun.

Bruce tapped his glass against his teeth and glanced at the thigh almost touching his own. He had to make sure nothing happened to Donna in San Francisco.

This was heaven, Donna thought. He'd stretched his strong left arm behind her back, rested the forearm lightly against her neck. He liked being with her. And he was becoming aware of her as a woman, she was sure. She hadn't missed his scrutiny. He really cared what happened to her, and he'd fall in love before he knew what hit him. And he'd never regret it. Neither of them would. Her silly blunder over Raymond Sung could prove a nuisance, but Bruce would forgive her when she explained. She wouldn't think about that now.

"You haven't tasted your drink, Bruce?"

"What? Oh, no." He took a bite of the fresh pineapple wedge garnishing the glass. "How did you know I'm crazy about mai tais?"

"I—"

"Good grief," he spluttered and coughed. "What is this?"

Donna took a long appreciative swallow from her own glass. "Carrot-and-celery-juice smoothie. I put lecithin granules in it for the blood and—"

"Don't explain." He handed her the drink and slid from the swing. "Don't tell me, thanks, Chickie. I really don't want to know. I think I'll just go see if I can scare up Mark. See you at the office tomorrow."

"And Wednesday night." She felt slightly sick as she

watched him leave. She shouldn't have added that last remark—it made her sound too much like an eager little girl. He wouldn't have forgotten.

"Right," he called, without turning back. "Wednesday night."

Donna waited until his footsteps faded away, and curled into a ball at one end of the chaise, a glass in each hand. Bruce Fenton had lived too long without someone to take care of him. How long had it been since his divorce? Almost two years now? And how badly had the episode really hurt him? With Bruce it was difficult to tell. They usually communicated well about any number of things, but if Bruce did not want to communicate he had a way of avoiding questions with his clever wit. He could so easily build a wall of laughter and hide behind it. She sighed softly.

WEDNESDAY EVENING, Bruce watched Donna settle gracefully in her chair. They had a table near the dance floor. Bruce was uncomfortably aware that conversation between the two men at the next table had stopped at the sight of her. Well, they could bug off. She hadn't even noticed them. At least she hadn't appeared to...

"Remember years ago," he said, "when I took you to Chinatown for the first time—remember the limiest punch in the world?"

"I guess," she said doubtfully.

"It was a drink I bought you to go with hot dogs, and I told you it was poisonous." Reminiscing about the past helped him hang on to their old relationship. But he couldn't shake the tension he felt around this changed Donna.

Her lissome body, too much of it exposed in a skimpy red dress, relaxed visibly and she laughed. "I do remember. You said to be careful where I dumped it or it'd rot the concrete. Bruce, I was scared to death that day, and you made it all right. You were always so good to me. I've never forgotten you holding my hand. And you know what?'' She leaned toward him, and his gaze flickered to the tops of her high breasts, then quickly back to her eyes.

Looking after her was going to be a full-time job. "What, Donna?'' he said, more soberly than he'd intended.

"I still have the doll you bought me that day. She's so beautiful.''

He felt oddly wistful. Time passed too quickly, and innocence with it. Donna was still an unspoiled young woman, but the girl he'd known was gone. "Did you keep what the lady in the store gave you, too?''

"The tiny ivory tiger with a thousand tigers inside—all too small to see, of course. Wait.'' She opened a small, beaded black purse and took out a worn leather pouch with a drawstring. "Look in here.''

Inside, wrapped tightly in tissue, lay the intricately carved little tiger. "The old lady said you were very beautiful, Donna,'' Bruce murmured. "And that the tiger was very lucky. She wanted it to be lucky for a lovely child. Back then you were just a shadow of what you've become. And I hope you'll always be very, very lucky, Chickie. But you've got a lot to learn about life.''

He recoiled from the veiled expression that slipped over her features. Caution was essential. He mustn't risk doing or saying anything that might make her close him out.

"I know a lot more than you think, Bruce.'' She turned sideways again and crossed her legs. Her high, slender-heeled black shoes, held on by narrow straps crisscrossing her feet, caught and held his attention. One toe swung pointing downward, flexing muscles in her calf, and her thigh was visible through the thin silky fabric of her dress.

Some baby-sitter he was proving to be. He focused on a point just beyond her perfect chin. "Donna, I'm not trying to come on as the heavy. It's only that I've been around a long time, and I want to look out for you while you're here. There are a lot of wolves in this town—"

She laughed. "There are a lot in any town. I appreciate you caring about me, but I can handle myself."

"Well, I get the feeling you…you think this is some sort of adventure. I don't want you to…oh hell…I'm no good at this. But you know people do things too quickly sometimes…get involved too fast…" He stopped, unsure how to go on. The drinks they'd ordered arrived, and he twisted the stem of his martini glass around and around.

"And then the getting uninvolved can be pretty painful, can't it?" Donna asked softly.

He glanced up at her sharply. She knew, somehow, that he was thinking about his own marriage.

"Damned painful," he said after a moment. "It all started out like a dream. Everything seemed perfect. Then the cracks began to appear. Things began to fall apart. And I couldn't stop it." Why was he telling her this?

"I'm sorry." And he could see she was. In fact, he was seeing again the total absorption she'd shown toward him at lunch the previous week. She reached across and placed her hand on his. She looked close to tears. He swallowed. She pressed his hand, then withdrew hers. "Do you ever hear from her?" she asked.

Donna liked him a lot, that was all. To her he was still the good friend who'd helped her out when she was a kid. "No," he said. "Not directly, that is. One of her cousins plays tennis at my club. I see him from time to time. I try to keep track. Anne's such a featherbrain, and it isn't easy to totally stop caring about someone who's been that close. I like to be sure she's okay.''

Donna seemed to steel herself. ''Would you…do you think you and she will ever…'' She hesitated, flushing slightly.

He helped her out. ''Patch it up? No. It was wrong from the start. The unworkable marriage. And neither of us had sense enough to know it.'' He paused, and silence settled between them. She looked so sad. He shouldn't have dragged in his personal problems—his dead history now. Donna expected a good time, a gala evening. He grinned, and leaned forward. ''That's not to say I won't try again. It hasn't soured me on the marriage institution as such.'' He was rewarded by a perfectly brilliant smile. He started to say something else, but the maître d', gliding to his side and bending low, cut him off.

''Sir. You're Mr. Bruce Fenton?'' He was holding a cordless telephone.

''Yes.'' Bruce looked up, grateful for the interruption. The conversation was getting too sticky.

''You have a telephone call. Do you wish to take it here, or in the men's lounge?''

''Here is okay. Thanks.'' Bruce reached for the phone.

Donna watched Bruce as he listened, watched his brows lift slightly and his mouth curve into a faint grin. He didn't look at her, but down at the tablecloth.

''Well, yes,'' he said. ''No, that's fine. And I'm glad you called here. I don't mind my date being interrupted for this. Good work, Joey. I owe you one.'' Still smiling he hung up.

Donna watched and waited, vaguely irritated; Bruce's eyes glowed with some secret amusement. She moved restlessly, making circles on the tablecloth with the base of her glass. Bruce continued to grin and say nothing.

"Would you like to dance?" she asked, expecting and instantly getting the reaction she'd hoped for. Bruce's smile disappeared.

He looked startled, but then an infuriatingly tolerant expression settled on his face. "Yes, I would," he said, and got up.

She could feel her heartbeat while she slid into his arms as if she'd done so a million times. This was the first time she had ever danced with Bruce—odd as it seemed. This was their first date. She smiled her own little secret smile as the pink lights dimmed. She felt his warm breath close to her ear, his hand at her back, watched the clean line of his jaw. She was aware of everything about him. Being in his arms felt so good, so right.

"I love dancing. Hey—are you lost in a dream?"

"Yes," she murmured, "a very nice dream."

He settled her more snugly against his body, and she found they danced together beautifully, as if they were of one mind.

"Have you looked around the room?" he whispered. "Did you notice I've got the most beautiful date here?"

She squeezed his shoulder. "Go on. You're terrific for my ego. Am I also clever, intelligent, reliable, a hard worker and a good cook?"

"I don't know about the last. We may have irreconcilable differences about veggies and their place in my life."

She laughed and moved fractionally closer. For long, silent minutes they circled, following the insistent rhythm of the music.

"I can see the pulse in your throat," he said. "You like this, don't you? You're having a good time?"

"Oh, yes," she breathed. "This is a beautiful place. Beautiful music. Everything is beautiful." She made an effort to share his light mood. She wanted to slide her arms around his neck and cling to him, but she didn't dare. If she made any sort of advance he would, as Laura had said, run like hell. Donna closed her eyes and leaned against his chest, nestling closer. She must be satisfied with this much for a while. She could afford to wait until he got more used to having her around before she let him know exactly how she felt. Bruce wasn't ready yet. He was still getting his emotions sorted out. What couldn't wait was her confession that she didn't want to search for her mythical father.

"Donna? Come out of your dream for a minute, will you? I've got some news that's just too good to keep to myself. I've got to tell you about my phone call."

She glanced up. "Well, good grief, what is it? You look as if you're going to explode."

"I may if I don't get this out right now, Chickie. You know when you gave me the dope on your father?"

"What dope? What about Daddy?"

"No, the original father, your natural father."

She missed a beat. Guilt overwhelmed her, guilt and embarrassment. "You mean Raymond Sung?"

"You gave me the wrong spelling, love."

"Wrong spelling? What do you mean? How many ways can there be to spell 'Sung'? S-U-N-G, right?"

He tightened his arm around her waist for a moment, clearly delighted about something.

"Absolutely wrong. There are multiple ways of spelling Chinese names. It's T-S-U-N-G."

Nagging uneasiness caused her to miss another beat. "What does that mean?"

"It means I found him, Donna. I found Raymond Tsung for you. I found your father."

"What?" She fairly shouted, coming to a dead stop. "You did what?"

"Donna, for Pete's sake, don't yell. Everybody's looking." He pulled her almost roughly back into his arms. "Dance," he said through his teeth. "Smile."

CHAPTER THREE

DONNA DID HER BEST to resume dancing and prayed the room's rose-tinged lighting would mask her burning cheeks. A fixed smile settled on Bruce's face, and the couples around them either grinned or pretended they hadn't noticed her outburst. Donna lifted her head and took a deliberate step—onto Bruce's foot. He stumbled.

"Donna, for Pete's sake, I'm the guy. I'm supposed to lead."

"I'm sorry," she mumbled. "I'm sorry. I…can we sit down?" Bruce had actually found her father? Oh, no surely not!

"Sure, let's go. But what's up?" Keeping his arm around her, he shepherded her back to their table. "What's the matter?" he asked with obvious concern as she sank into her chair, her knees wobbly.

He couldn't have found her father. Nobody could. Prairie had tried. Poor, vague, ineffectual little Prairie. Suddenly Donna realized that Prairie had probably never known the correct spelling of the man's name. Donna wanted to cry. There was a sick lump of dread in her stomach.

Mom and Dad. A wave of horror rushed over her. What would Mom and Dad say? They hadn't really been comfortable with Prairie wandering in and out of their lives all these years. They'd simply been too kindhearted to stop her. The missing father had been conveniently out of it, lost, destined never to turn up and trouble anyone. What a fool she had been to try such a childish trick. Her mouth was dry. She picked up her water glass, and Bruce reached for her hand at the same time. The water sloshed over the edge.

Bruce took the glass and set it down, then lifted her wet hand and blotted it with his napkin. "Look, honey. I'm sorry I sprung my news like that. I should have prepared you. But, Donna, I had no idea you'd be so...so deeply affected. I had no idea it meant so much to you."

She wanted to scream at him, "It means nothing to me. I don't even know him. I don't want to know him. He was just a nobody who passed through Prairie's life and disappeared. Let him stay disappeared." She felt an upsurge of tears. She mustn't cry here, out where everybody could see. She'd already caused people on the dance floor to stare.

"Well, it's true, Donna. I did find him for you. That's what the phone call was about." His voice was so gentle that she had to blink against the tears. "Donna? You okay?" He was looking at her and frowning, looking worried. He had clasped both her hands in his on the table. Never in her life had Donna felt so guilty, so utterly rotten and devious.

"Yes. I'm okay," she said carefully; she felt the pressure of his warm hands clasping hers.

"Good girl. I guess it's my fault for telling you so quickly, without any buildup. Forgive me, okay?"

"There's nothing to forgive," she murmured, looking away. And that was the understatement of the year.

"You must be a good lawyer—I mean detective," she added, feeling that it was a vapid remark but the best she could do for the moment.

"Not really," he answered, releasing her hands. "I got

a crash course in Chinese names when I was doing a summer job once during law school.''

''I'm sorry about making the scene on the dance floor. I was just…uh…shocked for a minute.'' That much was true, at least.

She had to have some water. Donna picked up her glass again and drained it. Somehow or other, she'd have to protect her mom and dad. They must never know what she'd done. She must face up to this, find a way out without hurting anyone.

Something unpleasant hovered in the back of her mind for a moment before she identified it. She'd have to meet the man. And what kind of man was he? Was he like Prairie, an aimless drifter? Any time now, tomorrow, the next day, she would be face-to-face with him. What on earth would she say?

''What…what's he like?'' she asked, her voice hollow.

''Well, good, you can still speak. I thought you'd be pleased. It was your idea.''

''It was my idea,'' she agreed dolefully. ''Have…have you met him? I mean, have you told him about me yet?'' She had the half-formed idea that it could still be avoided somehow.

''No. I haven't met him yet. He's in Hong Kong.'' Bruce sounded irritated.

She reached over suddenly and placed her hand on his arm. ''I'm sorry,'' she said. ''I appreciate what you've done, really I do. I know you put a lot into it. It's just that I…I…'' She paused, ''Hong Kong? You said he's in Hong Kong? You mean he isn't…er…here?''

''No.''

She waited a moment, expecting him to continue, and when he didn't, she prompted him.

''No what? Tell me about him, Bruce.''

"Are you sure you want to know? Well, forgive me, of course you do. That wasn't fair. He's due back in San Francisco in three weeks."

"Oh," she said in a small voice.

"He lives here. He has all his life. From what I gather, Prairie Crawford was a momentary diversion. I doubt he's given her a thought since—if he remembers her at all." He laced his fingers through hers.

"What is he like? I mean, what have you found out about him?"

He waited a moment, as if choosing his words carefully. "Well, I'd say this: don't get your hopes up that he'll welcome you with roses, a dinner party, and a big parade. My educated guess is that he may not."

"Why do you think that?" A small hope began to stir within her. Maybe the man didn't want to have a lost daughter in his life.

"Let me give you the facts as I've gathered them so far. First, he's married," Bruce began.

"You mean he's got a wife?" Donna asked blankly, rejecting the idea. A strange man was somehow beginning to take shape, just outside her line of vision.

"That's what married means, dear. And he has two kids, both boys. You have two half brothers."

Donna gulped. She didn't want this, any of it. She didn't want two half brothers. There was a whole family she didn't want. The man was taking clearer shape now. There was no shutting him out.

"I don't understand. What's he doing in Hong Kong—just traveling?"

"No. He took his wife and kids there. He's done what a lot of prominent third- or fourth-generation Chinese-Americans do. Taken the wife and kids back to the old country to sop up their culture. He, and his whole family, live here in San Francisco. His wife will keep the boys overseas for a couple of years, learning the language and customs of their ancestors. It's a good idea, actually. There's no point in being a product of a rich culture if you can't hang on to that along with your new culture.''

"Mom tried to get me interested in my Chinese background a couple of times," Donna said faintly. "But I just wasn't that enthusiastic. I guess I'm just middle-class Canadian through and through.''

"Now here's another thing. Your father—Tsung, that is—is pretty well to do, financially, I mean. He's the president of the First Bank of Cathay in Chinatown. And he's big in civic things for the city. Last month he dedicated a new playground. And he gets invited to the governor's ball every year. Are you beginning to see the man?'' Bruce was observing her carefully.

"I'm beginning to see the man," Donna admitted, not liking what she saw. All of this information was too real, too immediate.

"All right. I'm doing this for a purpose. I'm not going to spring anything else on you suddenly. I'm giving you this profile so you'll know that as solid citizens go, this guy is very solid. Have you got that?''

"Yes. That's pretty clear." At least her parents wouldn't end up having to give him money, the way they had with Prairie.

"Do you know why I'm going into this detail?''

"No.''

"So you'll be prepared, Donna. We have here a very solid citizen. Fourth-generation Chinese-American. Pillar of society. This is not exactly the type of individual who would welcome unexpected children turning up. See what I mean?''

"You mean he won't want to see me?'' Donna asked

thoughtfully. Of course. The man probably wouldn't even want to know about her.

"Exactly. I'm afraid, Chickie, that Raymond Tsung will not be exactly overjoyed that you've suddenly rolled into his life. What I'm saying is, it could go either way," he added, trying to soften his message.

"Yes, I can see that. Bruce, will you do me another favor?" Little shivers of tension ran up and down her back. She felt as if she might burst. Everything had gone wrong.

"Of course," Bruce said, smiling. "Didn't I just locate your missing parent for you? You name it, you got it."

"Stop calling me 'Chickie,'" she said evenly. "I hate that nickname. I really hate it. I've always meant to tell you that I hate it." She stopped, staring at Bruce's astonished face. She was shaking. What a crazy thing to say. She hadn't intended to speak so harshly. "I'm sorry." She carried on as calmly as she could. "I didn't mean to…to say that. I…"

"That's okay," he said after a moment. "So you don't want to be called Chickie. Okay. I won't do it. I always thought you liked it. When you were little, you did."

"I'm not little anymore, Bruce," she said, then closed her mouth firmly. She'd better stop there and not get in any deeper. Another second and she would say something that would completely shatter her relationship with him. All he needed was for her to announce that she was a woman and in love with him. That would send him screaming from the restaurant.

"Donna?"

"I'm thinking ahead," she said miserably. "Trying to, anyway. This…this father, Mr. Tsung, he'll be back in three weeks, right? And you think it's really iffy that he'll even see me?"

"I would say very iffy, Chic—uh—Donna. You'll just have to prepare yourself."

She could imagine it. Mr. Tsung would come back from Hong Kong. She would go to see him—possibly at his home, wherever that was, or at his bank. He would be horrified. He would doubt her. He would cross-examine her. He would deny ever having known Prairie Crawford. He would call his lawyer. She would be humiliated.

"You're not going to cry, are you?" Bruce asked nervously.

"No. I won't do that to you—not after all you've done for me."

"Nonsense." He was smiling the smile she loved. "I was glad to find him for you. What are friends for? When he comes back, we'll go and see him. He will either want to meet you or he won't. It's no big deal, Donna. If he's pleased you showed up, well, you can get acquainted— that's what you wanted. If he wants no part of a long-lost daughter, okay, we say 'sorry' and bow out. You've lived your life so far without him, haven't you? It isn't as if you didn't have great parents."

"Yes." Another feeble hope surfaced. "Bruce, you said 'we.' You mean you'd go with me?"

"Of course. I intend to see you through this, Donna. We go back a long way, you and me. We're buddies, remember?"

She sighed. She had had just about enough of being his friend and buddy.

"Why the big sigh, honey?"

"You mentioned my great parents," she improvised. "Those great parents are going to take a dim view of my going ahead with this without talking it over with them first. And I wouldn't blame them. I should have done that, Bruce."

"True. But it's too late now. You think they're not going to like it?"

"Mom's going to go all tight-lipped and reasonable. She does that. The madder she gets, the more reasonable she makes herself sound."

"And Evan, your dad?"

"Dad usually placates her, tries to smooth things over. I'm his darling. But in this case, with another father image—I don't know. He's got an awful temper when he lets go. It isn't that…it's that now…after the fact…I'm realizing how much I dread their being hurt."

"We'll have to guard against that, certainly," Bruce agreed, but his reassurance was small comfort.

"You know, since we're buddies," she said, trying not to sound sarcastic. "You could go one step farther with this fiasco."

"Now, it's not a fiasco yet, Donna. What's the step?"

"I have a feeling that Raymond Tsung is going to tell me to get lost. I have enough pride not to want to have him do it to my face. Could you…could you contact him first? Maybe by phone or something to…to…"

He grinned. "To see if the coast is clear? Sure. I'll do that. Then, if we get the green light, you can come in."

"Thank you, Bruce," she said fervently.

"That leaves three weeks," he said.

"Three weeks for what?"

"For you to get some Chinese culture, Donna. If Raymond is so gung ho for his ancestral beginnings that he's leaving his family in Hong Kong for two years, what's he going to think of a long-lost daughter who can't use chopsticks?"

Donna responded with a shaky laugh. "I'm going to take a crash course in chopsticks?" she asked.

"Sort of. For the next three weeks you'll think, eat,

sleep and act Chinese. Can you do that? While I was in
law school, I did a lot of work in Chinatown, and I do
know something about Chinese culture, even if you don't.
And I have friends who will help fill in the gaps.''

"Oh, Bruce, you are good.'' She should stop this charade right now. She should simply confess, tell him the
truth before she got them both in any deeper. He hadn't
had a chance to speak to Raymond Tsung yet.

"Sure,'' he continued enthusiastically, sliding his hands
over her forearms. "I'll even map out your program for
you, how's that? You know what? You should get a couple
of those Chinese *cheongsam*. You know, the sheath with
the high collar? I always thought that was the sexiest-
looking dress ever devised.''

Small tremors of excitement rippled through Donna's
body at the sensation of his warm hands caressing her
arms. She swallowed hard. She should tell him the truth
at once, push behind her the wild temptation to spend the
next three weeks closely involved with him.

"The museums,'' he continued. "The DeYoung has a
whole room of Chinese treasures—we'll spend hours there.
And I have some books. I was really into Chinese history
at one time. I'll give you a key to my place so you can
go in any time you have a spare hour, even if I'm not
there.''

To be with him—in his house! Donna felt drowned in
a surge of emotion. She had a sudden vision of the two of
them poring over Bruce's books, having cozy dinners in
Chinatown, going on intimate little shopping tours. The
fantasy shimmered like a beautiful dream—but she'd have
to pass it up. *Tell him. Now!*

"If Tsung rejects you as his long-lost daughter, it won't
be because you don't know about your heritage. After all,

we've got three whole weeks.'' Bruce was laughing now, having fun. ''Anything can happen in three weeks.''

He looked so wonderful. He looked so *dear*. It was too much. She couldn't resist.

''Yes…'' Her voice was unsteady. ''Anything can happen. Anything at all.''

CHAPTER FOUR

FROM DAY ONE of her "Asian Appreciation Course," as Bruce called it, Donna had a good time. She started out determined to tell him the truth at once, but made the mistake of allowing herself just one more day before facing his wrath, or whatever reaction her confession would bring.

She granted herself the day when they were in the DeYoung museum, as Bruce escorted her leisurely through the huge collection of Asian art.

"We may as well start at the top," he had said, pointing out the minute carving on a statue—or perhaps he'd been explaining the symbolism of the painting on a screen. Afterward, Donna couldn't recall the exact moment of her decision to wait before confessing the truth. He'd been so knowledgeable and funny and patient, and she had come to love him more, if that was possible, with every passing hour.

The next evening, one more day became two more days. He came home late from the office and found her sitting on the floor of his study, surrounded by books about Chinese history. She was so absorbed that she didn't hear him come in.

"Hi, bookworm," he said from the doorway, and she jumped.

"Good grief, I didn't hear you. What time is it?" she asked, and belatedly added, "Hi, Bruce. This is fascinating stuff. They invented the compass. Three...four thousand years ago? Imagine that?''

''Oh yes.'' He strolled into the room and went down on his knees on the floor opposite her. ''They were great travelers.'' He reached over and picked up another book. ''I think there's a better picture of the compass in this one. Theirs pointed south, though, instead of north. But it worked just as well as our modern one does. You haven't got to the rockets yet, have you?''

''Rockets? Don't tell me the ancient Chinese had rockets.''

''They sure did. The regular blast-off type—not so far removed from the type we have today. After all, they did invent gunpowder, you know.''

''Yes, I did know that.''

And as he bent studiously over the book, searching for a better picture of the compass, she thought, *One more day. Just one.*

Yet another day was added while they shopped in an expensive Chinatown dress shop. *I'm weak, I'm weak!* she railed at herself in the dressing room while she ran her hands down her hips over smooth turquoise satin. The straight sleeveless dress had its own timeless elegance. She had to have it, even if it took her whole summer's salary to pay for it.

Back in the showroom, she asked Bruce, ''What's it called again?''

''A *cheongsam*,'' he answered, leaning forward in his brocaded chair and flicking the long narrow skirt slightly in order to straighten the hem. ''All it really means, literally, is 'long dress.' Foreign words always sound so exotic until you get the exact translation.''

''Right. I remember I was so disappointed when I found out that all 'baton' meant in French was 'stick.'''

"Look in the mirror there, Donna. Move a bit to show that slit up the side. Now, wasn't I right? Isn't that the sexiest garment ever invented for a woman?" He gave a low whistle. It was the whistle that did it. Weak or not, she knew she had to have one more day with Bruce.

He was so wise. He was so knowledgeable. He was so clever. He also spoke quite a bit of Cantonese, which was the dialect most Chinese-Americans in the San Francisco area seemed to speak. He was also proficient in the use of chopsticks. She tried to be an apt pupil, to follow his lead, and—most of all—to please him.

Her one dismal failure—and she was ready to admit it by the next day—was in the use of chopsticks. She couldn't seem to master them. She, who had always had such superb control of bodily muscle and movement, found these little sticks treacherous and diabolical.

"No, no, Donna. You're gripping them too tightly again. Loosen up, will you?" he would caution. "See. Watch my hand." And he would lift his hand and the chopsticks would move magically between his lean fingers. "Now, watch this." Next he would pick up a morsel of food. It stayed put. He could even pause and wave it around as he spoke and it still stayed put. He could eat big morsels and small morsels without sending them flying across the table, and his little clots of rice didn't fall to pieces in midair the way hers did.

"You arranged to get shatterproof rice," she accused him once, and he traded rice with her.

"You have better chopsticks than I have, Bruce. I think yours are—"

"No. You said that before. And there is no such thing as double-jointed chopsticks. I have regular restaurant issue, the same as you have. Now try again. Try with that big prawn."

And she did try, as valiantly, as stubbornly, as gamely as she knew how. She, who could do a double back-flip without half trying, couldn't get a drippy piece of food to her mouth without dropping it, with a splat, on the table-cloth.

Her chopsticks seemed to have a will of their own. They projected bits and pieces of food so they landed any place but where she wanted. A snow pea flew into the rice bowl. A water chestnut leaped into her teacup.

"They close up like scissors," she would wail. "See, they did it again!" Donna became really embarrassed. "I do marvelous needlepoint," she added grimly. "Did you know that? Very intricate needlepoint. I'm very good with my hands. You should see the pillow covers I made for my aunt Christine."

Bruce began to laugh. "I don't understand it, Donna. You're half-Chinese, but I don't think you're even going to get one chopstick right. Look, watch me again, carefully this time—"

"One!" She seized upon the idea. "Of course, I'll start with one and work my way up," she said, tossing one stick aside.

"No, Donna, no! One won't do, and...no! Don't hold it like a dagger, for Pete's sake. That's not the way. I don't believe this." He was leaning back in his chair laughing at her now.

"Well, I got that piece of pork," she said, waving the impaled chunk around in triumph and popping it into her mouth. "A person could starve at this rate," she remarked, talking around the pork while she chewed.

"Donna, please don't talk with your mouth full," Bruce said, laughter still in his voice. "And when we leave here tonight, don't apologize again to the waiter about the spots on the tablecloth. They expect to have the cloths laundered. It's part of the regular overhead.''

The next day, she and Laura laughed about the debacle while they ate lunch. They'd decided to have lunch downtown together at least once a week, just for the fun of it.

''It looked as if we'd been playing Ping-Pong with the egg rolls,'' Donna said, and then fell into a pensive silence.

''What's the matter?'' Laura asked gently after a moment.

''I'm thinking about the message in my fortune cookie last night.''

''What'd it say?'' Laura asked, putting a pickle in her mouth. She had splurged and ordered the double burger with barbecue sauce, determined to ''hang the calories.''

''The message was, 'be honest in all your dealings and you will go far.'''

''You're kidding. What did Bruce's say? 'Watch out, the girl across the table is putting you on'?''

''No. I kind of wish it had. It's got to be easier when I get this out in the open.'' Donna pushed her salad aside. ''Laura, I'm dying for a bite of your burger. I am fed up—no pun intended—with the food of my ancestors. I mean half my ancestors.''

''Oh, you poor darling.'' Laura laughed. ''Here, you take this half. I can't eat it all anyhow. There must be a pound of beef in here.'' She gave half the burger to Donna. ''Watch out, it's messy.''

''Oh, heaven,'' Donna said, biting into it and chewing ecstatically. ''This is heaven. I needed some real no-nonsense junk food.''

''When are you going to tell Bruce?'' Laura asked. ''I think the longer you wait, the angrier he's going to be.''

''I know.'' Donna became pensive again. ''I think,

sneaky rat that I am, that I'll tell him tomorrow night instead of tonight.''

''Why tomorrow night?''

''Because tonight we're going running in Golden Gate Park.''

Laura paused, her hamburger in midair. ''Bruce is going running? Good grief…but I've missed something important, haven't I? When you come out of your burger trance, will you explain what I'm missing?''

''Sorry. I got carried away.'' Donna wiped her mouth with her napkin. ''I can't say when I've enjoyed anything this much. The point is, tonight when I'm running, I'll be wearing a sloppy sweat suit. Tomorrow night I'm wearing my turquoise *cheongsam*. Somehow I think I'll be more appealing in the *cheongsam*, don't you think?''

''Donna, you wretch. Bruce simply hasn't a chance against such conniving. That is a lovely dress. Donna, what's the matter? I didn't mean really conniving—'' Laura reached over impulsively and touched Donna's arm.

Donna blinked rapidly. ''Sorry. Dumb to get all teary. Your words hit home, that's all. I'm having an acute attack of guilt complicated by terminal remorse, I think. If only he wasn't so nice, so kind, so—''

''It's because he's all those things that you fell in love with him, Donna,'' Laura said softly. ''If he was a loser you wouldn't have looked at him twice.''

''But I am…I have been…conniving, Laura. I deliberately roped him into this run in the park tonight. Do you know why?''

''Because you're athletic and like to run, of course.''

''No. Because yesterday Bruce said one of the most wonderful things about me was my vitality, my energy. See? So I immediately hook him into a situation where I can be energetic and vital. I'm rotten. Utterly rotten.''

"No! I don't accept that," Laura said. "If you were really conniving and rotten you'd never tell him the truth, and you're going to."

"Right! Tomorrow night I tell him." Immediately she really wanted to do it, to get it over with.

She was less eager to clear her conscience when the next opportunity arose, and she was somewhat glad that Bruce was late arriving home the next evening.

Whatever his differences with Mark, he certainly did work hard. He had called, knowing she'd be at his house waiting. She had another half hour to kill. He was cutting it pretty fine for their dinner reservation, since he still had to dress.

Donna paced the lower rooms of the house as she rehearsed her opening gambit. "Bruce, let's wait a minute. I have something important to tell you." No, that sounded too grim, as if she were about to inform him of a catastrophe. "Bruce, there's something I think I should mention." No, that sounded as if she might be going to tell him his shirttail was out or his socks didn't match. "Bruce, there's a little matter we ought to discuss." That sounded better. But "discuss?" Yes, that was okay. "Bruce, we still have a couple of minutes. I'd like to briefly discuss a little matter with you." That sounded pretty good.

She paused in front of the white mantel and ran her fingers across its smooth edge. She loved this house, which was a good thing, because she planned to spend the rest of her life in it.

Donna turned, and glanced back at the polished floor in the hallway and the old-fashioned flowered rug in the living room. Rose vines with blurred cabbage roses twined all over it in a never-ending tangle. Across from her stood the stately white damask-and-fruitwood sofa. Stately or not, it was marvelously comfortable, with its down-filled seat and back cushions. Flanking the fireplace was Bruce's concession to true Victorianism, two pale green velvet chairs with high curved backs, the gentleman's chair with arms, and the lady's chair with just a suggestion of arms near the seat, to accommodate the ladies' skirts of the time.

"Bruce, we still have a couple of minutes. I'd like to discuss a little matter with you." *Well, that's got to go when we're married,* Donna vowed perversely. She was looking at a three-panel Chinese screen in the corner. It depicted two men, swathed in swirling silk and dust, fighting to the death, their faces pallid, grotesque masks. Unless, of course, the screen was dear to Bruce's heart for some sentimental reason. Then she'd just have to learn to live with it.

Maybe she could put her problem in the form of a question: "Could we briefly discuss a little matter?" That sounded even better. She jumped as the front door slammed.

"Hi, Donna! You here?" Bruce charged into the room. "Wow! The dress looks great!" He paused, dropping his briefcase on the floor and staring at her. "You're a knockout. But I guess you've been told that before."

She extended her arms and turned slowly, to let him take in the full effect of the dress.

"I'd like to stand and look at you, but I'm later than I thought I'd be. I'll just grab a shower and change. You amuse yourself for a few more minutes."

"Right," she said to the empty room, as Bruce disappeared. She heard him pounding up the stairs, then, somewhere a door opened and banged against a wall.

She'd make them a couple of drinks! That would help. Donna pushed open the big sliding doors that separated the living and dining rooms and opened a stained-glass cupboard door. This was where she'd seen Bruce get liquor. Vodka, vermouth. A vodka martini. That would do it. Glasses? Clutching the bottles, she hurried into the kitchen.

When Bruce came clattering down the stairs, she had everything ready. He entered the living room, smoothing his tie.

"Hey, what's this? We're running awfully late, sweetie. Have we got time for this?" He crossed the room and took up the short, squarish glass she offered him. He looked down into it, then sniffed it. "What am I looking at?"

"A vodka martini. That's probably the wrong kind of glass. I couldn't find any with stems, but it's exactly the same drink I saw you make one night when you said you needed a lift."

"True. As I recall, I offered you a carrot-juice-on-the-rocks or something to give you a lift and you said you didn't need one. That was the understatement of the month." He took a cautious sip. "Good girl. Perfect. Live well. That's my motto." He lifted his glass in a toast. "Here's to us, kiddo."

"I'll drink to that," she said, taking a tiny sip from her own glass. Boy, would she drink to that! "Bruce, we've got a couple of minutes. There's a little something I wanted to mention to you." Dammit, she'd said her line wrong.

"Okay, shoot." He was standing there, his drink poised halfway to his mouth again, waiting. A small silence developed, during which the glass-domed pendulum clock on the mantel ticked loudly. "Well," Bruce pressed, "mention it. That was a very attention-getting opening remark, but where do we go from there?"

For a full minute Donna simply couldn't think of a thing to say. Why hadn't she rehearsed a second line? Oh, stupid, stupid!

"Maybe you'd better sit down for this." She tried to keep her tone light, but failed. "I have a couple of things to..." She quickly rejected the word "confess." "...to clarify with you. I want you to know I've loved all this running around we've done, this digging into my Chinese ancestors' past. And I've really had a grand time. I can't thank you enough for all the effort and..." Good grief, this sounded like a farewell speech. She swallowed hard.

"Donna. Sometimes you have a problem communicating. Did you know that? Just pause, take a deep breath, and say it."

Feeling like a robot whose correct button had been pushed, she took a deep breath and started again.

"Bruce, the reason I'm having a problem with this is that I've done something I'm not exactly proud of."

He gave a quick laugh. "Don't we all?"

"Well, this is something that may upset you a bit, possibly make you...annoyed with me." She had hastily substituted "annoyed" for "furious." She would prefer not to think of Bruce as furious. She had paused again.

He gave a gentle sigh. "The minutes are passing. We have a reservation for eight. Just thought I might mention that."

She smiled a tight little smile. "You see," she said, scarcely moving her lips and speaking rapidly, "I had a hidden agenda for this summer in San Francisco. And I have the feeling that now is the time to...to...to...get it all out in the open." Her mouth had gone as dry as paper. She tried licking her lips, but it didn't help. "I have been completely selfish in my use of Raymond Tsung." She took another tiny sip of her drink and realized she was clutching the glass tightly.

"Use of Raymond Tsung?"

She sipped again, keeping her face down while she tried

to quiet her thoughts. She wasn't doing this well. He wasn't going to understand. "Yes," she said, nodding, still staring down into the glass. "Raymond Tsung…and you, too…in a way."

"I don't have any idea what you're talking about. Donna, look at me."

The vodka burned her throat. She hated the smell, too. Why hadn't she made something else?

"Donna?" He sounded exasperated now.

"Oh, Bruce." She raised her chin, then pushed back her hair. "You aren't going to like what I'm going to say, at least not all of it. If you think about what I'm telling you, you'll agree…well…you'll have to think about it, but you'll know I did what was best for both of us. It's just…"

"Donna! Stop this. You're driving me mad. Spit out whatever you have to say, *now*."

He was angry. She'd managed to do what she'd been so afraid of doing; she'd made Bruce angry. "I'll tell you." She pulled herself up as tall as she could and met his eyes. "The first thing we have to get straight is Raymond Tsung, I suppose. The way I've taken advantage of him."

"This isn't making any sense. In what way could you have taken advantage of the man? You haven't even met him yet."

"Yes. Right. True. And I don't want to. There's no need to. I'd rather just…level with you." Then, as if uncorked, the words came out in a rush.

"You see, I wanted to make sure I could see you this summer. I mean see you all the time. Constantly. So I chose to tell you about my biological father and I said that I wanted to find him. I don't want to find him, Bruce, not really. But I had to stay near you, you see? And I thought that was one way to do it."

He looked utterly blank. Donna plunged on recklessly.

"I never expected you to actually come up with the man. I thought it was a safe way to be near you. I did it because I love you. And I think you'd love me too if you would just stop and think about it a minute. We've been together, well, in a manner of speaking, for years and years. I thought if you and I had a summer together, really together, you would…uh…get the message. I love you, really love you. And to make you…uh, aware of me, I used this silly Raymond Tsung idea. I regret that. I apologize for it. I should have been more up-front with you.

"And you love me, Bruce. You've proved it in a million ways. For years. Look, we're both mature adults. I don't know why I made such a production of telling you this, when it's really such a simple thing, two people loving each other. I love you and you love me. It's just as simple as that, isn't it?" She paused, breathless, waiting for an answer. "Well, isn't it? Isn't it, Bruce?"

CHAPTER FIVE

THE GLASS STARTED to slip through Bruce's fingers. "You've got to be..." As his voice trailed off, his incredulous blue eyes darted from her face to the glass, and he adjusted his grip. Donna saw his Adam's apple move before he looked at her again. Despite his tan, he looked pale. "You've got a strange sense of humor, Donna. I don't think I want this drink." He set down the glass, then picked it up again when the liquor slopped on the table.

"I'm not joking," Donna said, disgusted with the tremor she heard in her voice. She'd unnerved him completely, and now she had to help him, settle him down, convince him that what she'd suggested was right for them both. "We have to talk, Bruce."

He fished an immaculate linen handkerchief from an inside jacket pocket and mopped up the droplets on the polished mahogany. He's stalling, Donna thought, almost amused. She'd really knocked him off his horse. Good. Now she'd close in for the kill.

She arranged herself on the couch. The turquoise satin of her dress, the long expanse of her tanned leg visible at its slit side, glowed against the ivory damask. "Come here," she beckoned persuasively. "Sit by me."

Bruce crumpled the handkerchief and stared at her. The usual warmth in his eyes had turned frosty. "Knock it off, Donna. This act doesn't suit you. Is that your first drink, or did you get a head start?"

Donna's skin stung, first cold then fiery hot. "I'm perfectly sober, Bruce," she said deliberately, "if that's what you're asking. I'm also quite calm, which is more than you appear to be. I'm sorry if I've shocked you. But it's easier for me to be honest about all this because I'm not the one who's supposed to be safe and sane. Spontaneity's expected of someone my age...I..." *Damn.* She shouldn't have taken that approach. Suggesting that he was the mature one while she was the flake wasn't the thing to do at all.

His mouth came together in a harsh line, and he yanked his tie loose, then unbuttoned his collar. "All right," he said slowly. "Let's take this one point at a time. First, Raymond Tsung. You don't really expect me to believe you were only pretending to be interested in the man, do you?"

Donna took a long swallow of her drink, and coughed. Making Bruce see things her way wasn't going to be easy.

"Donna," he said, with a frightening intensity, "I asked you a question."

"Hmm, yes." Donna cleared her throat. "Well, actually, yes, I did pretend." She held up a hand as he opened his mouth. "Please don't stop me. I was wrong. It was a dumb approach. Laura warned me that this would happen—that you'd be mad—"

"Laura knows about this?" he exploded. "She knows and she hasn't told me? God damn it. Wait till I get hold of her."

He lifted the telephone receiver, and Donna shot from the couch to stop him. "Don't," she ordered. "Laura had nothing to do with my decisions. I'm an adult. She knows better than to tell me what to do."

"In that case, she knows wrong. Someone should have told you before you made fools of both of us."

Donna eased the phone from his fingers, setting her drink on a coaster at the same time. "What do you mean, made fools of both of us? I may have made myself look foolish with you, until you accept the truth, but that's all. It was the only way to make you face up to the obvious."

"The obvious," he snorted. "It's all so simple, isn't it, my little friend? You really take the cake." He shook his head, muttering, and put his glass down. Still talking indistinctly to himself, he shrugged off his jacket and tossed it, over one of the Victorian chairs by the fireplace.

"Bruce," Donna said tentatively. She'd kicked off her shoes earlier, and when she stood close to him she had to arch her neck to meet his eyes. "We'll work everything out, you'll see. I know this is all a bit of a shock, but you'll get used to it."

He rested his chin on his chest and his hair fell forward, catching light from the last shafts of sun coming through the tall windows.

She put a palm on his chest.

"No!" Bruce drew back. "I don't know what's gotten into you, but it stops here."

But she'd felt the thud of his heart, the slight trembling in the solid muscle beneath her fingers. Bruce Fenton wasn't immune to her. "Could we do what you said, take this one step at a time? I'm sorry I pulled the stunt with Raymond Tsung." She meant it, truly meant it. "I don't know what made me do that, except that I was desperate for a way to be with you."

He laughed bitterly, and turned away to rest his head on his arms atop the fireplace. "And it worked. Jeez, I can't take this in. What happened, did you and some of your little friends dream up a summer's entertainment? Let's make a fool of Bruce Fenton this summer? Something to laugh about in years to come? Hey, Carla, remember when we came up with that number to pull on Bruce?'' He rolled his forehead on the backs of his hands. "Well, kiddo, you've gone too far."

Donna sucked her lower lip between her teeth. He still saw her as a kid, one of the group of kids he'd met on his visits to her family in Vancouver.

"This wasn't anybody's plot but mine, Bruce. I'm the one who's been in love with you forever."

He straightened as if she'd shot him, and stared at her, stricken, in the mirror over the fireplace. "Don't...don't say that again. You're just a child, only nineteen. You don't know what love is."

"I'm not a child, and I do know about love," she responded deliberately. "Fight it, if you like, but you'll give in in the end."

"Oh, my God," Bruce whispered. "This is awful. What the hell would Evan say if he could hear this...and Sara?" He swung around and grabbed her shoulders. "Laura already knows. Does Mark? Donna, so help me, if Mark knows we'll never hear the end of it. You'll come to your senses eventually, but Mark will never let any of us forget it."

Sickness gathered in the pit of her stomach. In her worst nightmares, she'd never imagined Bruce reacting so strongly, so negatively. "Mark doesn't know. Laura hasn't told him."

Bruce seemed to digest this information. Then he brushed past her and strode about the room, pushing back his hair, shoving his hands into his pockets. He dragged his tie all the way off and threw it on top of his jacket.

"All you have to do is forget Raymond Tsung and give yourself time to get used to the idea of having me around all the time," Donna said, her wavering confidence making her voice crack. "Honestly, Bruce, that's all—"

"It's not all," he snapped. "It's out of the question. Now, listen to me. Get over here." He took her elbow and hustled her back to the couch. "Sit there." She thumped onto the seat. "And listen. Don't interrupt. Don't say a word." His eyes narrowed warningly.

Donna folded her hands in her lap and sat rigidly upright. She regarded him steadily.

He faltered, lifted his hands, then resumed pacing. "I *can't* forget Raymond Tsung. It isn't possible."

What had Laura said? That he was like a dog with a bone when he was onto something? Donna sighed. "I didn't expect you to actually find Raymond Tsung," she said quietly. "My mother and father both tried and failed. I didn't think anyone would ever find him."

Bruce turned the full force of a glare on her. "You mean Evan and Sara tried to find Tsung? That's another little point you failed to mention. Why would you do this to me?"

She studied her hands. "Because I love you."

"No." He shook his head. "No, no, no. This is crazy, it isn't right. You don't know what you're talking about. You've done what a lot of us do, translated one kind of…of…affection into another. We are still just friends, very special friends, and we always will be, if you don't insist on pushing for something that can never be."

"Why can't it? You're a mature man. I'm a mature woman. We liked each other the minute we met, and we've never stopped liking each other. Now we love each other. Or at least I love you, and you'll learn to love me. The best love affairs come from friendships. Bruce…" She let the rest of the sentence trail away. He was watching her with deepening concentration, and in his eyes Donna thought she saw a mixture of fascination and…fear? Bruce couldn't be afraid of her.

"You hit it," he said slowly. "In all you said, somewhere, you hit it. You said you were mature."

"I am."

"Yes. Well, Donna. In that case you're ready to face up to what you've done and accept the consequences, aren't you?"

Her scalp prickled. "Absolutely."

"Good." Bruce sat beside her and turned sideways, so that he could look closely into her face. "Listen carefully. I've already contacted Raymond Tsung in Hong Kong—"

"But—"

"*Listen.* I have an appointment to see him when he returns to San Francisco. I contacted his secretary and made an appointment."

Donna rubbed her moist palms together. "Cancel. You didn't say what you wanted to see him about. Just call and cancel."

"I can't." He lifted her wrist, then dropped it as if it burned him. "Raymond Tsung is an important man. You don't just call up his office and say you want to come in for a chat. You have to make it sound imperative that you see him—life and death, understand? I gave Fenton and Hunt's name. I made it sound like this was the most important meeting the man was likely to have—ever. I really rubbed it in, Donna. For you, dammit. And now you're going to hold up your end."

"I can't," she whispered, sagging. "I absolutely can't, Bruce. I don't want to see him, even if he does want to see me. I've really done it, haven't I?" She ran a finger over her mouth.

Bruce turned his head away. Donna lifted her hand letting it hover inches from his shoulder, and her resolve crumbled. She just wanted to be with him. She leaned against him, pressing her cheek into his chest.

He was suddenly very still. "Please sit up, Donna. I've got a few things to say, and I want to make sure that you're listening."

She didn't move. He couldn't be this hard, he couldn't.

Bruce gently gripped her upper arms and pushed her away. He brushed her hair back from her face, and for an instant she thought she saw a softening in his eyes, but he patted her cheek awkwardly and leaned forward, resting his forearms on his knees.

"You say you're mature, Donna. Now you're going to have to prove it. The first step is for you to face up to how stupid this little game of yours is."

"Bruce—"

"Stupid, Donna. It is stupid. I'm twelve years older than you and divorced, and not looking for any kind of commitment. And if I were, I wouldn't be with the daughter— the nineteen-year-old daughter—of some very old and dear friends."

"You don't like me?"

He shook his head. "Of course I like you. Don't interrupt. And don't listen selectively. Right now, we're going to deal with the immediate mess you've gotten us into and try to forget the ridiculous suggestions you've made."

Donna felt the first stirrings of anger.

"You asked me to find Raymond Tsung and I did," Bruce continued. "I've made arrangements to see him, and I'll keep my appointment when the time comes. And if he says he'd like to see you, you'll see him, Donna. Got it?"

She clutched the edge of the seat.

"Got it?"

"Yes," she said softly.

"Good. Then we understand each other. Next. When we've dealt with Tsung, you'll finish out your summer job with the firm. I want you to have a good time. I intend to make sure you have a good time, with people your own age. Since Laura's been in on all this, I'll put her to work helping me find some suitable companions for you.''

"Suitable companions?"

"That's right. Young people."

"Not has-beens like you?"

His face came up, the beautiful mouth set in a humorless cast. "Rudeness doesn't suit you, Donna. But, yes, you've got the picture."

The room, the very air around her, took on a sharp clarity. All her senses came alive. She'd let him finish, then decide what to do next.

Bruce got up and went to the window. He pulled aside a lace panel and ducked his head to peer at the trees outside.

Donna waited. His back was even broader than she'd realized, and his biceps filled out the crisp white fabric of his sleeves. She tossed her head, opening her mouth to take a deep breath. Nothing had changed. Nothing. She wanted him more and more.

"At the end of the summer," Bruce said without facing her, "regardless of what happens with Raymond Tsung, you'll go back to Vancouver and enter college as your parents expect you to do."

Vague anger became barely suppressed rage. He was pulling the old overbearing father-figure routine, and she wasn't about to put up with that—least of all from Bruce, who'd taken his own sweet time to settle down.

He braced himself against the sash. "And as far as you and I are concerned, none of this conversation ever happened. With any luck, you can meet Tsung and not rile your folks. You'll get over the rest of this…this schoolgirl infatuation. And now we'd better leave or we'll be late for our dinner reservations."

Donna moved silently on stockinged feet. Bruce turned from the window and jumped when he found her within inches of him. His strained smile faded instantly.

"How did you used to feel when people tried to tell you what to do with your life, Bruce?"

He glanced behind him, then back at Donna. The only escape would be an obvious sliding past her—unless he climbed out the window. That didn't seem all that hilarious right now, Bruce thought, or such a bad idea. And if only she weren't so damned lovely.

"How did you feel when Mark and Laura, and Irma, went on at you about how you should grow up?"

He could smell her perfume. It was something with sandalwood in it, something exotic. It suited her. He pursed his lips. The perfume was far too sophisticated for someone her age.

"You ran a club or something, didn't you? And you were how old, twenty-two? It was called the *Blue Concrete* and some cult brought in vegetarian casseroles, and your partners were a couple of hoods."

Bruce felt the blood rush to his face. Someone had been having a field day with his personal history. "That was a long time ago, Donna. And it was pretty damned stupid. I caused a lot of trouble for a lot of people—Mark and Laura particularly. But it's over, and I'm not proud of any of it." He looked at the ceiling and grinned wryly. "I was lucky not to land in jail—or end up dead."

"So I heard."

He regained his composure. "I'm sure you did hear. If nothing else, I gave his family enough to talk about for the next century. But, to get back to your original question, when someone told me it was time I got my act together and went back to school—Mark did that for me—I had enough smarts to agree. If I hadn't, I'd probably be a middle-aged failure by now like your mo—'' *Oh, no.* ''I mean, I'm grateful someone gave me advice I needed.'' He paused. Her beautiful eyes registered her hurt. He should never have started to put down her mother. ''I didn't mean to belittle Prairie, Donna. We're both worked up. Okay?''

''It's okay,'' she agreed very softly. ''The truth often hurts. And my mother is a middle-aged failure. Now, do I get a chance to talk?''

''Well, I guess.''

''Thank you.'' Donna slid her small hand into his and walked with him to the middle of the room. She twined his fingers in hers. ''I'm going to give all this to you point by point. One, I do love you. That's never going to change. Two, regardless of how much I love you, you're not going to tell me what I'm to do with the rest of my life. On the third point, and I've already admitted this, I was very, terribly wrong to send you after my father. I'm sorry, and I'll do what I have to to get us both out of this.''

She reached across to hold his other arm, and pulled him in front of her. ''Last of all, Bruce, the decision to go to college will be my own, and I will go eventually. After you and I are married.''

He knew his mouth had fallen open, but the muscles in his jaws wouldn't work to close them. ''Married?'' he heard his voice crack.

''Married,'' she confirmed, nodding. ''When you and Anne got together, I decided I'd just imagined there was meant to be something permanent between you and me. Bruce, that was a miserable time for me. But then, when you divorced, I knew I'd been right in the first place. This is exactly what was meant to be.''

When you felt faint, did little black flecks dart in front of your eyes? She couldn't mean what he thought she meant. ''Before Anne,'' he said slowly, struggling to understand. "You mean you've been planning this for years? How old were you when you decided we'd...when you started..."

"About fifteen," she said calmly.

"Fifteen," he echoed, and instantly remembered her then. Hadn't that been the year when she'd finally talked Evan into letting her get her ears pierced? Evan. He refused to let himself think about Evan and Sara. They couldn't possibly know any of this. And they wouldn't, he'd see to that.

Donna rested her hands on his shoulders and looked intently into his face. "Remember when I was fifteen," she said. "You came up to Vancouver and stayed with us. And you took me to the zoo in Stanley Park." She was smiling, a little wryly, he thought. "As if I was still the little girl who needed outings to make her feel good."

He felt a small flash of chagrin. "Fifteen is a kid. And I thought you enjoyed that day."

"I did. I would have enjoyed anything you took me to do. All I wanted was to be with you, anywhere."

"And while we were looking at polar bears and I was buying you popcorn, you were plotting this?" He tried for an amused tone and failed.

"Not really plotting." Donna's lowered lashes hid her eyes. "Not then. I just knew I had to do something about the way I felt when I was with you...and the way I always thought about you when you were here in San Francisco. But I didn't know what it was going to be."

And, Bruce thought, when she had come up with a plan, it had certainly been a mind-boggler. "That's where you went wrong then, Donna. You followed some adolescent whim. But don't feel bad, or embarrassed. We all have some ideas we think are terrific at the time, then later, we find out we were way off base."

"I do know this all sounds bizarre, Bruce. But I'm not the first woman to fall hopelessly for a man and then make up her mind to do something about it," Donna said. Bruce almost groaned aloud. She hadn't been listening. "I don't expect us to march up the aisle this week, or anything," she continued. "We've got a couple of months to get to know each other properly."

"A couple of months?" He couldn't seem to form complete thoughts.

"Before the end of the summer. I figure we should be ready to let my parents know our plans by then." She was smoothing her palms over his chest now, running her fingers along his jaw. And the sensation low in his gut was happening all by itself.

"I want you to stop this, Donna, now." Her wrists, when he held them, were tiny. He closed his hands more tightly around them. "When you think about what you've said you'll know how out of the question it is." He continued to hold her until she slipped her thumbs under his and placed his hands behind her neck. "It really is out of the question." Her body, flattened to his, was slender and soft. He looked down into her eyes, at her mouth.

She stood on tiptoe. "Kiss me, Bruce."

He shook his head.

"Mmm. I want you to." She left his hands where they were and slid her own under his arms, up his shoulder blades, into the hair at the nape of his neck. The pressure brought his face down until he felt her breath on his lips.

"Donna," he said weakly. She kissed his chin. "Donna." He repeated her name against the corner of her mouth. His arms were crossed over her back. "You don't want to do this."

She turned her head, brushing her lips slowly across his.

"But I do want to, Bruce. I just said so. I always mean what I say."

Her body was supple, arched upward to press against him. The sensation of her breasts on his chest made it impossible to keep his attention focused. "Donna, please—"

"Shhh," she whispered into his neck. "Don't think, Bruce. Just kiss me."

And he did. His mouth met hers. He drew back a fraction as his brain registered shock; then he sighed and covered her lips again.

He kept it gentle. He was managing to control the kiss; he was doing okay. The worst thing now would be to humiliate her. *No,* his conscience protested. "This isn't right, Donna, honey. Believe me, we can't do this." The worst thing would be to allow one more second of this torture— for either of them.

"We can." Her eyes were closed, her face still upturned and beckoning.

He clasped her elbows. "Let's sit down and talk some more about this," he said, knowing she wasn't paying attention.

She edged him backward with her strong gymnast's thighs, her smooth, golden thighs....

Bruce gritted his teeth, squeezed his eyes shut, and felt his calves collide with the couch. *Damn it all,* he silently cursed as they collapsed, Donna on top of him, onto the satiny seat. Where was his willpower when he needed it?

CHAPTER SIX

THE WILLPOWER IDEA was a fallacy. There was no such thing as willpower. Donna's lovely face hovered inches above his, her lips parted. Her body on top of his had a seductive bonelessness which made Bruce move instinctively to accommodate her subtle curves. *Watch it, Fenton!* He couldn't give in to this.

"Donna, honey…" Bruce moved his hands down and grasped her waist, ready to lift her off him. But he'd waited an instant too long. Her lips came down on his. Another instant, and his arms encircled her, holding her close. He let the kiss continue, not as long as he wanted to, but as long as he dared. Then, gently but firmly, he lifted her and rose to a sitting position, putting her down beside him. Her arms still clung to him, and her lips. She made a small sound in her throat, something between a sigh and a sob. He had the sudden feeling that if he made one false move he could damage something precious in her. She was so young, so vulnerable. Never had he felt so old, so jaded. There was such simplicity about it, her offering to him. And it was an offering, showing an absolute trust in him that left him shaken.

He reached back and pulled her arms from his neck, held both her wrists immobile, his thumbs moving from time to time to caress the backs of her small hands. He had the sick fear that the next word he uttered was of paramount importance to this child-woman whose face was upturned to his, whose eyes held a love older than time. Somehow he must deal with this, her defenselessness, her unconscious provocativeness—the fact that she couldn't know what this was doing to him.

He had waited long enough. He didn't have to speak first. Donna said, swallowing hard, "I guess I ruined it. I guess I made you angry." Her eyes shimmered with the tears she was struggling to hold back.

"No," he said softly. "Not angry. Not at this."

She twisted her arms slightly and he let go of her wrists. She didn't reach out to him again. Her hands lay limp on the shining turquoise satin of her dress. He felt a lump like a rock in his throat.

"I was wrong," she said, her voice low. "I love you, but you don't love me." A shiver went through her and he longed to take her into his arms again, but he didn't dare.

"Oh, but I do love you, Donna," he said gently. "I've loved you for years, you know that."

"Yes," she said shakily. "Best buddies and all that. What happens when best buddies isn't enough any more? Is that the end?"

"I'm not saying that, Donna. But what I am saying is that if you're right—and that's very iffy—maybe we are meant to be together. But not yet, not this way. And not without answering a hell of a lot of questions first. We've got to think some long thoughts—"

"I've already thought long thoughts. I've been thinking about us for years."

"But I haven't, Donna. For me, this comes like a thunderbolt out of the clear blue sky. Totally unexpected."

Despite all her efforts, a tear brimmed over and fell down the curve of her cheek. She brushed it away hastily. "About a minute from now you'll say, 'Oh, this is so sudden,' and run from the room." Her attempt at humor fell flat, and she looked completely miserable.

"No, I won't run. I learned a long time ago to face problems head-on. It's better that way."

"Yes, I'm a problem for you. I'll concede that." The depth of bitterness suddenly evident in her voice startled him. He wanted to touch her, to comfort her.

"Nothing the two of us can't resolve together." He smoothed the sleek black curtain of Donna's hair as she bent her head forward.

"I'm not the big bargain you think I am, for one thing," he said, "I'm older than you are. And it's more than just years, honey. And I've already had one failed marriage. I'm not what you'd call a real good risk as a husband prospect."

"But if I'm willing to take the risk—Bruce, these are things I've thought through a hundred times!"

"But I haven't. Humor me. For me, this is all new territory. Look at it from my point of view for a minute, if you can. For one thing, there's our longtime family connection. Of all the girls—women—I'd ever get involved with, the daughter of an old family friend would be the last. What kind of guy do you think I am? The family connection in itself presents one hell of a problem. Surely you can see that. What do I say to your parents? 'Hi, Sara. Hi, Evan. By the way, I'm sleeping with your nineteen-year-old daughter.' What do you think they'd say?"

"You make it sound cheap," she said tightly.

"Leaving that aside for the moment, we have the problem of your future being unresolved."

"You're my future."

"Assuming for a moment that...some day...I may be, what about now? What about the next few years? You're going to forget the whole idea of going on to university? What about your own abilities? Your own talents?''

"Oh, Bruce, you sound like a lawyer.''

"I am a lawyer, and thank heaven I've had some training in logical thinking.'' He got up and crossed the room, and immediately wished he hadn't. She looked so small and forlorn, alone in the middle of that pale expanse of couch.

Donna leaned her head back and watched Bruce from beneath her lowered lids, loving every inch of him. She had handled this badly, very badly. Would she ever be able to set it right again? Well, not right, exactly. It hadn't been right before. That was the problem. She'd grown up, and he hadn't been aware of it.

But he was aware now. She felt a rising sense of something like triumph. He was fully aware of her as a woman now. She had stirred his senses, and deeply. He had responded to her as a man, not as her friendly buddy. She had that much anyhow. Something deep in her, something purely womanly, reveled briefly in the knowledge.

All right, she told herself. *He knows. At least he knows now.* She had to start somewhere, and that much, at least, had been accomplished. But she must draw back a little. She'd tried to go too fast, and consequently had made some mistakes. She had sense enough to recognize all the problems—she'd certainly thought about them long enough. But this was all new to Bruce. So Donna decided that she had to withdraw a bit. Retreat. Let him sort it out at his own speed. A line from a half-remembered poem passed through her mind: "And what is mine shall come to me.'' She closed her eyes for a moment, remembering the kiss and cherishing the memory.

"That leaves the immediate problem, doesn't it?'' she asked softly.

"What immediate problem?"

"The reservation for eight o'clock for dinner. Do you want to cancel it? It's okay if you do. I won't mind."

"No, no. Of course not. We can't…we can't waste that gorgeous outfit." He was definitely uncertain, obviously feeling his way with her. "Or don't you want to go? Are you still with me?"

"Oh, yes, yes." She got up from the couch in a single fluid motion. "I'm with you. I'm in the game to the very end." And as she spoke Donna made several rock-hard resolutions. She wouldn't mention the subject of love again for the rest of the evening. She would be vivacious and charming. She would put him at ease, make him feel good about himself, make him laugh. She knew him well enough to know that laughter had always been his shelter, his hiding place.

"There is one thing we ought to settle," he said tentatively.

"Only one?"

"We've got to distance ourselves for a while, not see so much of each other. In view of this, I have to—we'd—better cool it, that's all."

"You're probably right," she said meekly. "I'll go along with that." And she spoke with a brilliant smile that cost her every shred of control that she had. "From here on, you call me. I won't call you. Fair?"

"Fair. Come on, let's go."

DONNA WAS AS GOOD as her word. At the office, she no longer rushed to get Bruce's coffee, or waylaid him in the hallway. She simply gave him a cheery wave as he walked by, the way she did with anyone who passed her desk. She didn't call him or go to his house.

Perversely, Bruce missed her marked attention. Each

time his phone rang he snatched it from its cradle, and was acutely disappointed that the voice at the other end was not hers. He hated coming into his empty house after work and not stumbling over her sitting on the floor surrounded by books. He began to miss—and this was ridiculous—her bright, eager, idiotic suggestions about his nutritional intake, or his nonexistent physical-fitness program.

He even began to wish, heaven help him, that they could go running again in the park. He thought he must be losing his mind. He hated running in the park. Then he remembered her comment, ''I won't call you. You call me.'' And—laughing at himself for being every kind of a fool— he began to think of reasons—legitimate reasons, certainly—to call.

Slowly, Fenton. Think it through! he cautioned himself, and decided that seeing her amid crowds of people would be the best solution for them both. So he searched the datebook section of the *Chronicle* to find places to take her.

His first selection, a scruffy little street fair in the Haight, was not exactly a big success, but she seemed to enjoy it. He thought the vendors looked tired, weary, perhaps, of an endless succession of street fairs. Their long tangles of slightly greasy hair, the old and deliberately quaint clothing, all seemed somehow out of date and a little ridiculous to him. Their wares—jewelry, leather goods, handicrafts of all sorts—looked shopworn, as if from having been unpacked and spread out for sale once too often. Bruce felt suddenly apologetic. Donna was so young and so vibrantly healthy that she contrasted oddly with these shoddy surroundings.

''Do you want to go? Had enough street fair?'' he asked after they had examined a few stalls.

''No,'' she said quickly. ''Not yet, please not yet. We

haven't even looked at the other side of the street." And she burrowed her way through the crowd to cross the street. He followed her with the uncomfortable feeling that he was too old for this. *Enjoy, Fenton!* he admonished himself as he detoured around a guitar player who wasn't very good. He thought disgustedly, *Forget it, Fenton. You're past it. This sort of junk is for the young in heart.* Grimly, he followed her to the end of the street, waiting patiently while she listened to a singing zither player, while she bought a shell necklace, while she stood entranced before a juggler; and as he watched, it seemed to him that the juggler improved. It didn't matter that the flying ninepins needed a fresh coat of paint. Some of Donna's enjoyment communicated itself to him.

"You really liked this, didn't you?" he said as they left. "Come back in October, and I'll show you a real street fair. We'll go down the coast for the annual Pumpkin Festival." Then, as he saw the quick leap of eagerness in her eyes, he drew back. *Back off, Fenton. Cool it.*

Next Bruce found a kite-flying contest at the marina during a long summer evening. It had been one of San Francisco's brilliant, windy days, and he and Donna were stretched on a blanket on the grass, gazing up into the kite-filled sky. The green water of the bay was full of whitecaps. The sun was going to set in a little while in a blaze of color.

Because of the capricious wind, each kite seemed to have a mad life of its own, straining at its cord, leaping, dipping and soaring.

"I never saw such kites!" Donna said with delight. "Look! Oh, I wish my little brother Jimmy could see this. Oh, look at that fish! Look at those silver-and-purple boxes! Look at that man! Bruce, it's a kite shaped like a man!"

"I see it, I see it," he laughed. Oh, it was good, Bruce thought, lying here beside her, laughing at the kites. And truly, the kite makers had outdone themselves this year. There were a number of flying wind socks, and on the same principle, many of the kites were of different shapes and wind-filled, so that each had a realistic form. Together, Donna and Bruce watched, marveling at a string of great boxes in rainbow colors that bobbed and swooped in the upper air currents like some curious cubist dragon. They watched the fat gaudy fish with fluttering fins and waving tales tugging at their lines. They watched the flying man, his winged arms spread out at his sides and his trousered legs trailing behind him, looking exactly like a hang glider over the dancing waters of the bay.

"Oh, I wish I had my camera," Donna groaned. "I could get some pictures of them for Jimmy. He's into kites now. He'd love to see these."

And Bruce found himself approaching a perfect stranger who had a Polaroid camera. *What's the matter with you, Fenton? You going soft, or something? She should have remembered to bring her own camera.* But he made a deal with the man on the spot for pictures to send home to Jimmy McGrath.

One of the best times they had together was not something he had found in the *Chronicle* datebook, but simply a happy accident. They were driving down Geary Street, headed vaguely in the direction of the beach, not quite sure what to do with the rest of an afternoon. They had dressed up for a dutiful appearance at one of Laura's benefit luncheons. Suddenly Bruce made a right turn and circled around the block.

"What's the matter? Are we going back?" Donna asked. "Aren't we going to walk along the seawall?"

"We just passed the Russian Orthodox Church. Didn't you see it?"

"Of course I saw it," she laughed. "How could I miss that gorgeous golden dome? Except, since neither one of us is Russian—"

"But they're having a wedding," Bruce said. "Didn't you see the wedding party coming out?"

"A wedding!" she cried, as Bruce pulled the car to a stop near the entrance to the church.

"Yes. Look at the way all the cars are decorated. And since we are dressed up for Laura's do, we're far too grand to walk along the seawall. We'll go to a wedding reception!" He eased his car into an impossibly small and thoroughly illegal parking space, and felt a glow at her quick response.

"Oh, what luck that you know someone getting married here," she said, walking beside him into a dense crowd of wedding guests.

"I don't know a soul here, Chickie," he said, smiling at several unknown faces and receiving answering smiles. "Oops, sorry, the word Chickie just slipped out. I don't know these good folks from Adam, but who's to know that in a crowd of two hundred or so people? Ah, here's the entrance, I guess. It's where everybody's going." He took her firmly by the elbow and led her into the large recreation room of the church.

They came into a fairyland of pastel streamers, balloons and hundreds of floral arrangements. Vast tables were spread out, some covered with a lavish display of wedding gifts, some loaded with Russian food on ornate silver platters and towering silver urns spouting little puffs of steam, redolent of spices.

"You mean you don't know them," she hissed. "You mean we're...crashing?"

"Yep. It's the only way to go. Look, here comes the bride!" And they melted back into the crowd, over which a kind of hush fell. The newly married couple passed, the woman very young, very flushed and bright-eyed, with that sparkling aura all brides seemed to have. Her new husband was much taller, his arm draped possessively around her shoulders, his other hand clasping hers tightly. Then they moved on, and a babble of voices arose. Next, cries rang out. There was the clink of silver on china, and the throbbing of Russian music welled over them all.

"Let's eat." Donna grinned, raising her shoulders as if she half expected to be caught. But they worked their way slowly to the tables. They weren't hungry after Laura's luncheon, but they sampled one or two of the more exotic dishes pressed upon them by smiling caterers. They stood there, munching delicious unnamed morsels. They talked and laughed with friendly strangers. They wished the radiant bride happiness. They congratulated the beaming groom.

Then they fell back again as the dancing began, and wild dancing it was. The young men were especially eager to show off their skill. There was a pattern to it all, probably based on ancient customs. A little clearing would magically appear on the dance floor, leaving room for a solitary dancer. The man would go down gracefully almost to the floor, clasping his arms in front of his chest, kicking his feet, first one, then the other, out before him in perfect rhythm to the beat and moan of the music. He would kick his way across the room until he came to a place in front of the bride, and there he would dance for her, offering her this moment of grace and agility, strength and skill, in brief tribute. It was a gesture of love. The phrase "dance at my wedding" came and went in Bruce's mind. This was a wedding dance to remember.

When a dancer could continue no longer, he would bounce upright, bow to the bride and kiss her extended hands while laughter rippled through the room. Then another man would take his place. There was a warm, flowing, give-and-take among these people, and Bruce found himself responding to it. When he looked down into Donna's flushed face, he could see that she was utterly entranced by it all.

"It's beautiful," she breathed. "It's beautiful." Her wide dark eyes took on a sheen of tears.

Fenton, you jackass! Why did you bring her to a wedding, of all things? And he hurried Donna outside as quickly as he could, saying goodbye right and left to people he hadn't known a few minutes before.

Outside again on Geary Street, the lights were just beginning to come on.

"Oh, Bruce, that was wonderful. What a marvelous idea to stop," Donna said eagerly as they walked to the car. "Why didn't you join in the dancing? Those men were really good, weren't they?"

He gave a hoot of laughter. "Looks too strenuous for me. I'd break a leg in the first minute. I can't imagine kicking a thousand times from a low squat. Come on." He unlocked the car door. "Well, come on." He turned, and she wasn't where he expected her to be. Then he lowered his eyes, and there she was.

"Come on," she cried. "Try it!" She was down almost to the sidewalk, and clasping her arms in front of her, bouncing and kicking, she began dancing her way down Geary Street.

"Get back here!" He took off after her, slid his hands beneath her arms, and hoisted her upright again. Smiling people had stopped to stare, and he burst out laughing.

He hadn't had so much fun in years. It was a wonderful summer.

The laughter caught in his throat, but he kept smiling. He must be careful, so careful.

"This has nothing to do with my Chinese heritage, does it?" she asked, her eyes sparkling, as they drove away from the church.

"Not a thing," he agreed blandly. "I just thought you'd like a change of pace. San Francisco is a chameleon. It's anything you want it to be. You come on Columbus Day and everybody's an honorary Italian. We have another big parade then. We always have a parade." They laughed together, and things were almost as they had been. Almost.

When he wasn't with Donna, or working, Bruce doggedly pursued his research into Raymond Tsung. Who was this man who was Donna's biological father? He had to find out. Since he'd been the one to insist she follow through with what she'd started, he had to make sure that, somehow, Donna wasn't going to be hurt. He got the man's financial report and studied it. Whew! The guy was loaded. Bruce felt uneasy. Would this sort of man be receptive to seeing an unknown daughter?

He sought out an old friend, Edison Wong, with whom he had worked on the project to help Hong Kong newcomers adapt to the city.

"Well, what's new, man? Haven't seen you around," Ed said over a beer in a small Chinese restaurant.

"Oh, busy. You know, this and that. Say, do you know Raymond Tsung? Over at Cathay Bank?"

Ed pursed his lips in thought. "I know him by sight, of course. Everybody does. He's a wheel. I don't know him personally. I don't travel in his circle. This is pretty good. Is this Hong Kong beer we're drinking?"

"No. American. They don't have any Hong Kong. What

do you know about him? Tsung, I mean.'' Bruce put his glass down, making little wet circles on the bare table.

"Well, I don't know. What are you looking for? I think he's a nice enough guy. That is, I never heard anything bad about him. He's an overachiever, that's for sure. He's top dog over there at Cathay. He's into all the big stuff, you know, cutting ribbons, laying cornerstones, always first on the list to contribute to something. Why d'you want to know?''

"I'm looking into the backgrounds of a number of Chinese-American overachievers,'' Bruce improvised.

"Chamber of Commerce or the city going to give him another award or something, I'll bet. Well, let me see. He's married. Her name is Helen Chow. Nice lady. Kind of pretty. They've got kids. Two, I think. Boys. I tell you who might be able to give you something. See Gertrude Wong, no relation to me, over at Cathay Bank. She works for him. I went to Cal with her.''

Gertrude Wong met Bruce on her lunch hour. She had been shopping, and carried a large Macy's bag full of purchases.

"You wanted to talk about Mr. Tsung?'' she said briskly. "Can we talk while we're walking? I'm going to be late otherwise.'' She seemed a little too old to have gone to college with Edison Wong. Maybe she'd gotten a late start. Bruce reached over and took the heavy shopping bag, and they walked along together, dodging in and out of the crowds on Grant Avenue.

"Eddy said something about some sort of award committee or something. Are you going to give Mr. T. an award?''

Bruce coughed and said, "I'm really not at liberty to say.''

"Oh, sure. Of course not,'' she agreed quickly. "Lemme

see, what can I tell you about him? He's a nice enough guy, a family-man type. You understand, I don't know him that well. True, I'm a loan officer at his bank, but I'm not exactly buddy-buddy with the president.''

Bruce made an understanding noise while he prayed she never compared notes with Raymond Tsung's secretary, who would wonder why Bruce Fenton found it necessary to investigate the man he'd made an appointment with. She might wonder enough to mention something to Tsung on the phone and reveal Bruce's hand before he was ready.

Gertrude Wong was looking at him.

''What's his wife like?'' Bruce asked.

''Mrs. Tsung? Beats me. I know she wears designer suits, because she's come into the bank a few times wearing them. Oh yeah, they're very family, if you know what I mean. Close-knit. Always at some family do. Plenty of brothers, sisters, cousins. And businesswise, he's up on affirmative action. Watches to see that women get an even break. I like that about him.'' She was panting a little from exertion. They had come to the door of the bank building, and she reached over for her bag. ''Thanks.''

''Thank you.'' He handed it to her. ''Christmas in mid-summer?'' He grinned and she grinned back, her eyes suddenly laughing.

''You might say so. One of my aunts is visiting from Taiwan, and she's going back Tuesday. Going back means taking presents to everybody. We're all helping her get them together.'' She paused a moment. ''I'm sorry I can't seem to offer much help, but I just know him in that busi-ness-employer way that doesn't amount to much.''

''Everything helps. Let me give you my card. If you think of anything else, give me a call. I'm interested mainly in character delineation—what sort of man he is.'' That sounded pretty good, he thought.

"You might talk with Father Fu over at Old Saint Mary's. That's Nathan Fu, the younger Father Fu. I think he's nephew to the older one. Anyhow, I know he's worked with Mr. Tsung on a lot of civic committees and such, you know, for community improvement and so on. Do you want me to give him a call and introduce you?"

"Yes. Would you, please? I'd appreciate it."

Later in the day, at Old Saint Mary's, Bruce handed his card to a slim, middle-aged Chinese in a cassock, carrying an armload of paperback music books. They stood in the dim, lofty nave of the church itself, where Bruce had been sent by a girl in the office.

"How can I help you, Mr....ah..." Father Fu glanced down at the business card Bruce held out. "Mr. Fenton?" Then recollection dawned. "Oh, you're the man Mrs. Wong at the bank telephoned me about. Let me get rid of this stuff, will you?" The priest dumped the books onto a nearby pew. "We can sit over here, if you like."

They sat in a pew, and Bruce ran his hand over the old wood while he looked up at the altar. "Quite a landmark, this old church," he said.

"Oh yes. Not as well attended on Sundays as it used to be, but surviving. Let's see, you needed information concerning Raymond Tsung?" The priest's face was tranquil, but his eyes were sharp and alert. "Was this in the nature of...ah...a legal matter, Mr. Fenton?"

"Not at all," Bruce said quickly. "Just a casual inquiry. I'm trying to get a line on the man's character, if I can."

"Something about a possible award, Mrs. Wong said. I understand that you must be circumspect, since the recipient is not yet selected. Raymond and I have had dealings together working on various committees set up by the city. He's received a lot of awards, as you will see if your inquiry takes you as far as his office. You have only to look on the walls there.''

"The nature of the man,'' Bruce said, somewhat desperately. What he wanted to say, but couldn't, was, "Would he be nice to a lovely young girl who suddenly showed up claiming to be his daughter?''

"You mean is he kind to his mother and does he refrain from kicking stray cats?'' the priest asked, his eyes glinting with amusement.

Bruce had to laugh. "That's close.''

Father Fu was silent and thoughtful for a time, his thin hands resting motionless in his lap. Finally he spoke.

"Raymond Tsung is, above all things, a doer. He gets things done. He is a remarkably competent man, in many areas. He is, or appears to be, a devoted family man. He is a fourth-generation American, but with a strong sense of his Chinese culture. He speaks both Cantonese and Mandarin fluently. He is currently in Hong Kong, but will be back in a couple of weeks. He will leave his wife, Helen Chow, and their two sons there, probably for a period of two years. He's closed up their house temporarily. They live out in the Richmond, on the avenues. The address will be in the phone book if you don't already have it. He will stay temporarily with his sister and her husband, the Nicholas Huangs, also in the Richmond. That sounds like Wong, but it's spelled H-U-A-N-G. This is inconvenient for him, but he wants the boys to use their original language in its pure form and to appreciate their original culture. So this way nothing is lost, you see?''

"Yes. And it's a good idea.'' Bruce was almost startled by the priest's question. He had been lulled by the gentle monotone of the man's voice.

"I'm not sure there is anything else I can tell you.''

"Thank you. You've been very kind. I wondered about

this—'' He paused, not sure how to proceed. ''This feeling Mr. Tsung has for his Chinese culture. Would you say he is something of a racial purist?'' *What I mean,* he thought, *but can't say, is how is Tsung going to react to the appearance of a half-Chinese daughter?*

''Are you asking me if Mr. Tsung is a bigot?'' Father Fu's face split into an engaging grin. ''Offhand, I'd say no.''

Bruce laughed at himself. The good father was aware of his intensity. He had overplayed his hand, and he knew it.

''You might talk to Malcolm Gee, the realtor. He and Raymond have been active for years in both the Rotary and Lions clubs. They've done a lot of good in the community. I'll get Gee's number for you if you stop in with me at the church office before you go.''

It was almost sundown when Bruce finally left Chinatown and headed home. He was discouraged. What had he found out, actually? Not much more than he had known already. From Malcolm Gee, Bruce had learned that Tsung was a sometime Sunday painter, but didn't work very hard at his craft any more. Probably his artistic hobby was the last vestige of his fling at being an artist in his youth. Suddenly, Bruce wanted to see Donna. He wanted very badly to see her. As soon as he got into his house he dialed the Hunts' number. His luck held. She answered the phone.

''Have you eaten yet?'' he asked without preamble.

''No. The Hunts are going out, and E.J. is over at Mark's mother's for the evening—I think Irma's even keeping him overnight. I'm on my own. I haven't gotten around to eating yet.''

''My housekeeper won't like it, but I don't feel like eating alone. Why don't I come over and get you and we'll eat out together?''

"Why won't Violet like it?"

"I told her this morning I'd be home, so she'll have made something."

"Maybe you should eat it."

Her indifference stung him. "I just thought you might enjoy going somewhere."

"Why not? Okay," she said, sounding pleasant, but definitely not eager.

Suppose her great declaration had simply been a teenage fantasy? Suppose she was over it now? He had a quick, intense, recollection of the pressure of her mouth on his.

"I'll pick you up in ten minutes," he said, his voice a little thick.

"I'll be ready, but you know, I'm not that hungry. Maybe something light, okay? No big deal."

"Right." He set the receiver back in its cradle and discovered that his palm was moist. What the hell was wrong with him? *Crowds,* he was thinking, *we should be with lots and lots of people.* The way he felt at the moment, he knew better than to be alone with her.

Half an hour later, they were walking down Fisherman's Wharf among teeming hordes of tourists. It was the most crowded place he could think of.

"I thought you didn't like Fisherman's Wharf," she said, dodging two portly people in Hawaiian shirts. "You always said it was too touristy. Are we going to eat down here?" She looked into the restaurants they passed, at the stalls of cheap goods, the vendors selling hot dogs, popcorn, balloons. She stopped at an open-air counter full of tourist trinkets.

"This is a good year for ceramic cable cars marked Souvenir of San Francisco, isn't it?" she asked.

Bruce picked one up and turned it over in his hand. A nearby mime imitated his action perfectly.

"Do you like crab? You said you weren't hungry. Maybe we could just walk around and eat some crab."

"Fine." Donna had noticed a number of people eating out of plastic containers with small plastic forks as they walked along in the gathering dusk. Lights in the restaurants and along the street were beginning to come on.

They stopped at one of the large brick crab pots, and a man in jeans, torn T-shirt and large rubber apron fished a big cooked crab from a cauldron full of boiling water. He slammed the crab onto a stack of newspapers and began cracking the shell with a mallet. Then he broke it into pieces and put great chunks of the succulent white meat into two containers.

"Mmm, good," Donna said, taking her first bite. "This is the way to eat crab. It doesn't need a lot of gooey dressing."

They walked in companionable silence for a time, weaving their way through the crowds. There were a few benches, but all were filled, so they sat on the edge of the wharf, their legs hanging over the greenish water that slapped at the pilings below. At a little distance, there was a small fishing boat, old rubber tires hanging from ropes over its sides to act as shock absorbers.

"You seem a little glum tonight," Donna said after a time. "Today not go so well?"

"It's Raymond Tsung. I've been doing my homework. The only new things I came up with today are that he's an intermittent Sunday painter. Water scenes mainly. And he speaks Mandarin as well as Cantonese. The other stuff I'm finding out is...is..."

"Is what? He's Jack the Ripper in disguise?"

"No. Anything but. He's Mr. Perfect. The more I hear about what a great solid citizen he is, the more I wonder how..."

She poked at the uneaten remains of her crab, looking down, her silken hair hiding her face.

"You mean you don't think he's going to welcome me with any big parade, right?"

"Oh, you could get your parade. He might be overjoyed with an unknown daughter. But...well...it could go either way, Donna. You might get your parade. Or..." He poked savagely at his own crab. "Or he may just call his security men and have us thrown out. It's a toss-up."

CHAPTER SEVEN

THE NEXT MORNING Donna and Bruce crossed paths briefly in the employees' lounge at Fenton and Hunt. Both were taking a late coffee break.

"Hi. You coming or going?" Bruce asked.

"Going. It's time for me to get back. She gave him a bright smile, dumped the remainder of her coffee into the sink, and tossed the plastic cup in the trash.

"I haven't forgotten I promised you a trip around the bay in my boat," Bruce said, filling his cup.

"Great. Thanks. But I haven't figured out yet how you're going to get all those other people on the boat. What have you got? A liner?"

"What other people?" He glanced up from his cup in surprise.

"The other nine hundred and ninety-nine."

"What are you talking about?"

"I haven't missed the fact, Bruce," she said, smiling as if to remove any sting from her words, "that ever since I tried to seduce you, you've always made certain never to see me except in the midst of intimate little groups of at least a thousand people. I didn't miss that, you know."

He gave a shout of laughter, but his color heightened. "Oh, you picked up on that, did you?"

"Yes. I'm taking it as a compliment on my degree of seductivity," she said demurely.

"I don't think there is such a word as seductivity, but I get your point." He stirred his coffee with a plastic stick.

She wanted him to mention the boat trip again, but instead he said, "I just had a call from my old friend, Edison Wong. He had another bulletin about the Tsungs."

Donna braced herself, and tried to look pleased. "And what's new with Mr. and Mrs. Tsung?"

"Eddy's wife's sister goes to the same hairdresser as Mrs. Tsung. The story is that Mrs. Tsung wanted to have more children, but it just didn't happen. Apparently, she's a real hard-core mother type. She was after Mr. Tsung to adopt, but he vetoed that."

"Oh? Did Eddy's wife's sister find out why?"

"I asked Eddy, and it turns out he had asked his wife that, and she said, her sister said, that Mr. Tsung is very family-oriented. Said he is very proud of the family name, etcetera, and only wanted their own kids, not someone else's. So Mrs. Tsung had to be satisfied with the two kids they have." He glanced up at the clock. "Good grief. I've got to beat it. I have an appointment about now."

At home that night, in her lovely green-and-gold bedroom at the Hunts', Donna lay sleepless for a long time, staring at the light and dark shadows that played across the coved ceiling, as the sheer window curtains blew in and out. She smelled the slight scent of salt air, and in the far distance, thought she could discern the faint sound of two or three foghorns in mournful conversation.

She knew, beyond a shadow of a doubt, that the coming meeting with Raymond Tsung was gong to be a difficult one. She tried to imagine, but couldn't, how he must have been during his time with her mother, Prairie. She had learned some time ago that Raymond and Prairie had lived together for a time, sharing a single room with another couple in a crummy district of "the city."

"It was rather nice," Prairie had said long ago. "There was a little stove and fridge down at the end of the hall, and we all had sleeping bags. And Ray got the prettiest paper fans from Chinatown, and we tacked them on the walls. And Ray painted two pictures of boats."

Donna felt a creeping sadness, as she always did when she thought of Prairie. What would Prairie think if she knew what Raymond Tsung had become? He'd come a long way from a sleeping bag in that crummy room with paper fans on the walls; from riding his motorbike up and down San Francisco's hills with Prairie behind him, her flowered peasant skirt billowing in the wind. Did Raymond Tsung regret his brief wild period? Was he ashamed of it? He didn't, she was sure, even know that she existed, because by the time she'd been born, Raymond had been replaced by Donald something-or-other, after whom she was named.

And when this strange man who was her father found out she existed, what then? She didn't want to think about that. She crawled out of bed and struggled into her robe without turning on any lights. Clutching the robe tightly around her, she went to the window and pushed aside the filmy curtain. The garden below was in darkness, and she felt a cool damp mist against her skin. She shivered.

And what about Mom and Dad? The unwelcome thought was suddenly in the front of her mind. What were they going to say when they found out what she had done? What were they going to think, to feel? Would they feel somehow betrayed? Abandoned? They didn't deserve that. What was Mom doing now, this minute? What was Dad doing? What was Jimmy up to? The thought of her little brother brought a lump to her throat. They were probably all in bed, without a worry in the world. Vancouver was in the same time zone. Yes, they'd all be sleeping peacefully. They didn't know about Raymond Tsung yet.

And when they found out, what then?

Mom had taken her in, given her love, a home. And when she'd married Dad—he had married them both, taken on a complete family.

"Well, your mom said it was a package deal or no deal," he had joked with her. "So I was stuck, you see?" She felt her eyes stinging when she remembered how desperately she had wanted her mother to marry Evan McGrath.

And they had done it. They had given her everything she had ever needed and wanted. Hers was a far cry from the half-life she'd had with her own mother, in and out of foster homes with Prairie drifting back into her life at midterm to take her out of yet another school for some reason, or for no reason at all. She had been a frantic little girl with bitten fingernails. A torn, divided little girl. Overjoyed to see Prairie again—because she did love Prairie, and always would—but heartsick at the idea of missing school, once again losing whatever friends she'd managed to make. Six- and seven-year-olds should not have to endure anxiety attacks.

Then Donna thought about Sara Fletcher, her new mother—her true mother, regardless of which woman had borne her—and about Evan McGrath, the kindness they'd shown her, the fun, the security, the priceless stability they'd given her, so freely, and with such love.

How could she have forgotten that? Why had she started this stupid quest for Raymond Tsung? She might have known that Bruce would find him.

"I'm sorry. I'm sorry," she murmured to the empty room. She suddenly realized that she was crying. She stood by the open window, both hands pressed to her mouth, her open robe moving in the night wind. She needed—desperately—to talk to Bruce. Right now. She hurried to her bedside phone, stumbling a little over the hem of her gown, and picked up the phone with unsteady hands to dial his number.

"Hello?" His voice when he answered sounded as if he was wide awake.

"Bruce? Bruce." Donna gulped out his name and swallowed hard. What an idiot she was. She had reverted to her little-girl custom of calling him when she needed a friend. Her glance passed over her bedside clock. Even as a child she hadn't called him in the middle of the night!

"Oh, I'm sorry. I...didn't realize the time."

"Donna? For Pete's sake. That's okay. I'm accustomed to women calling me in the middle of the night. That's the story of my life. I just can't fight them off."

"Oh, Bruce—" She laughed shakily.

"You're crying, Donna." His voice was suddenly gentle. "What's wrong, Chickie? Sorry. I forgot you don't—"

"No, no. It's all right. You can call me anything you want. I really shouldn't have phoned you, but I—" Her control wavered, and she said in a small voice, "I'm homesick."

"Oh, good Lord! That's serious! That could be terminal. I'm coming right over with my little black bag. Donna? Donna?"

"Yes." She gulped. "I'm still here. Bruce, you don't have to do that. I'm just being foolish."

"No, that's quite all right, miss. I make house calls. And I'm a well-known specialist in foolishness. Tell you what, I guess the Hunts are asleep, right?"

"Right. You can't come. It's okay." She was feeling better, just talking to him.

"Nonsense. I don't mind missing my well-earned rest.

But wait ten minutes and go out back, will you? By that tree. We can't talk on the terrace. It's right under their bedroom.''

"Okay. Right. I'll be there," she said, suddenly breathless. She went into the bathroom, splashed her face with cold water and toweled it dry. Her eyes would be swollen. Well, it didn't matter. It was pretty dark out there. Bruce wouldn't even notice. She was about to hurry into the hall, but stopped. She couldn't meet him in her nightgown and robe! He'd think she was trying to seduce him again. She rushed to the closet and groped wildly among the clothes there. She grabbed the first things at hand.

It seemed awfully dark and empty at the bottom of the garden. The hammock and the chairs were shadowy white shapes. She stood close to the tree to be in its shadow in case she heard footsteps coming down the nearby alleyway. She heard nothing until the soft scrunch of Bruce's car tires on the driveway. He was so sweet, so kind. Not many men would come out like this in the middle of the night on a silly whim; and that was all it was, a whim. She felt choked with gratitude when she heard the back gate squeak faintly as he came in, then the metallic sound of the latch falling back into place.

"What in God's name are you wearing, Donna?"

"Oh." Bruce was suddenly beside her, peering at her in the darkness. "I...just grabbed these. Just jeans and a sweater and...this...poncho thing."

"You're planning a trip to the Antarctic? A turtleneck and poncho on a night in midsummer? You're mad. Absolutely mad. I've always said so."

"It is too warm!" she said with a sudden sense of discovery, pulling the poncho over her head. After it came the turtleneck sweater.

"Hey. Wait. Not everything. It's not that warm!"

"No. It's all right. I've got a shirt on underneath. See?" She flung the sweater onto a chair on top of the poncho. She stood before him, arms spread wide.

"Well, you sure messed up your hair. And your shirttail is out now. Pull yourself together, woman, and sit down."

She sat on the edge of the hammock, swung up her feet and stretched out, patting the space beside her. Oh, it was nice being with Bruce.

"Come on, there's room for two."

"Not without a bundling board, there isn't," he responded with a laugh, sitting on the edge of the nearest chair and reaching for her hand.

"What in the world is a bundling board?" She slipped her hand confidently into his. It felt so good, so right.

"An early-American device. Made from wood. They were hinged and fitted up into the high headboard of a bed so that they could be let down as a partition."

"You mean a wooden board that pulled down to the mattress?"

"Right down the middle, like a fence. It was for courting couples in winter in New England. The guy could still come to court the girl, but thrifty New Englanders weren't about to burn a fire all night. So the couple got into bed under the covers and pulled the bundling board down between them. That way they could at least talk without freezing to death."

"I don't believe it. You're kidding." Donna had to laugh. She felt better and better. She wanted to ask, "Are we a courting couple?" but didn't. He had been nice enough to come over in the middle of the night. She would keep it light.

"Is this the beginning of a course in American history?" she asked instead. "Well, if we have to do history tonight, it'll be a relief to get something besides Chinese anyhow."

"Makes sense," he said, caressing the back of her hand. "Our Mr. Tsung is Chinese-American, isn't he? So we do both. Two hundred plus years of American history, and a mere seven thousand years of the Chinese variety. Not a bad balance, certainly. Now, miss. Tell me your symptoms." He dropped her hand and sat back in his chair. She was sorry, because now his face was hidden in heavy shadow.

"Oh, I got to thinking about what a dumb stunt I've pulled, and what Mom and Dad would say if they knew, and...I don't know. Thinking how great they've been to me all these years, and how much I owe them..."

"Guilt. Classic case of guilt. I'm a shrink, too, in my spare time. Incidentally, as I know Sara and Evan, I think they would be horrified to hear you say anything at all about 'owing' them."

"Oh, well, yes," she amended hastily. "But I know what I owe, Bruce, and I'm doing a bum job of repaying it. And then there's that Mr. Tsung, all primed for a summit meeting with a prominent San Francisco attorney. Boy, when you tell him the truth it's going to go over like a lead balloon."

"We don't know that, Donna. We just know in very vague, general terms what kind of guy he is. He may surprise us."

"Yes. We may be surprised right out of his office. He can't have somebody arrested for something like this, can he?"

"Of course not, don't be an idiot. The worst he can do is tell us to get lost."

"Oh, how awful. How embarrassing. Bruce, you don't have any idea how much I want to get out of this."

"On the contrary, I have a very good idea. You've been

wiggling on the hook ever since I set up the appointment with him.'' He sounded very matter-of-fact.

''Can't you cancel it? Can't we get out of it? Can't you just call up and say it's a mistake, you wanted some other Mr. Tsung?''

''No. I cannot. We're in this, and we're going to see it through.''

''Oh, Bruce.'' She lifted her arms and covered her face, moving her head from side to side.

''Please, Bruce?''

''No.'' Bruce cleared his throat. ''Donna, you don't know it, but most of the buttons on your blouse are undone.''

''Oh! I'm sorry!'' Her hands flew to the buttons, and she began fumbling at them. ''What must you think?''

''Plenty, love, but not for your ears. It wouldn't be so noticeable, but you're sitting—lying, I mean—right in the middle of a damn moonbeam.''

Donna sat up, too quickly, causing the hammock to rock wildly from side to side. She tried desperately to regain her balance, but Bruce had to leap up and grab her flailing arms to keep her from falling.

''Okay,'' he said, as the hammock settled down. ''Okay, now? You don't know a hell of a lot about using a hammock, do you?''

''Not...not very much.'' She clung to his forearms, unconsciously straining toward him, her face turned up toward his. Silence fell, a silence that was not silence. It was filled with night sounds, the distant guttural croak of a frog in the pond next door, the sound of a cricket clattering in the nearby shrubbery, invisible birds twittering sleepily in the leaves above their heads. *He's going to kiss me,* she thought, almost in wonder. She slid her hands over his shoulders, closing her eyes, waiting. It came with incredible sweetness, his firm lips gentle, tentative, almost hesitant, brushing hers softly again and again. His arms went around her, and she was pulled up against him. He buried his face in her neck.

"Oh, Donna, Donna. What am I going to do with you?" Sighing, Bruce pushed her back down into the hammock, one hand gripping both her wrists and holding them against her chest.

"I didn't do it on purpose," she whispered. "I didn't, really."

"You sound like a little kid."

"I'm not a little kid!" She struggled to rise, but he held her down.

"You could have fooled me, love. That's what gets to me. One minute you're a rational, mature adult, the next minute you're ten years old. It's driving me nuts." Silence fell between them again. "Now I suppose I've made you mad," he added, letting go of her wrists and standing up to look down at her.

"No," she said quietly. "Because what you say is true, I'm afraid. I guess I've still got some growing up to do." Her voice was unsteady.

"Well, hey, that's no crime. It takes a while, you know. I know it. I was the original perpetual juvenile delinquent—but you've heard all that."

"What did you do? How did you get a handle on things? When did you know you'd crossed the line—become an adult? I mean, really an adult?"

"I'm not sure I have," he said slowly. He went down on his knees beside the hammock and sat back on his heels. "I don't think it's a sudden thing, Donna. I think it kind of comes by stages. As we live. As we cope."

"And how did you start going through these…these stages?" She didn't mean to sound so forlorn.

"I can tell you that. I turned the corner when I decided to face up to things. I decided to confront things. It was time to stop ducking problems and meet them head-on."

"I'm going to do that," she said after a moment. "It'll be a start, anyhow. Maybe the start of the beginning of the first stage."

"Who are you going to meet head-on, honey?" he asked gently.

"Mr. Tsung."

"Good girl!" He stood up and brushed the knees of his slacks. "Look, are you okay now? I'd better push off. If Mark or Laura wake up and start wondering what's going on at the bottom of the garden, all hell could break loose."

"We're just talking." She sat up gingerly and swung her legs over the side of the hammock.

"Yeah, but I can just see Mark storming down here, bathrobe flying, to tell me off for compromising little Nell. And Laura, well, I love my cousin, but Laura is sometimes a real mother hen. What's the matter? Are you laughing at me?"

"It's funny."

"Sweetheart, lemme tell you, there is nothing funny about Mark in a rage. I know."

"No. Not Mark. My parents. You didn't know me when I was little. I mean, really little. I was the most miserable kid. I had a single part-time parent. What I wanted most in the world was to have a set—two parents. A mom and a dad. I used to make wishes when I saw a new moon, and on a dozen other things. I wished, and wished, and wished, always for the same thing, and now—"

He caught her meaning immediately. "Now they're all coming true. The answers to all those wishes. You've got sets of parents coming out of the woodwork. You've got Sara and Evan. You've got Laura and Mark. And in a couple of days you may well have the Tsungs." He was laughing, too.

"It'll never end. They'll keep coming and coming and coming. You don't know how many of those wishes I made." They clutched each other, laughing helplessly.

When the laughter was spent, he walked her to the terrace door, his arm around her shoulders, holding her close against his side and waited until she stepped inside and locked the door behind her. Then he made a little Okay sign with his thumb and forefinger, and turned to walk away.

Donna stood just inside the door for a long moment, her heart pounding. He hadn't wanted to let her go. He hadn't wanted to. She knew it. She had seen it in his eyes, felt it in the slow, reluctant way he had released her on the terrace. *Don't fight me, Bruce,* she thought. *Please don't fight me.* But he was fighting her, holding back. He wasn't giving in easily. It was going to take time to destroy his barriers, a lot of time.

She went swiftly and silently to the stairs. "I've *got* time, Bruce. I've got as much time as it takes!"

CHAPTER EIGHT

DONNA PEERED THROUGH one of the panes in the greenhouse door. A hazy film blurred the shapes inside, but she could see the bright blue of Laura's dress moving at the far end of the center aisle.

"You really gonna do it?"

E.J.'s stage whisper made Donna jump, and she glared down into the boy's round golden eyes. He'd sneaked up on her, and he must have felt her nerve failing. "I'm going to do it, E.J., if you get lost—now. If your mother catches sight of you and figures out this wasn't my idea, well…" Donna made a slicing motion across her throat.

"Okay, okay." E.J. retreated, scowling; then he turned and zigzagged, brown legs flashing, through the flowerbeds to the house.

Donna tapped the greenhouse door and turned the handle slowly, gritting her teeth like a latecomer entering church. Once inside, she felt foolish. Laura was a reasonable woman, a good friend, so she wouldn't mind Donna asking if she could take E.J. out.

"Laura," Donna called. Her resolve fled again as the other woman turned clear eyes on her. "Um…it's lovely in here. Smells so good." She sniffed the moist, heady air. "Like a greenhouse…"

While Donna cringed at her own awkwardness, Laura smiled benignly, saying only, "Yes, I love it here, too."

"I was wondering…" Donna began.

Laura carried on as if Donna hadn't spoken. "How are things with you and Bruce? Any more progress with Raymond Tsung?"

The sense of dread that seemed to linger in the pit of Donna's stomach lately rushed upward. "Bruce is making wonderful progress with Raymond Tsung. Any day now I expect to find out what the man eats for breakfast."

Laura looked up sharply. "What's the matter? I thought you had everything under control."

"Well, I don't." Donna spread her hands and sat down with a thud on an upended crate. "Good Lord, Laura, I'm trying not to think about it at all. One day at a time and all that, but I can't remember what a full night's sleep feels like. I've really screwed this up."

"It wasn't such a hot idea," Laura remarked mildly. "But we all do things on the spur of the moment. You'll work it all out—Bruce'll make sure of that. You and Bruce, you spend a lot of time together, but you don't say anything about…well, you know."

Donna knew. She was in limbo with Bruce. He'd done exactly what she'd planned, become very much aware of her as a woman. And the awareness had scared the hell out of him. "I'm miserable, Laura," she said at last. "Absolutely miserable. I love him more and more, and I just feel more helpless."

"Meaning what? The helpless bit, I mean?"

"Well, I think he cares for me." She twisted the delicate emerald ring her parents had given her for her high-school graduation. "But you were right at the beginning when you said he'd been scared to death of getting involved with me. Sometimes I catch him looking at me like I'm a bomb about to explode."

Laura noticed some mud on the toe of one low-heeled white pump, and she moaned. "Look at that. I'm going to have to change shoes." She checked her watch. "And I'm going to be late for lunch. Look, sweetie, hang in there. For what my opinion on romance is worth, I think old impervious Bruce is cracking a little at his well-glued seams. You're getting to him. I probably should be discouraging this. In fact, I know I should. I'm a disgrace. But I believe in love, real, honest-to-goodness, head-over-heels love, and you and Bruce might just have the makings of some of that. I know how I felt with Mark. Nothing would have stopped me wanting him once I..." She paled and closed her mouth firmly.

I know how I felt. Laura had used the past tense. A deep sadness and confusion almost overwhelmed Donna. Yet Mark and Laura did still love each other very much; Donna's every instinct told her that they did. But something was steadily eroding the foundation of that love, and if they didn't get help, their world would crumble, or simply freeze into separate compartments under one roof, revolving around each other but never touching.

"When does Raymond Tsung get back?" Laura asked. She scraped her shoes on the metal rack near the door.

"In a couple of weeks," Donna replied. "Bruce has an interview all set up. I'm terrified."

Laura smoothed Donna's hair. "Don't be. Bruce can be Mr. Diplomacy when he needs to be. You should see him in court."

Donna instantly wished she could do just that. She wished she were with him right now.

"Come on." Laura waved Donna to her feet. "I'd better go see what condition E.J.'s in."

There was no mention of Mark, who was working at home today. "Laura, I was wondering...I was wondering...would you teach me about plants sometime? The way you can make things grow fascinates me. It must be a great hobby." She couldn't chicken out now. E.J. was counting on her.

Laura, dressed in an expensive linen dress and jacket, wiped a muddy hand across her forehead, then pulled the hand away and frowned. "Damn. Now I'll have to redo my makeup. Why did I agree to go to one of Dollie's never-ending fund-raisers?"

"What's this one for?" Donna asked conversationally. She pulled the hem of her T-shirt lower over her jeans, grateful she didn't have Laura's busy social schedule.

"I can't remember." Laura found a rag and wiped her hands. "Can you believe that? I give up a perfectly wonderful afternoon when I could be getting some good work done out here, and I don't know why. Dollie Winthrop never stays interested in anything long enough for me to know what her pet project of the moment is. I'd better look at my appointment book or I'll be asking her how she's doing with preserving bay squid when she's already moved on to motivational programs for privileged kids."

Donna sucked in her lower lip to suppress a smile. "You could just not go."

"I paid my five hundred dollars a plate for something-or-other salad, and I'd better show up or there'll be an empty space at the table with my name in front of it."

"I bet they won't mind as long as they've got the money," Donna said. She wished Laura were less preoccupied—and happier. Her blue eyes were so often distant and unfocused, and the corners of her beautiful mouth turned down. Donna remembered her mission. "I shouldn't have thought a thing like this luncheon would be a place to take E.J. Why not leave him with me?"

Laura paused, the rag between her hands. "E.J. likes to go places with me. Dollie's grandchildren will be around somewhere; he'll be in the game room with them."

"They're all teenagers." Donna shifted awkwardly, kicking clods of earth beneath a bench loaded with flats of cuttings. "I don't suppose they're too thrilled with playing nanny to a six-year-old, and since I've got a day off work, I'd like to have him with me. I thought we'd go to the park and try out that baseball I bought him."

"I meant to talk to you about that," Laura said. Donna saw the muscles in her cheeks tighten. "Those balls are so hard. If he got hit on the head he could get a bad concussion...or worse. I really think he's too young for baseball yet. Anyway, Dollie's expecting me to bring him." She pressed the rag down on a bench in a tight wad and examined her nails. "I'll have to redo these as well." She looked up abruptly. "Is E.J. dressed properly, do you know? I asked Mark to remind him, but if I know Mark, he forgot." A corner of her mouth twitched.

Donna's stomach squeezed together. What was wrong here? What was happening between Mark and Laura? On the surface they were polite. There'd never been any open hostility that she'd heard. But the undercurrent of tension was as tight as a bowstring.

Before she could press her case, Laura walked briskly out of the greenhouse, and Donna had to hurry to keep up. Mark was sitting at the kitchen table, reading a newspaper and drinking coffee. E.J., still in his tank top and frayed cutoffs, his bare feet swinging, sat close to his father with his nose almost touching the cartoon page in front of him.

Mark glanced up as the sliding door scraped open. He smiled at Laura. "Hi, hon. How does your garden grow?"

"Whew." Laura headed for the sink. "Pretty good this year. But it's hot out there."

"You're dressed too warmly," Mark responded. He got up and went to put an arm around Laura's shoulders. "Why are you wearing a dress—and a jacket, for Pete's sake—to garden in, love? Go change. We could take an ice chest with cold drinks and buy fried chicken for lunch—dinner too, if everyone wants. Or we could stop for pizza somewhere later. How does that sound?''

Water splashed loudly from the faucet into the sink. Without turning off the faucet, Laura shrugged free of Mark's arm and stared up at him. ''What are you talking about?''

He glanced at Donna, faint color sweeping over his high cheekbones. ''I thought it might be nice if we took a day off, completely off. You and I could go to the park with Donna and E.J. and play baseball.'' He grinned tentatively. ''You're the star athlete around here. You'll show us all up, but we can take it.''

''Mark, I told you this morning I had to go to lunch at Dollie Winthrop's. And I asked you, not more than an hour ago, if you'd make sure E.J. changed.'' She shot an exasperated look at the top of her son's lowered head. ''I guess you didn't think it was important, since it was something I asked you to do. I should have asked Mrs. Cooper—''

''Laura!''

Mark's voice, raised as she'd never heard it raised before, shook Donna. She wished she could disappear.

''Don't shout at me, Mark,'' Laura said, and her voice shook. ''Please don't shout.''

''I'm not.'' He shook his head. The handsome lines of his face were deepened by more than fatigue, Donna realized. Mark Hunt was a sad man—a disappointed man? ''I'm not shouting,'' he continued. ''I'm sorry, Laura. I thought since Donna and E.J. were going to the park to play ball, that you and I could go too. We don't do enough of those things anymore.''

''Whose fault is that?'' Laura snapped. She pressed a

hand over her mouth, and Donna saw tears glistening in her eyes.

"Mine, I guess. Is that what you're saying? Well, fine. Go to lunch, if it's so damned important. I thought you couldn't stand Dollie Winthrop and her causes."

"And I thought I was helping you by doing the things everyone else's wife does."

Mark closed his eyes for an instant, then pulled her rigid body into his arms. "You are, sweetheart, you are. I'm sorry. I guess I just got the wrong impression about what you wanted to do." He didn't look at E.J., who clearly longed to be somewhere else.

Laura did look at the boy. "E.J., you know you're coming with me. I suppose you sent Donna to persuade me to get you out of it, and assumed I'd say yes. Go and change."

E.J. left the room without a word.

"Laura, honey," Mark said quietly, pushing back the cloud of dark hair from her face. "Don't you think E.J. would be better off at the park? Donna will take good care of him."

Tears slid silently down Laura's cheeks, and she pulled away from Mark. She turned to Donna. "Sorry about this, Donna. Even happy families have their moments, huh? I bet your mom and dad blow up from time to time. I do have to take E.J. with me. Dollie expects him, and... and...I do have to take him."

"Okay," Donna said. "I understand. I shouldn't have suggested going to the park."

Mark reached out to brush the tears from Laura's face, and then circled her neck lightly. "You're right. Dollie will be disappointed if you don't take E.J. I was just being selfish. I wanted my family to myself for a while. It's been a long time since we did anything just by ourselves." He smiled at Donna. "And Donna counts as a borrowed member of my family, right, Donna?"

"Yep," she agreed, too emphatically.

"Go on, then," Mark told Laura. He kissed her mouth lingeringly, looked into her eyes and stepped back. "Give my best to Dollie and the rest of them. Try not to volunteer for any more projects."

"I won't," Laura said. "I promise." She almost stumbled as she left the kitchen, but hurried on.

Mark stared silently out the window for a long time while Donna tried to decide what to do, what to say.

"Laura worries about E.J.," he said distantly. "She's a good mother, the best."

"Yes, she is," Donna said quickly. "I'm sorry I caused a flap."

Mark laughed. "E.J. caused the flap. The little stinker. He thought he could hedge his bet by making me behave as if the arrangements were all made, only his plot backfired."

"He's a good little boy."

Mark looked at Donna over his shoulder. "Yes, he's a good boy." He laughed again, bitterly this time, his amber eyes clouding. "We're all good, aren't we?"

"THESE ARE THE BOOKS Sam promised me—Sam Chong. This one discusses Chinese territorial adventures since 2,000 B.C. There are a lot of very interesting maps and charts showing how the country changed over the centuries as far as its sphere of influence went. And it gives some accurate material about government structure, the philosophy of the people, eras of discontent, and on and on. It's something."

"Sounds like it, Bruce."

"You'll find Chinese economics and government fascinating."

Bring back the rockets, Donna thought, *give me the exciting stuff.* Four thousand years of government and economics should be enough to kill any interest she'd acquired in her father's homeland. This hadn't been a sparkling day. First there'd been the disturbing events of the morning at the Hunts', followed by a depressing afternoon in her room—the only place she'd felt comfortable—while Mark holed up in his library. Now the time she'd looked forward to spending with Bruce was turning into yet another of his fact-feeding sessions.

"Are you listening to me?"

Donna looked up guiltily. "Yes. Yes. I was just looking at the cover of this book. The countryside looks beautiful."

He narrowed his eyes at the tone of her voice, and made a tutting sound of disapproval. "That's Bavaria. It's mine. Shove it over there and concentrate."

She put the book on the rug beside her and pressed her hands between her knees. "When's the last time you had your eyes checked?"

Bruce raised his head and squinted at her. "What?"

"When's the last time you got your eyes checked? You squint and peer all the time."

He sighed, and flopped against the couch. "Can't you concentrate for just a little while? I don't remember when I last saw someone about my eyes. I don't spend a lot of time worrying about any aspect of my health. I do have a pair of reading glasses around here somewhere, but I never remember to use them."

Donna jumped to her feet. "That's irresponsible, Bruce. If you need glasses, you need them. It isn't wimpy to take care of your health. Lots of people need glasses, so they simply use the things. Big deal. Eyes deteriorate some-times.''

"Mmm," he agreed, smiling faintly. "Particularly as one gets older, my dear.''

"You're not…oh, Bruce, you deliberately say things like that just to goad me. You can be two years old and need specs.''

"Maybe I should wear them—all the time. I think there's an old saying, 'Men don't make passes at girls who wear glasses'?''

Donna couldn't help laughing. He looked so mischie-vous, and so pleased with himself. "And you think it might work the other way around and save you from me?''

He shrugged.

"Let's find the glasses and give it a try.''

Bruce straightened hastily. "I don't think so. China has always had a monumental problem feeding its people. I told Sam we needed something concise; a quickie course in foodstuffs, supply, agricultural methods…you know what I'm talking about.''

"Bruce, am I going to have to study how my ancestors planted crops?''

"Good grief." He expelled a long breath. "You're de-veloping the worst possible attitude toward all this. I thought you might be getting interested. You should want to know everything about where your father came from and what his people were like. This total disinterest of yours is unnatural.''

"Says you. What if I've discovered I definitely gravitate more toward the Caucasian part of me? I was born here, my biological mother was Caucasian, and I grew up as part of a Caucasian family. I'm still part of a Caucasian family, and I intend to…'' She stopped herself from adding that she intended to marry a Caucasian, but the glint in

Bruce's eye let her know that he'd guessed what her next statement would have been.

"You could just as well have had a Chinese mother and a Caucasian father, Donna. Everything could have been reversed. Then it would have been normal for you to want to know about the white part of you. You're being deliberately difficult." The room was hot. He stood up and took off the tie and the jacket of the suit he'd been wearing when he'd picked her up on his way home.

Donna watched with dreamy concentration as he rolled his sleeves back over his muscular forearms. Sun-bleached hairs glinted along the moving tendons in the backs of his hands and on his arms. He looked marvelous in his suits—indolent, carelessly elegant—but she preferred him in shorts and an old T-shirt. He had the kind of legs that should always be seen...long, well-shaped, narrow at the ankles, and his feet.... She picked at the seam in her jeans. Did most women get turned on by a man's ankles and feet? Amy Dross, who lived next door to their old house in Vancouver, would have said something original, like, "Kinky, Donna." But Amy had never been in love, really in love. The overgrown basketball player she'd been seeing was a passing interest; even Amy said so. Donna expelled a huge sigh. The boys in school had never interested her: she recalled awkward kissing, pawing that always went further than she wanted it to go. Boring.

"Hey. Hi. Come back, please."

Bruce's voice penetrated her thoughts, but distantly. Donna smiled up into his face. His face was so perfectly made. The way his eyebrows stretched straight above his eyes and winged upward slightly at the ends, the very regular bridge of his nose and his clearly defined nostrils, his clean-cut jaw, shadowed by beard now, the shallow cleft in his chin, and his mouth.... Bruce had the kind of mouth movie stars had, wide, turned up at the corners, with a fuller lower lip.... She sighed again.

"You understand about the Pacific rim, Donna?"

"Mmm? No."

"The trading arena created by the U.S. and the Pacific— China, Japan and so on. It's thought that China could be our greatest trading partner someday."

He was really serious about all this. One way or the other, he was going to pound some of this information into her skull. "That's interesting, Bruce," she said, crossing her legs and concentrating on his eyes—his very blue eyes.

"It is. Very. We're living in interesting times. And this trading business is one of the reasons your father's likely to become even more successful than he already is."

Donna slumped. *Raymond Tsung again.* She leaned forward and rested her chin on her hands.

"Look, Donna, you're making too much of this." Hitching up the knees of his pants, Bruce dropped his loose-limbed body to the rug beside her. "I'm not asking you to become Princess Tsung complete with bound feet. I just don't want you to come off as nothing but a brainless All-Canadian cheerleader."

She bristled. "I'm not brainless."

"I know, I know." He looped an arm around her shoulders. "That didn't come out right. What I meant was, I want to feel proud of you and I want him to be proud of you, even if you aren't going to be more than passing acquaintances. Possibly only related ships that pass in the night. Is that wish so wrong?"

Donna leaned against his chest and closed her eyes. He was finally loosening up with her. And being with him felt so good, so right. "It's not wrong, Bruce. I'll do whatever you want me to do."

"Terrific." He leaped up and hauled her to her feet. "I

want you to take all these back to Mark and Laura's.'' He gathered the books under one arm and, his other arm around Donna's waist, strode into the hall and out the open front door. ''I've got an appointment, so I can't spend any more time with you this evening. I'll run you home. Spend every spare minute seeing what you can assimilate, and we'll have another summit meeting in a day or two.''

They reached his car, and he let her go while he opened the passenger door and tossed the books behind the seat. She climbed in, feeling vaguely numb.

Bruce drove fast enough to make Donna cling to the window rim, and squealed into the circular driveway at the Hunts'. When they stood by the steps, he presented her with the books, a charmingly satisfied grin on his face.

''That should keep you going for a while,'' he said, glancing up at the house, clearly anxious to be gone. Donna had wanted to talk to him about Mark and Laura, but he hadn't given her a chance.

''Anything wrong, Donna?''

What sort of appointment could he have at eight in the evening? she wondered. ''Why would anything be wrong? I've got to shut myself up with piles of dusty facts I don't want to know. Everything's wonderful.''

''Oh, Donna.'' He gripped her shoulders and rested his forehead on hers. ''I don't want to harp on this, love, but you did start something, and now we simply have to finish it. I'm sorry you aren't more interested. I'll tell you what. How about having our little cruise on the bay on Saturday? We could relax and go over some of this in comfortable surroundings. I think you need to unwind.''

She had to close out the clean, faintly lime smell of him, and the feeling of his hair on her brow. Saturday on the bay, with Bruce, in that beautiful boat she'd heard about but had never seen. Saturday. Less than two days away.

"Don't you like the idea? You said you wanted to go out on the boat."

"What time should I be ready?"

"That's my girl." Bruce threw back his head and laughed, showing off perfect white teeth. "I'll call you tomorrow, or talk to you at the office. Plan on leaving fairly early in the morning, though. Do you like to watch the sun come up?"

Watching the sun come up with Bruce appealed more to Donna at this moment than anything had ever appealed to her before. "Yes, I do," she replied demurely. He was already climbing into the car. "I'll be on this spot at four on Saturday morning."

Bruce grimaced, and yelled over the sound of the engine: "Make it four-thirty, sweetie. Some of us still need our beauty sleep. See you on Saturday."

Donna opened her mouth to shout back, but the car was already in motion. "Saturday," she murmured against the pile of books in her arms, and hopped from one foot to the other when gravel spewed from Bruce's tires onto her sandaled feet.

CHAPTER NINE

BRUCE HIT A LEVER on one side of the control panel and
Donna heard a rumbling, bumping noise at the stern. She
leaned over the cockpit rail and watched a chain creep
steadily through a brass-rimmed opening. The anchor sank
into the clear waters of San Francisco Bay. "Jeez. Everything on this boat's automatic. I bet even I could run it
single-handed."

Bruce gave her a withering glance. "I told you this tub
wasn't for the purist. As far as I'm concerned, a pleasure
craft means just that—a craft designed for pleasure, not
something to sweat over." He cut the engines and added,
"I can't believe how few people are out this morning."
He shaded his eyes and looked directly into the sun.

"They'll catch up with us later," Donna remarked, considering, then discarding, the idea of taking off the terry
cloth wrap she wore over her swimsuit. "It's still a bit
early for mere mortals."

"And we aren't mere mortals?" He did something to
fix the wheel and dragged a deck chair farther aft.

Donna positioned another chair beside Bruce's. "We are
definitely most unusual. We know what's worth effort, and
that sunrise was worth getting up in the middle of the night
for." She sat down, but he was still checking the sky and
the sea and the steadily rising sun, as if making sure he'd
selected the best spot to heave to.

"I'd have to agree with you there." He flopped down,

slid forward, and stretched out his long legs. "All that purple and gray and gold."

"In stripes," Donna added.

"The water was fantastic too, wasn't it?"

"Yep. Mauve silk and steel. Fantastic."

"You win."

Donna closed her left eye and looked at Bruce with the other. "Win what?"

"The description contest. You're better at it. Silk, steel. I wouldn't have thought of those." He tilted his floppy white bucket hat over his eyes and crossed his arms.

"You aren't going to sleep, are you?" Donna asked.

"Mmm. Just a nap. Got to make up for last night. You nap, too."

Donna opened her mouth to say she didn't want to nap. Instead, she smiled and rested her cheek on the back of her chair. Bruce's tanned chest, most of it exposed beneath the thin cotton shirt he hadn't buttoned, already rose and fell steadily. He'd fallen asleep. Just like that. Donna got up and prowled the cockpit of the fifty-foot motor-sailer. A lazy man's toy, Bruce had called it while they were driving to the marina. A vessel guaranteed to be sneered at by any self-respecting sailing purist. Donna climbed halfway up the ladder from the cockpit to the main deck, and studied the boat's elegant lines. The sails were furled, and the mast soared cleanly into a steadily brightening sky. Oak and brass gleamed. *Lake Lady* might be a lazy man's toy, but she was also very beautiful, and worth a fortune, Donna guessed.

She returned to the cockpit, and found a spot where she could rest her elbows on the rail and face Bruce. He sighed and crossed one ankle over the other. This was the way he should always look, she thought, relaxed, young. Today he'd "dressed up" he said, which meant that a khaki shirt and shorts had taken the place of the customary T-shirt and cutoffs. Donna crossed her own arms and narrowed her eyes. He was too good-looking to be on the loose, and too appealing. She wished he'd wake up. She wanted to talk to him, and look at him…and swim…and look at him. Well, she could look at him, anyway.

"Is my fly unzipped or something?"

Donna jumped, and felt her cheeks flame. "I wasn't…" *Damn him.* He hadn't been asleep at all!

"A figure of speech, my love." Bruce pushed back his hat and grinned innocently at her. "I just meant you were staring as if there was something wrong with me."

"There's nothing wrong with you, except your foul sense of humor." She turned to lean on the rail and stared back toward the marina, a distant green strip flanked by pale stucco houses and apartment buildings.

She heard the deck chair creak. "I didn't mean to embarrass you," Bruce said, and he wrapped his arms around her shoulders and pulled her back against his chest. "But you were staring at me pretty hard, young lady. And it wasn't the stare of a kid at a surrogate uncle, was it?"

Donna's heart beat hard. "We already know you passed the surrogate-uncle stage with me a long time ago, Bruce."

His chin rested on top of her head. She wished she'd taken off her robe; she wanted to feel his naked skin on hers.

He took a deep, ragged breath that moved her hair. He smelled wonderful, warm and clean. The salty air whipped their clothes.

"I wish I didn't like holding you, Donna."

She slid her hands over his forearms, afraid he'd let her go. "There's nothing wrong with one human being liking to hold another. It's healthy."

He hummed a tune she didn't recognize, his throat vibrating at the back of her head, and rocked her more firmly against him. They were becoming closer; despite Bruce's reservations, the magic she'd known existed was working.

"This is just about my favorite spot in the world," Bruce said. "I've loved the water and boats as long as I can remember. When I was a boy, my father used to bring me out here to fish."

"Your father was George Fenton."

"Yes. And my mother's name was Rhea. Everyone saw her as an iron lady, and she *was* tough—but she could be a marshmallow."

Donna kissed a flexed muscle in his arm. "You loved your parents. Laura lived with you, too, didn't she?"

Bruce ran a thumb along her jaw. "Yes. I didn't appreciate her then. She must have been a saint to put up with me. I was a horror, but she was forever covering up for me with the folks."

"What happened to her own parents?"

Bruce became still. "I'm not sure I should..." He hesitated, then resumed his swaying motion. "Laura would tell you herself if you asked. Her mother was my father's sister, a bit flighty, my mother always said—whatever that meant in those days. Anyway, Laura lived with us from the time she was a baby. Actually, she was already with my parents when I was born. Later we heard her mother had died. I don't know anything about her father."

"I see." Donna sank into deep thought. Laura was gentle, reflective. She'd always been kind and understanding toward Donna. Maybe her own precarious childhood was the reason. She knew what it was like to feel tolerated and unsure, the way Donna had before Sara and Evan had adopted her.

"I guess you would relate well to one another," Bruce

said after a while. "I never thought about it, but you and Laura have quite a bit in common."

Donna thought about Laura and Mark and the charged atmosphere pervading their home. Now didn't seem the appropriate time to discuss the subject with Bruce. "Laura lived in Seattle while she ran her clown troupe, didn't she?"

"Yes." Bruce unfolded his arms and rested his hands lightly on Donna's shoulders. "That's where she and your dad met. But you already knew that."

"Then I have Laura to thank for my meeting you." She craned her neck and smiled up at him. But Bruce wasn't smiling.

"Laura had a rough time for a few years."

The burgeoning sun lost some of its tender warmth. "Nobody ever explained exactly why, Bruce."

"It's not very pretty. Mark's father walked under the wheels of a car Laura was driving. It was early in the morning after her high-school prom, and her date was too drunk to drive."

Donna shuddered. "Oh, how awful."

"She was delivering papers to the office, papers she should have taken to the Hunts—Bill Hunt—the night before, only she forgot." He sighed, and rubbed his face. "Anyway. It was raining heavily, Laura may have been driving a little too fast, and she was tired, and Bill didn't look where he was going before he barged off the curb. Then it was all over, and by the time Mark had finished hounding Laura, she went to live in Seattle. I didn't see her for six years, until my father died and left his share of Fenton and Hunt to Laura and me jointly. I'm glad he did. It brought us all back together."

"Maybe that's what he intended."

"I'm sure he did. Wherever he is now, he's got to be

smiling. His wayward boy ended up in the firm after all, and Mark and Laura are happily married—perfect.''

''I don't like thinking what it must have been like for poor Laura. She's so gentle, and she loves Mark so much.'' Donna ducked around Bruce and went to the port rail. Everything wasn't as perfect with Mark and Laura as Bruce thought, but she wasn't about to ruin the moment. ''That's Tiburon and Belvedere over there, right? The houses hanging onto the hillside?''

''You've got it,'' Bruce responded. ''And Sausalito. You're becoming quite the informed native, Donna. We'll have to drive up around there some day. I've always had a thing for all those little lagoons in the Belvedere area. If I wasn't already entrenched in Pacific Heights, I might consider moving to Belvedere.''

Donna felt an internal pressure, and tried to stifle her longing. The mood was right, and the surroundings, yet she didn't know what she should or shouldn't say to Bruce about their situation. ''I'm going for a swim,'' she announced, slipping off her blue robe. She avoided Bruce's eyes, knowing well that her white suit did wonderful things for her slender, always-golden body.

His hand on her wrist surprised her. He held fast. ''It's cold as hell in there. I thought you were only going to sun yourself. No one swims in the bay.''

She stared into his eyes, then at his mouth, and the sharp movement in his throat. ''Of course they swim. It's perfect. Clear.''

''It's freezing, I tell you. The Japanese currents don't come up this far, and the water's rarely even slightly warm.''

''It'll be warm as soon as I'm in.'' She pulled free, clambered up to balance herself on the side, and made a clean dive. She rose to the surface, breathless, blinking, slicking back her hair while she shivered. Bruce had been right. The water was icy.

"You nut!" Bruce leaned far out, hatless now, his blond hair blowing this way and that. "Now do you believe me?"

The shock of hitting the water was already fading, and Donna smiled. "It's wonderful. You don't know what you're missing." She struck out in an easy freestyle, putting some distance between herself and the boat.

"Come back," Bruce hollered. "You'll cramp up or something. Women!"

Donna heard a splash and rolled onto her back in time to see circles spreading on the surface. Seconds later, Bruce's head popped up, his mouth open to let out an anguished howl. She grinned and approached him, side-stroking lazily.

"Argh," Bruce wailed, "This is awful, Donna. That little run the other night probably took ten years off my life. This'll finish me. I'm going to have cardiac arrest."

"Give yourself a minute or two to adjust," she shouted. "You'll love it. And quit making so much noise, or they'll call out the coast guard."

He snorted, and dived again. Donna paddled in place, smacking water into sheets of sun-dyed drops. She turned her face up to the sun. The next instant she was sinking, dragged down by iron hands on her ankles. Bubbles rushed upward around her head, sweeping into her nose and mouth and ears, and she flailed until strong arms surrounded her and carried her back to the surface.

Bruce, sunlight glittering on his wet hair and lashes and the streaming rivulets on his face and shoulders, held her tight and grinned delightedly. Donna scrubbed at her stinging eyes, choked, and spat brine. Then she pummeled his shoulders. "You lousy rat," she sputtered. "Why'd you feel you had..." She coughed again. "You didn't have to get even. I never asked you to swim with me."

"No, you didn't. Got carried away, I guess, and in my best shorts, too. It's a good thing I've got a spare pair aboard."

His grip hadn't loosened. They bobbed and circled slowly. Donna pushed back her hair, then Bruce's. His smile slowly faded.

"It isn't so cold when you've been in a while, is it?" Donna said, swallowing. He'd moved a hand to her waist. Their bodies were pressed together, and she felt sharp little thrusts of heat in her breasts and belly and thighs. Bruce's hand was spread wide over her bottom now.

"I've never seen another face like yours, Donna," Bruce murmured. "Do you know, I can't sleep sometimes, and I think it could be because of your wonderful face."

She couldn't look away from his eyes. "I've been seeing yours in my sleep for longer than I want to admit."

"This isn't right."

"Why?"

"It...isn't." Bruce kissed her lips softly. Donna tasted salt and closed her eyes, going limp in his embrace. There was something she wanted to tell him.... Then his tongue opened her mouth and she looked at him, startled. She'd been kissed before, they'd kissed before, but not like this. Bruce moved his mouth wildly over hers, and she wound her fingers in his hair.

She gripped his legs between her own and instantly felt the effect she was having on him. When she slid her hands around his waist, he pulled away and put several feet of water between them.

Humiliation sickened her. He thought she was promiscuous, that she was deliberately trying to trick him into seducing her.

"Donna," Bruce said indistinctly.

She couldn't answer.

He swam close enough to reach for and hold her hands. "You never asked why I called the boat *Lake Lady*."

She shook her head.

"Didn't you ever wonder, since she's oceangoing and moored in a bay?"

"I guess I did."

"After our wedding, Anne and I honeymooned on the lakes in northern Italy."

Donna's stomach dropped. "I think I heard that."

"I bought the boat after we got back, when I still thought of Anne as my lake lady. She liked the name. I really loved her, Donna—or I thought I did. I wasn't very mature in some ways. The failure of the marriage wasn't all her fault."

"Takes two, huh? They always say that." Her legs were numb now.

"I'm making you uncomfortable."

She wanted to agree. Instead, she said, "I'd like to talk about the things that matter to you. I want to understand."

"Let's go back aboard. I don't trust myself in this water with you, and I need a clear head."

They boarded by the fixed ladder to the cockpit. Donna toweled off, rubbing harder than necessary, concentrating on the sensation of the rough fabric on her skin. She put her robe back on over her wet suit, and found a brush and comb. Bruce had climbed aloft, saying he wanted to change, and by the time she'd wrestled the tangles from her hair, he'd returned in dry shorts and slipped his bare feet back into tennis shoes.

"You didn't comb your hair," Donna remarked when he'd settled in his deck chair. She leaned over him and ran her own comb through his hair. She half expected him to stop her. Instead, he held her waist tightly and let her finish. For a few seconds, she looked down on the top of his head, at his broad, deeply tanned shoulders, and wished there were no impediments to their loving each other. "There. Done." She bent swiftly to kiss his neck, then retreated to her own chair.

A speedboat roared by, leaving *Lake Lady* rocking in its wake. More and more sails dotted the bay. The early-morning peace was gone, but Donna had no desire to leave.

Bruce watched her through half-closed lids. He was going to tell her some truths he hadn't confronted himself until today. They'd been there, carefully guarded deep inside him, and now he had to drag them out. In those few minutes with her, in the water, he'd come face-to-face with just how powerful his feelings for Donna were. He couldn't allow those feelings to get out of hand, not without a lot of thought, and not without knowing that he could be what she needed him to be.

Where did a thirty-one-year-old man start when he hoped to explain to a nineteen-year-old woman why he thought they shouldn't have a relationship? With the obvious? "I'm too old for you, Donna." As soon as he'd said it, he knew the argument didn't hold up.

"No, you're not, Bruce. Age is relative, we all know that, and it doesn't have anything to do with what we feel for each other."

Her hair was slicked tight to her head and formed a V between her shoulder blades. Her face glowed, clean and devoid of makeup. Thick lashes made her dark eyes even more unreadable. Bruce glanced down at her robe, but saw in his mind her spectacular body in the sleek one-piece swimsuit. He looked away.

"Tell me why you think you contributed to your divorce, Bruce. That's what you were going to do."

"I'm not sure I can, now. Anne left, and everyone said she was too immature, and I agreed. I never explored what happened very deeply. It was easier that way. But I was deluding myself. I'm not sorry the marriage didn't work out, but I haven't been honest about all the reasons it didn't. You can't go on until you make peace with what's gone before, Donna. Do you know what I mean?"

"I think so."

"You'll understand what I'm saying if you try. I'm saying there's a lot about some of the things I've done and the way I've done them that I haven't looked at objectively."

"Do we have to analyze everything we do? I don't think so." She leaned toward him, then gripped his knee. "Isn't it okay to let go of what we can't change and just carry on?"

He covered her hand. She made life sound so simple, but he supposed life had seemed simple to him at nineteen, too. "Some of what we do can be forgotten, Donna. I've forgotten more than I remember. I don't give a damn about hiring cult members to make health-food casseroles, or that whole episode. I was young and stupid, and I did stupid things. But I wasn't so young when I married. I was twenty-eight, and I still did stupid things."

Donna turned her palm to twine their fingers together. "Laura said Anne was a spoiled kid who took you for a ride."

Bruce felt old and tired. "Laura said, Mark said, like I told you—everyone said. But I knew Anne was young, and I don't mean in years, although she was…about the same age as you are now." He looked at her sharply and bit his lip. She'd closed her eyes. "Sweetheart, she was young in every way, but she was lovely, and I wanted her. I never once stopped to think that I was marrying a beautiful woman only because she turned me on physically, and because she was the kind of decorative addition to my possessions that I'd always dreamed of having around permanently. Do you hear what I'm saying?'' He tightened his grip until she looked at him. ''I'm telling you that at twenty-eight, only three years ago, I had never really looked at what it meant to truly love another human being—or at the truth that to make a relationship work there must be friendship and interests and philosophy in common. I hadn't considered that there had to be more to marriage than a fantastic body ready and willing in bed at night, and a woman on your arm that every other man would wish were his.''

Donna wetted her lips. When she raised her eyes to his, he realized she was close to tears. He was laying too much on her, he thought.

''Nobody starts off in marriage with all the problems ironed out,'' she said slowly. ''I always thought that you were supposed to spend a marriage getting to know each other. When there's nothing else to learn, that's got to be dull. Even when you've been together for years, there has to be some little surprise that keeps cropping up. If Anne had stuck around, you'd have learned the other elements you needed to make your marriage whole. You're blaming yourself because it didn't work, when it wasn't your fault.''

''It wasn't all my fault.'' As he said the words, Bruce wanted to believe them and forget the rest. But he couldn't. ''I didn't help her to grow. When she said she was bored, I bought her another diamond, or took her on a trip. I treated her like a pretty, empty-headed child I could placate with presents. And for a while it worked—until someone with more expensive presents and a more exciting life-style came along. She's somewhere in Europe now, probably still accepting some bauble every time she gets depressed.''

''And that's your fault?'' Donna asked, shaking her head. ''I guess I don't understand.''

''I said what happened wasn't all my fault. But if I'd thought more, earlier, I probably wouldn't have married her, or at least I'd have waited until we were both at a point where we were ready to work on a worthwhile marriage. And even after I'd made the first mistake and gone through with the white-lace-and-rice bit, I could have taken a longer look at what was wrong—what was missing—and tried to do something about it.''

''Okay, okay.'' Donna stood up and bent over him. ''So you've come to some valid conclusions. And you didn't know them then, when they could have made a difference in your relationship with Anne. But you obviously know them now. It's time to move on, Bruce. Time to stop blaming yourself for what you can't change.''

He itched to take her in his arms, to kiss her wonderful, serious eyes, her lovely mouth. ''You're partly right, Donna,'' he said carefully. ''Only, before I get into another supposedly forever situation, I've got to be sure it's with the right person. I'm going to be damned certain the next—the only other woman I ever intend to marry—is right for me and that I'm right for her. We're going to like each other, even when she has a headache four nights in a row—or I do. I'm going to love her as much with crow's feet as I did when she didn't have a line on her anywhere. And she's going to like and love me, as well as want my money—for good. This woman and I are going to be dotty over each other's minds.''

''And you don't think I can be that woman?'' Donna

had turned away, and he hardly heard what she said. "I've still got a long way to go, haven't I?"

He buried his face in his hands. He *wanted* her to be the right one, dammit, for both their sakes.

"You were probably right when you said I should do what my parents want and go to school in the fall. The trouble is, I do love you, Bruce, and that isn't going to change. And even though part of my mind tells me that I'm not as grown up as I need to be, the other part says I'm as old as time in some ways. I don't think I could have any stronger feelings than I do."

"I know how you feel. I think I feel it too. But I think you may have some maturing to do before you can honestly be sure what you want in…in a husband." He inhaled deeply. "And I don't know how long that's going to take, any more than you do."

Donna sat on the deck and leaned against his legs. She rested her head on his knees and stared at the bright sky. "I wish you didn't make so much sense, but you do. Bruce, if I have to examine my brain under a microscope, I will, but I know what I'm going to find. Today, tomorrow—ten or twenty years from now, I'll still want to be your wife."

He put his hand on her shoulder beneath the terry robe. "I'm going to do some of that examining myself. But I do know I'm not ready for another commitment yet. Right here, like this—the sun, the water, you, exactly as you are—everything feels right, and I want it to be. But I know I'm still not ready for another marriage."

CHAPTER TEN

DONNA LOVED DRIVING alone in San Francisco, and Laura was generous about lending her small BMW when she wasn't using it. Driving by herself had always given Donna a feeling of freedom, but San Francisco's hills added the sensation of taking off into space as she topped the crest of each hill. She had her favorites. Bruce had introduced her to the downward sweep of California Street as it approached Grant Avenue in Chinatown. If the signals were with you, you could go down, down, down for blocks before coming to a dead stop at Grant to let a flood of pedestrians cross.

And there was a block on Powell street going toward Market so steep that she had once seen a woman in very high heels turn around and walk down backwards to keep from toppling over. But her favorite was the block on Filbert so perpendicular that the sidewalks alongside were in steps. She might detour over to Filbert now, she thought. There was plenty of time. She knew Bruce wouldn't get home until about seven.

She was dressed in a new sweat suit, teal blue with white striping down the pant legs. She wasn't about to wear the same mottled gray outfit Bruce had seen her in the last time they ran. She was sure she could persuade him to go with her again tonight. She'd worked overtime, typing to help out because they were shorthanded due to vacations. She felt tense. She needed a good run. She always felt marvelous after running. There was something about a good run that left her relaxed and exhilarated at the same time. She must try to get Bruce involved in a fitness program on a regular basis.

When she'd mentioned it before leaving the Hunts', Laura had burst out laughing. "Forget it, Donna," she'd advised. "Bruce is blessed with good health—through no effort of his own. He's far too lazy to deliberately move a muscle he doesn't have to."

"Well, he goes sailing," she had said in Bruce's defence.

"Sailing. You know perfectly well all he does is push buttons. That boat does all the work. You might as well give up, Donna. He wouldn't bother to learn a new sport. The only reason he plays tennis sometimes is because we took lessons together when we were growing up, and he was too competitive to let me beat him at anything."

"Tennis, huh? I play tennis. We could play together."

"Like once every six months? That's Bruce's nod to physical fitness. He belongs to a club. But you wouldn't like it, love."

"Why in the world not?" Donna couldn't imagine disliking anything to do with Bruce.

"He plays one set and then heads for the bar, where he has at least three drinks to get over the strain and eats all the nibblies in sight. Mark has often said that Bruce can eat more potato chips, Fritos and nachos than any other six living men."

"But he could run," she had persisted. "That doesn't take any skill."

"You got him out once," Laura said, smiling; then she handed Donna the car keys. "Maybe you should count that a victory and quit. Any coordination Bruce has is sheer luck. When he was little he could stumble over the pattern in a rug. He'll never go for running very often.''

"Well," Donna said, taking the keys, "I'm going to give it another try. Running alone in the park in the early evening, after work, is okay. There are plenty of people around. But I didn't like it the other night when I got there after eight.''

Laura caught her arm as she turned to leave. "You didn't run alone in Golden Gate Park at night, Donna!'' There was consternation in the blue eyes. "Mark would have a fit if he knew.''

"Well, yes, I did," Donna admitted. "It was that other night I worked late. You and Mark were out when I got home, and I just needed to get out and run.''

"Oh, don't do that again, please. It's just asking for trouble.''

"I'd already decided that by myself,'' Donna said ruefully. "Somebody followed me, and not just another runner, either. Fortunately, as Dad always says, I can outrun the devil himself, so I lost the guy.''

Laura grinned suddenly. "You know what? I know we've sworn off being devious since Bruce actually found Mr. Tsung, but why don't you tell Bruce you've been running alone in Golden Gate Park at night? He may just decide to come with you.''

Donna grinned. She tossed the keys up and down in her palm and turned to go without another word.

The sun was low in the sky when she pulled Laura's little green BMW to a stop in front of Bruce's house. The door was just closing behind him. It opened again immediately, and he leaned out.

"I thought I saw Laura's car. Hi. Come on in. I'm just figuring out what to do about dinner.''

Donna hopped from the car and sprinted up the short front walk. "What are you dressed up for?" Bruce asked.

"It's my new running outfit. Like it?"

"Ye-es," he said doubtfully. "But not what it portends. I have this gut feeling you're going to invite me for another of your famous runs."

"Bingo. We've both worked hard all day. We need to unwind."

"Look, kid, I never needed help unwinding in my life. My problem is usually the reverse." He strode ahead of her through the hall, dropping his briefcase on a table and yanking off his tie. As he placed one foot on the bottom step of the stairway, he paused for a moment. "My problem is winding up in the first place. I'll say this for you. You have a gift for it. You're wound up all the time."

"Why, thank you, Bruce. I think. Okay," she said lightly. "If you don't want to go, you don't. But I better get going. It'll be dark soon, and Golden Gate Park isn't very well lighted in places."

He was halfway up the stairs when he turned and clattered down again quickly.

"You're not going to run in the park alone at night! What are you, some kind of nut?" He stopped in front of her and grasped her shoulders.

She shrugged free. "Look, I've got to hurry. And listen, dear friend, I'm safe, believe me. There isn't a mugger alive who can outrun me. Why, the other night—"

He grabbed her shoulders again. "You mean you've done this before?"

"Bruce," she said with elaborate patience, careful not to smile. "There are two typists out on vacation and another one got sick. We're shorthanded down at Fenton and Hunt. You VIPs in your private offices never know what's going on. I worked until after eight the other night. And tonight...why, I only just got off a few minutes ago. This is the only time I've got to run today.''

He groaned. "Oh, all right, dammit. I'll go with you. This time, mind you. This time only. But I don't want you to get any crazy ideas about a fitness program. I'm already fit. If I were any fitter I'd be Superman. Wait here.'' He started up the stairs again, but turned suddenly three steps up.

"What happened the other night?''

"Nothing happened,'' she said blandly. "That's the point. There was some man following me, but I put on some speed and lost him.''

He groaned again, hollowly, and climbed the stairs like a bent old man. She couldn't help laughing out loud.

All the way to the park Bruce laid down various ground rules. He was a teeny bit out of condition, so he was going to set the pace this time. They were only going to run for a very short time, and then rest. They were only going to run on level ground.

"Bruce, lighten up, it's not going to kill you. It'll be good for you. You'll love it.'' She turned onto Fulton Street and drove beside the park until she reached the avenues in the Richmond district.

"Turn in here. It's pretty level here,'' Bruce commanded.

"Little bit farther,'' she said, driving on. "Let's get closer to the beach.''

Once they'd left the car and entered the endless green expanse of park, Donna felt an immediate rush of pleasure. The setting sun seemed to blaze in the tops of nearby trees, casting long shadows across the rolling lawns. There was a scattering of green slat benches along the winding road, most of them empty. An elderly man, with an elderly cocker spaniel, occupied one. Halfway up a nearby slope was a spread blanket, the remains of a picnic, and a couple with a baby asleep in a carrier. It looked wonderfully peaceful and almost deserted. From the distance came the sound of traffic, lighter now than it would have been a couple of hours ago.

"Well, okay," Bruce said impatiently. "We came here to run, so let's run." He started off down the path at a dogtrot.

"Bruce," Donna called disgustedly. "Come back. Don't you remember anything about our last run? What I told you?"

He wheeled around, going onto the lawn to do so, then loped back and ran in place. "What's the matter with you? You're just standing there. You're the one who was so hot to run. Have you grown into the ground?" He was starting to breathe a little more rapidly, and came to a stop.

"Did you forget what I explained about stretching first?" she asked. "You don't just start running."

"Oh, yes," he said, clapping his hand to his forehead. "We do calisthenics first. I remember now. We stretch. We twist. We bend. We use a nearby tree and put our leg up it and push. We damn near tear out perfectly good leg muscles. How could I ever forget? You take that tree. I'll take this one, it's closer." He went to the tree and fell against it, hands outstretched, and arched his back in and out. "Look, Ma, I'm warming up."

"Oh, Bruce. This is serious. We're dealing with our bodies here. We want to do what's best for our bodies. We must listen to our bodies." She began her own series of exercises, starting slowly and working up to a more strenuous pace. She could feel her tight muscles loosening.

"My body wants to go home," Bruce grunted after a moment. "My body wants to sit down in my living room and have a drink."

"Bruce, knock it off, will you? Can't you admit that this is one thing I do know more about than you do?"

"Well, you said listen to our bodies, and mine is speaking very clearly regarding the point about going home."

She ignored his complaints, and continued her workout until she felt ready to run.

"Okay. I'm ready," she said, beginning to run lightly in place. "Are you ready?" She adjusted her white sweatband against her forehead.

"I'm ready to drop. Is that what you mean?"

She set out at a loose, steady pace, not too fast. She would increase her speed by easy stages as she went. She knew from long experience that she wouldn't really hit her stride for some time.

"Come on," she called over her shoulder. Then she gave herself up to the joy of controlled motion, her feet hitting the path lightly, rhythmically, her face bathed in alternating sun and shadow. In a few moments, she heard Bruce coming behind her. She stayed in front of him, knowing from experience that if she slowed to drop back and run beside him, he would also slow down. She did moderate her pace somewhat when she began to hear his audible breathing. She mustn't push him too hard. She must help him enjoy exercise if she could.

"When are we gonna stop?" He was panting now.

"Save your breath," she called over her shoulder, and almost stumbled over the first of a line of wood ducks waddling rapidly across the road. Donna sprinted and made it past the rest of the yellow-footed procession. "Look out for the ducks," she yelled.

Too late. Bruce either hadn't seen them or couldn't stop soon enough. She heard him shout, and whirled around just in time to see him plough into the birds. They scattered in a burst of outraged squawking, feathers flying, and

Bruce crashed headlong among them and sprawled face-down on the lawn.

"Bruce! Bruce!" She rushed to him.

He rolled over and sat up. "What in the living hell!"

"Ducks," she said, "just some ducks you ran over. We must be near one of the lakes. Are we?"

"I...don't...know," he said, in a measured voice. "And...I...don't...care." Then he groaned and lay back, spread-eagled on the lawn. "Well, at least those stupid creatures stopped this mad run. Sit down," he commanded. "Rest a while. I know you're not tired, but rest anyway."

Laughing, she dropped down beside him. It was clear the run was over, not long after it had started.

"You know something," she said after a moment, pulling off her sweatband. "We're not even wet."

"Should we be wet?" he asked testily.

"Well, runners usually work up a sweat. We didn't even do that."

"We did enough. We gave a thousand ducks cardiac arrest," he grunted. "Just be quiet and relax."

"This was a start, at least. It should show you something, Bruce. You are a little bit out of condition. If you would do this—just a little of it—working up slowly—you'd be in so much better health. Exercise has to be made a regular part of—"

"Donna, will you please shut up?" Bruce had closed his eyes.

"Admit it," she persisted. "Aren't you beginning to feel better already?"

"I am beginning to feel dead."

"But, Bruce—" She began to gather a bunch of white clover blossoms.

"And if you don't shut up and let me rest a minute, you are going to be dead."

She started making a clover chain, twisting each thin, pliant stem into a loose single knot and thrusting a bloom through it. When she had enough for a circlet, she joined the two ends. She'd been silent long enough.

"Are you rested yet?" she asked.

"No."

"When do you think you will be rested?"

"In twelve hours, I think. Approximately."

"Would you like a clover chain?"

"Donna." His voice was heavy with warning, but he sat up. "That's kind of cute," he added, as she put the chain on her head. "So that's a clover chain, huh? Well, nature girl, I think I have some news for you."

"What's that?" she asked eagerly.

"I think I busted my ankle." He gingerly stroked his left ankle.

"Oh, Bruce, no. And after only ten minutes running." She scrambled to her feet. "Can you...uh...move it?"

"Maybe. Give me a hand, will you?" Wincing, groaning slightly, he managed to struggle up on one leg.

"Bruce, listen," she said urgently. "Just today at the office, some of the men in the coffee room were talking about this great doctor at a big hospital. He specializes in sports medicine. You're laughing."

"I can't help it. The idea of me going to a sports-medicine specialist."

"You're not hurt at all!"

"Oh, hell." He had put both feet solidly on the ground. "I thought I'd con you into stopping this running non-sense." With that, he took off, racing back the way they'd come. She caught up with him almost instantly.

Back in the car again, she was still laughing. "You'd do anything to avoid some sort of regular program, wouldn't you?" she demanded.

"Practically," he said. "Give me the keys. You haven't eaten yet, either, have you? Shall we go to that wonderful junk food place?"

She sighed deeply. "What's that?" She dug in her pocket for the car keys.

"Only the best hamburger place in San Francisco." He clutched a handful of the faded T-shirt he wore with threadbare khaki shorts. "And they don't require a shirt and tie, my love. Incidentally," he said, turning to look at her, "you're going to run every day, aren't you, no matter what I say."

"Yep."

He sat for a moment, his hands on the wheel. "I'm not giving in, mind you," he said after a moment. "But I don't want you coming out here by yourself. Seriously. Can we make a deal?"

"Bruce? You're coming with me?" She felt breathless.

"Yes. But grudgingly. And not necessarily to run," he added quickly.

"Not to run? How could you keep up? What would be the point?"

"Oh, I'll run sometimes," he conceded. "But not if I don't feel like it. Understood? I may just drive along beside you in the car, okay? And your laurel wreath, or whatever it is, is crooked."

She burst out laughing, trying not to sound triumphant. "Any way you want," she agreed. "Whatever you say." She took the circle of clover off her head and twirled it around, chuckling to herself.

WHEN HE WENT INSIDE his house again, he accidentally let the door slam behind him. It echoed loudly, making the rooms around him feel even emptier than they usually did. He had a strong impulse to call Donna back, but crushed it. Well, she'd got her way after all with the damned phys-ical-fitness program. But there was no way he could let her roam around that park after dark. What had she been thinking of, the little dumbbell? Or else he was the dumb-bell, and she'd conned him—which was, he had to admit, entirely possible.

He picked up a stack of mail from the hall table and began to riffle through it. And she had looked lovely in that flower-halo thing she had put in her hair. He held the letters in motionless hands for a long moment, seeing her face, her smile. What it meant was that they would be together that much more. *You're a sap, Fenton,* he told himself. *She conned you. And you fell for it.*

He walked listlessly into the living room and sat in one of the chairs in front of the empty fireplace, the mail still in his hands. She was too damned seductive, that was the trouble. He'd just have to hang on to his big-brother act until the end of summer. And that, he thought, wasn't go-ing to be easy.

But at the end of summer—what then? Well, Donna would go back home to Vancouver, that's what, start uni-versity the way she should, the way her parents wanted her to.

Speaking of her parents, he hoped he could get Donna through the Raymond Tsung affair without too much has-sle. He didn't want her hurt by it. When he went to see Tsung, he'd make very sure of the man's attitude before he took Donna to face him. And maybe, just maybe, they could get the business finished without upsetting Sara and Evan.

Then…sometime…maybe…if Donna was right, and they did have a future together… He let the idea drift through his mind for a while as he began to go through the motions of sorting the envelopes in his hands, not even looking at them.

DONNA WAS CLEAR INTO the breakfast room the next morning before she realized the atmosphere was charged with suppressed anger. She paused behind her chair, wishing desperately that she was someplace else, anyplace else.

"Everybody else goes in the van," E.J. said through his teeth, his straight little back rigid with fury. "All the other guys…"

"Okay, E.J. That's it. Enough. It's just a little two-week summer school." Mark spoke sharply. "Your mother always drives you to school. That's the arrangement we've always had, and that's what she wants to do." He had started out firmly, but ended on an almost doubtful note.

"Always been." E.J. slammed down his spoon, dropping the bite of cantaloupe he hadn't put in his mouth. "Mom! I want to start riding in the school van!" He turned blazing eyes on his mother. "Are you gonna drive me to school when I get in second grade? Are you, Mom?" He was near tears.

"E.J. Don't talk to your mother in that tone. Morning, Donna. Sorry, we seem to be having a little domestic row. Now, be quiet, E.J. Don't spoil breakfast for everyone. Eat up, son. The sky isn't going to fall in just because your mother won't let you ride in the school van."

"But the other *guys*…" The little boy was pleading.

Laura crumpled her napkin in her lap. "What do you mean, his *mother* won't let him. You agreed, Mark! You agreed it was better that I take him to school and pick him up. Summer school is no different. Don't put all the blame on me." Her blues eyes were bright with anger.

Donna lowered her head and plunged her spoon into the half cantaloupe on her plate. Mrs. Cooper came in from the kitchen with a platter of scrambled eggs and small sausages in her hands. As soon as she saw they hadn't finished their melon, she stopped.

"That's all right," Laura said with an effort. "Put it down here, please. I'll serve."

Mrs. Cooper put the platter down, then went to the sideboard for the coffeepot to fill Donna's cup.

"E.J.," she said pleasantly, "Your little friend, Malcolm, is on the phone." E.J. shot a quick glance at his father. Mark nodded, and E.J. put down his napkin and hurried from the room, darting in front of Mrs. Cooper as she left.

"Thank you," Donna said as the kitchen door swung shut. She tried desperately to think of something—anything—to say to fill the silence.

Mark forestalled her. "Donna, I want to thank you for putting in so much overtime. Summer's a bit rough because of the vacations. I appreciate the help."

"Oh, it's nothing," she said hastily. "I don't mind work. Mom taught me that. And if it wasn't for Fenton and Hunt vacations I probably wouldn't have a summer job, right?"

Mark forced a tight little laugh. "Right. Anyhow, I'll sure give you a bang-up reference when you leave."

Laura broke in "You haven't answered my question, Mark."

He looked blank for a moment, and then, in a pathetic attempt at humor, added. "Will you repeat the question, please ma'am?"

But Laura was having none of it. "I said don't put all the blame on me for driving E.J. to school and back. You agreed, dammit. You thought it was the best thing to do." She was so angry she was shaking.

"I did," Mark said slowly, as if realizing for the first

time how angry his wife was. He turned to Donna. "Forgive us," he said with a weak grin. "Little lapse in communication, I guess. Yes, Laura, I did agree. When he was in kindergarten. He's completed the first grade now, and he's a fairly mature kid. And you didn't answer his question."

"Mark!" Laura flung her napkin onto the table and rose from her chair.

"Well," Mark continued levelly. "He asked if you were going to insist on driving him to school next year."

Without another word, Laura turned and left the room. Donna, terribly embarrassed for both of them, saw the sunlight flash on Laura's bracelet as she stepped outside onto the terrace.

"Sorry about that. I guess I shouldn't have said that." He watched as E.J. came barreling back into the room and took his seat. "You'd better get going on that melon, son. Or don't you want it?"

"Not really," E.J. said. Donna noticed, with a lump in her throat, that his brief chat with his little friend hadn't lightened his mood any. He still looked upset.

"Okay." Mark reached over and took away the plate. "Eggs?" he asked, but E.J.'s doleful look answered him. "Well, why don't you just drink your milk and we'll call it even. You can eat a bigger lunch today, okay?"

E.J. silently picked up his glass and gulped the milk noisily without further comment from his father.

Mark leaned forward, trying to see where Laura had gone. Then, with a muttered, "Excuse me, please," he too rose and left the table to go out on the terrace.

E.J. put down his empty glass and looked, wide-eyed, at Donna. She gave him a smile of encouragement. "You have a milk mustache. Do you want to wipe it off?" she asked.

An Important Message from the Editors

Dear Reader,

Because you've chosen to read one of our fine romance novels, we'd like to say "thank you!" And, as a **special** way to thank you, we've selected <u>two more</u> of the books you love so well **plus** an exciting Mystery Gift to send you— absolutely <u>FREE</u>!

Please enjoy them with our compliments...

Pam Powers

Peel off seal and place inside...

Lift here

How to validate your Editor's
"Thank You"
FREE GIFT

1. Peel off gift seal from front cover. Place it in space provided at right. This automatically entitles you to receive 2 FREE BOOKS and a fabulous mystery gift.

2. Send back this card and you'll get 2 brand-new *Romance* novels. These books have a cover price of $5.99 or more each in the U.S. and $6.99 or more each in Canada, but they are yours to keep absolutely free.

3. There's no catch. You're under no obligation to buy anything. We charge nothing—ZERO—for your first shipment. And you don't have to make any minimum number of purchases— not even one!

4. The fact is, thousands of readers enjoy receiving their books by mail from The Reader Service. They enjoy the convenience of home delivery...they like getting the best new novels at discount prices BEFORE they're available in stores... and they love their Heart to Heart subscriber newsletter featuring author news, horoscopes, recipes, book reviews and much more!

5. We hope that after receiving your free books you'll want to remain a subscriber. But the choice is yours— to continue or cancel, any time at all! So why not take us up on our invitation, with no risk of any kind. You'll be glad you did!

GET A *Free* MYSTERY GIFT...

SURPRISE MYSTERY GIFT COULD BE YOURS *FREE* AS A SPECIAL "THANK YOU" FROM THE EDITORS

DETACH AND MAIL CARD TODAY! ▼

Yes!

I have placed my Editor's "Thank You" seal in the space provided above. Please send me 2 free books and a fabulous mystery gift. I understand I am under no obligation to purchase any books, as explained on the back and on the opposite page.

PLACE
FREE GIFT
SEAL
HERE

393 MDL DVFG

193 MDL DVFF

FIRST NAME

LAST NAME

ADDRESS

APT.#

CITY

STATE/PROV.

ZIP/POSTAL CODE

(PR-R-04)

Thank You!

The Reader Service — Here's How It Works:

Accepting your 2 free books and gift places you under no obligation to buy anything. You may keep the books and gift and return the shipping statement marked "cancel." If you do not cancel, about a month later we'll send you 3 additional books and bill you just $4.74 each in the U.S., or $5.24 each in Canada, plus 25¢ shipping & handling per book and applicable taxes if any.* That's the complete price and — compared to cover prices starting from $5.99 each in the U.S. and $6.99 each in Canada — it's quite a bargain! You may cancel at any time, but if you choose to continue, every month we'll send you 3 more books, which you may either purchase at the discount price or return to us and cancel your subscription.

*Terms and prices subject to change without notice. Sales tax applicable in N.Y. Canadian residents will be charged applicable provincial taxes and GST.

He blotted it carefully with his napkin. "Are you going to have eggs and all that stuff?" he asked.

"Why?"

"Well, I have to brush my teeth before school, and I...well, if I go, you'll be all by yourself. Is that okay?"

"Oh, sure, E.J. You're sweet, you know that?"

He gave her a tentative grin and put his napkin on the table, his eyes quickening with interest at her next comment.

"Why are you going to this summer school anyhow, E.J.? You finished first grade all right, didn't you?"

"Oh yeah. Kid stuff. And so's this summer school. It's not really *school* school, it's more like painting pictures and making things. We're making puppet heads now. I'm making a clown head. For Mom."

"Oh, that's lovely. She'll be pleased."

E.J. heaved a sigh. "This is my second choice, summer school is."

"Oh. What was your first choice?" Her heart went out to the child.

"Summer camp." He barely breathed the words, his eyes shining. "I thought for a while I could go to summer camp, but...but..."

"Well, maybe six is a little young for summer camp," Donna said lamely. It wasn't. He could have managed it, she thought. He was a very competent six-year-old. At six, she had still been living with Prairie. She had transferred on buses by herself, going across Vancouver with the door key on a string around her neck. She had got up alone in the morning and lit the stove and put the kettle on for Prairie's coffee, and never once burned herself. Kids could cope, if you gave them half a chance.

"They had swimming," E.J. started, "and first-aid training and all. You go by the buddy system. Everybody has a buddy to look out for, and..." He continued telling her about the camp.

Donna caught the sound of Laura's voice, almost strident, from the terrace. Fortunately, E.J. didn't notice, he was so taken up with his own words.

"Parents are supposed to back each other up, Mark. You should never, *never*—"

Donna heard the low murmur of Mark's voice. His tone was reasonable, conciliatory, but his words were indistinct.

"I don't care! I'm not going to have him on that van. How do I know what kind of driver..."

Mark spoke again, this time somewhat firmer. Donna caught the words "competent" and "other parents."

E.J. looked at his watch. "Boy, the time!"

"Look," Donna said hastily. "Why don't you go brush your teeth. I'm fine here. I don't mind finishing alone."

Without a word, the boy tumbled out of his chair and shot out of the room. Donna heard him clattering up the stairs at a dead run.

Then, suddenly, she heard Mark's voice. His words were clear and blunt.

"Laura, you're going to have to let him go sometime— *let go*. I will not have him raised like a sheltered only child."

"Only child? He *is* an only child." Laura was fairly shouting now. "And whose fault is that? I ask you, whose fault is that?" Her words were cut off suddenly by a little choking sound, and Donna heard her add, "Oh, Mark, I'm sorry. I'm sorry." She was obviously trying not to cry. Her voice seemed closer, and Donna, terrified they would come back and find her there, leaped up and ran out of the room, taking the stairs as fast as E.J. had.

Oh, those poor souls, to quarrel like that, and in someone else's hearing. It told Donna that they had both reached the limits of their endurance over—over what? She was deeply shaken. Laura and Mark, along with her mother and father, were her ideals of marriage, a good, sound, happy marriage. What was wrong? Did Bruce know? She was shaking slightly as she went into her room and shut the door. She had to talk to Bruce.

DONNA DIDN'T HAVE a chance to speak to Bruce until after work, when she drove Laura's car to his house. She had called him earlier at his office and asked if he would mind another run in the park; after groaning deeply, he had agreed. She gave two little beeps on the horn and waited for him. In a moment he came out the front door dressed, she noted, in a new gray sweat suit, and loped to the car.

"All ready?" she asked, making herself smile, and added, "The sweats look great. They'll be more comfortable."

"Thanks," he said. "And I'm as ready as I'll ever be."

They drove in almost total silence until they got to the park.

"Are we not speaking or something?" Bruce asked as they left the car.

"What?"

"Usually I can't get a word in edgewise, and now you've gone silent on me. What's the matter? There is something the matter, isn't there?"

She looked at him for a long moment. How in the world could she talk about Laura and Mark's problems? She felt like an intruder, and somehow disloyal.

"Since when have you clammed up when you had a problem?" Bruce asked easily. "Unload it, sweetheart. You always have before. Here, let's sit down on the grass." He sprawled at the base of a drooping willow, its fronds moving slowly in the summer breeze.

She sat beside him. "It's Laura and Mark. I...that marriage is in trouble, isn't it?" she blurted out.

"What?!" He sat up straight and faced her. "You're out of your mind, Donna. Offhand, I'd say Laura and Mark's marriage is possibly the strongest relationship in the universe. Whatever gave you that wild idea?"

"I don't think it's a wild idea, Bruce." She bent over, worrying some blades of grass with nervous fingers. "There's something wrong there. They quarrel. I think quite a lot."

"Oh, Donna, you've gone off your rails, honey. I know my cousin, and when she went for Mark it was total, believe me. And I know Mark Hunt, better than I really want to, and believe me—"

"I don't mean they don't love each other.... I..."

"You're living in their house, right? You're going to hear some...well...differences of opinion between them—"

"Quarrels, Bruce," she persisted. "Plural." She pulled up a blade of grass and chewed it.

"All right, quarrels plural. There isn't a married couple in the world that doesn't have their fights. That's part of it. Surely your mother and father have quarreled on occasion?"

"Ye-es, not often, but now and then, I guess they have."

"Well, then..." He spread his hands. "Come on. Incidentally, what makes you think they have a lot of quarrels? Have you actually heard them, or what?"

"Yes. I have." She took the blade of grass from her mouth and stared at it. "When I think about it, it isn't really a lot of quarrels, Bruce. I don't know if I can explain it or not. But it's more like one long, long quarrel that goes on and on and never gets finished." Despite her effort at control, her voice was unsteady. Laura and Mark meant so much to her and her family.

"Hey, steady now. And stop eating grass. I know you're a health nut, but eating the lawn is too much." He reached over and took the grass away. "That was a joke. You're supposed to laugh at jokes."

She forced a smile. "I'm sorry. I sort of ran out of laughs today. Bruce, it's like there's something there, under the surface, spoiling everything for them. But they keep going through the motions. Mark is so polite, so smooth, and Laura is so...so careful about my feelings...my feelings, of all things. And they're hurting. I can feel the hurt."

Bruce looked at her a long time, quite serious now. "This long, long quarrel that has no ending, do you have any idea at all what it's about?" he asked gently.

"E.J.," she answered promptly. "It's always some disagreement centering around E.J. And this morning, I heard—I wasn't deliberately listening, but I couldn't help hearing—something about E.J. being an only child." She stopped, too diffident and too fond of Laura to repeat Laura's bitter accusation: "I ask you, whose fault is that?"

"Ah, little old E.J., is it?" Bruce clasped his arms around one raised knee and put his head down on it; when he spoke again, his face was hidden from view. "Yeah, you're right, honey. I guess that is an old quarrel. Laura lost a baby a couple of years ago, but you knew that, didn't you?"

"Yes."

"Well, Mark is dead set against her getting pregnant again. He's afraid he'll lose her, too, next time."

"But—she wants to try again?" Donna murmured.

"Having been reading between the lines myself for the last couple of years, I'd say yes, but Laura's never said anything to me about it. She wouldn't, probably thinking that it might reflect on Mr. Perfect himself. Make him appear stubborn—which he is—or something. But yes, I know in my gut that Laura wanted children, several of them, and they've stopped with E.J. That may be a point of conflict. But, Donna…'' Bruce reached over and took both her hands into his. ''They'll work it out.'' He drew her gently into his arms and held her against him with a slight rocking motion. ''Honey, they've worked out tougher things than this.''

She tilted back her head and looked up into his face, suddenly tremulous. Bruce was going to kiss her again. Laura and Mark faded to the back of her mind, and she slid her hands up his chest and around his neck. He did this sometimes. He was careful and guarded and wary, and then sometimes, when she least expected it, he kissed her, like now.

''Donna, Donna,'' he whispered against her lips. Then, ever so gently, he pushed her away.

She kept her eyes lowered to hide the singing triumph in her heart. He didn't want to push her away. He didn't want to! She felt it, knew it, as surely as she knew the sun rose in the morning and set in the evening. She let him push her away without resistance, and leaned forward on the lawn, balancing herself on closed fists. She wanted him, here, now, on the lawn beneath the willow tree, but she mustn't let him see. She mustn't.

She got up quickly. ''If we're going to run we'd better do our warm-ups,'' she said, trying to sound brisk.

''Frankly, my dear,'' Bruce said, getting up slowly, ''I don't give a damn about running today.'' He was trying to keep it light.

She made herself laugh, and spun on her heels to face him. ''What would you rather do?''

He gave her a lingering look. "Never mind, I'll settle for running, I guess." And Donna felt her face flame.

"I think I should mention one other thing before we start." His voice was grim.

"And what's that?" She made rather a business of adjusting the sweatband across her forehead.

"He's back. Raymond Tsung. His secretary called my office today."

"Oh, Bruce." There was a quaver in her voice. "Already?"

"Right. Already. And I'm going to see him tomorrow. So start bracing yourself."

"I am. I will. Now, listen, Bruce…" She stopped before he raised his hands.

"You said you'd go through with it, Donna. You promised."

"I will, only…only…"

"Don't sound so despairing. He may want nothing to do with you. He may—hey, Donna, wait." But she had already taken off, running as hard as she could.

When he returned home after dropping her off an hour later, Bruce shut his door and leaned against it for a moment. Did she have any idea how gorgeous she was? He pushed himself away from the door and walked slowly into his study. He stretched across the desk and flipped through his calendar. How much longer was this summer? How many more days were there? His hand, as it turned the pages, was unsteady.

CHAPTER ELEVEN

THE FOLLOWING MORNING Donna got to Fenton and Hunt early in the hope of seeing Bruce before the workday started. To her dismay, the receptionist was sick, and she was elected to be trapped at the front desk most of the day. She knew that would curtail her freedom sharply, but she watched for Bruce anyway. He came in while she was busy writing down a phone message. She signaled for him to wait.

"What's up? Why the frantic signals?"

She finished writing. "About today, Bruce," she began and paused, smiling until one of the secretaries passed. "I've been thinking, and I think you'd better—"

He reached over and covered her hand. "Donna. It's all settled what I'm going to do today, so forget it. Discussion is closed."

"But what time?" she whispered desperately. "What time are you going to see him?"

"Two-fifteen, Donna. Gloria Hu got me in as the first appointment after his lunch. And I have the feeling that he'd probably have a longer lunch hour if it wasn't for me."

"Who's Gloria Hoo?"

"His secretary. Now, are we through with this chat?"

"But, Bruce, I've been rethinking it and I can't...last night I dreamed about Mom and Dad, and—"

"Stop vacillating, Donna. One minute you're going

through with it. The next minute you want to chicken out again. Stop it. If he wants to see you, you're going to see him if I have to carry you in bodily. Clear?''

"Right, Chief!" She narrowed her eyes and gave him a smart salute; then she bowed her head over the desk, muttering to herself.

"I'm afraid I didn't quite get that," Bruce said. "Something about a macho male, wasn't it? Well, never mind. I'll report back to you this evening."

AT TWO-TEN, BRUCE opened the great glass door of the Bank of Cathay, crossed marble tiles, passed gleaming rosewood desks, and walked behind a polished railing toward the tellers' bronze grills.

"Pssssst. Mr. Fenton. Pssssst!"

He turned in search of the sibilant whisper and saw a broadly smiling and vaguely familiar face. He knew her, and struggled for her name. Gertrude Wong. Eddy Wong's non-relation. He had quizzed her about Tsung.

"Good afternoon." He smiled, hoping he wouldn't have to stop. He had cut it pretty fine, and he didn't want to be late. Tsung's secretary had been very specific about the time, and had even called his secretary this morning to remind him of the appointment.

"Did he get it?" Gertrude Wong had risen from her desk, and she hurried toward him.

"Get it?" he echoed blankly.

"The award, you know."

"Oh. Well, I'm just going up for an interview now," Bruce said.

She smiled benignly and crossed her fingers. "Take the last elevator. That's an express to the executive floor. Then a sharp left."

"Thanks." They waved crossed fingers at each other,

and he hurried on, practically skidding to a stop before the elevators.

He arrived on the executive floor at two-fourteen by the clock over Gloria Hu's smooth, shining head, which nodded to him gravely. She could, he thought, have traded her job for one as a model any time she pleased.

"Mr. Fenton? Mr. Tsung just got back. Give him a minute for one phone call, and then you can go in." She waved one perfectly manicured hand toward a chair, and he sat down, looking around the office.

Raymond Tsung was doing okay. Yes, indeed. Everything was expensively beautiful. Each fabric seemed to be in tones of gray with touches of gold or red or black. Black was picked up again in some of the Chinese wood pieces. Gold was repeated in a spectacular five-fold screen, which stood across the room from where Bruce sat. Even the equipment seemed to have class, he thought. When the telephone sounded there was no bell, just a gentle two-note musical tone.

"Mr. Fenton. You can go in now. Right through here." She pressed some hidden button, and a little gateway that separated Raymond Tsung from the outside world slid silently open. Bruce walked on bottomless carpet into a small anteroom. Feeling something close to his early courtroom stage fright, he approached the double doors facing him.

They opened as he approached.

"Mr. Fenton. Come in." A middle-aged Chinese held the door wide and gestured him in. It took Bruce a moment to realize that the great desk opposite was empty, and that Tsung himself had opened the door for him. It was a touch of graciousness he hadn't expected.

"Thank you." He extended his hand. The other's grasp was firm, and brief. He was a busy man, just back after several weeks' absence from his desk. He probably had a hundred things to do, but even so would not sacrifice courtesy because of his schedule.

"Sit here, why don't you?" Tsung pushed a gray leather chair closer to the black lacquer desk, then went behind the desk to seat himself. He was a shade above medium height, and somewhat stocky, but he moved with grace. His banker's gray suit was tailor-made and elegant. A platinum ring, set with lapis lazuli, gleamed darkly on one well-kept hand. "Now, what can I do for Fenton and Hunt? I recognize your name, Bruce Fenton, of course." He smiled, and his slightly crooked teeth gave his round face an impish quality.

"My name?" Bruce was suddenly nervous, and he wondered if some of the people he had questioned had told Tsung.

"Oh yes. You did quite a lot of work here a few summers ago, I recall. I've heard many good things about you."

"Oh, I see. Well, it was little enough, helping new immigrants settle in. Since we're a nation of immigrants anyhow, it seemed only fair."

"Nice viewpoint. It's good to remember that fact once in a while." His smile was genial, but he leaned forward in an attentive attitude. It was a subtle gesture that conveyed the message he really didn't have time for much idle talk.

Bruce took the hint. "I gave you my firm's name, Fenton and Hunt, so you wouldn't think I was trying to sell you something. Actually, this is not a legal matter."

Tsung's onyx eyes glinted with humor. "Then you did come to sell me something?"

Bruce laughed. "No. I came on behalf of a friend,

Donna McGrath. She's spending the summer in San Francisco and was thinking of looking you up.''

''Ah? I'm afraid I don't place the name.''

''Do you place the name of Crawford?''

''That rings a bell. Two in fact. I have a Crawford in my employ here in the bank, and the man who overcharged us for plumbing at the house is named Crawford. One of those?'' He gave that engaging grin again.

''Prairie Crawford?'' Bruce felt his mouth dry. *Damn it.* He felt like a first-year law student facing a judge. He could tell nothing from Tsung's face. It still held only polite interest.

''Prairie Crawford. No, I'm afraid I...wait.'' He sat back abruptly in his chair. ''I did know a Prairie Crawford once! Good heavens. You're going back quite a way, Mr. Fenton. Is she still—? Do you know her? Tell me, how is she doing?'' He laughed. ''What a free spirit she was. Don't tell me she outgrew it all and became a stockbroker or something. I did myself, and became a banker.'' He rocked in his chair, smiling in remembrance. ''I used to think of Prairie sometimes, and the old place where we lived— usually when I was bored out of my skull at a board-of-directors' meeting. I haven't done that lately.''

''Well, it's her daughter I came to speak to you about—''

''Her daughter! So she got married and settled down. What do you know! I'd never have thought it. Why does it make me kind of sad?''

''No, actually she didn't. Settle down, I mean. She's still pretty much a free spirit. Her daughter is nineteen now— almost twenty—and she was adopted by a Canadian couple named McGrath when she was about thirteen. Prairie couldn't care for her, so she had the sense to hand the child over to people who could. She visits Donna from time to time. They haven't lost touch, which is nice, of course.''

"And the girl, Donna, is nineteen, you say?" Tsung leaned forward again, the smile gone, the dark eyes intent.

How was he going to take this? Bruce felt the palms of his hands go damp, and he pressed them against his thighs. If Tsung rejected the idea of Donna being his daughter, Bruce might be tempted to poke the guy in the nose.

When Tsung spoke, his voice was deceptively soft. "Are you about to tell me, Mr. Fenton, that Donna McGrath is half-Asian?" Tsung was quick, no doubt about that.

This was it. "Well, yes, she is, but that's beside the point, she—"

Tsung shook his head slightly. "I differ, sir. It is decidedly *not* beside the point. Are you going to tell me that I have a nineteen-year-old daughter from my days with Prairie Crawford?" Both his well-kept hands were pressed flat on the desk, and he seemed about to rise from his chair.

"Yes," Bruce said. He went on quickly. "Please understand that Donna is, and has been, exceedingly happy with her adoptive parents. She makes no claim upon you. None at all. It is simply that she is spending the summer in San Francisco and, well, perhaps like all adopted children, she was a bit curious to meet you. There is certainly no obligation on your part to meet her, if you are at all reluctant—"

"Claim, Mr. Fenton? Obligation, Mr. Fenton? Of course she has a claim." He rose from his desk and stood behind it, a dull color coming into his face. "Of course there is an obligation. Reluctant? No way. We are talking about my daughter, Mr. Fenton. My daughter, do you realize that?"

Bruce stood, too, completely nonplussed. He watched as

Tsung pushed back his chair and started pacing about the office, pounding one fist softly into the palm of his other hand. "A daughter. A daughter! Think of that. Just think of it! I've got to call my wife! Please excuse me for a moment." He lunged for the phone and spoke a flood of Chinese into it before hanging up again. "I've asked my secretary to put through a call to Hong Kong. That's where my wife is, Hong Kong. Good grief!" He flopped into his chair, pulling a fine linen handkerchief from his pocket and wiping his palms, then his face. "Please excuse me, Mr. Fenton. I guess I'm upset. I don't suppose you've ever had anyone walk into your office and tell you…my God!"

"Look," Bruce said desperately, sitting down again. "Miss McGrath is a friend, and of course I also represent her, but I do assure you that—"

"You have no idea, Mr. Fenton," Tsung interrupted heedlessly, "how my wife and I wanted more children. We have two sons. No daughter. Never any daughter. My wife even wanted to adopt, but I… Mr. Fenton, this is the greatest day of my life. When can I see her, my daughter? Do you have a picture of her? But it doesn't matter what she looks like. My *daughter!*"

"Actually, I do have a picture, I think," Bruce said, fumbling for his billfold. Now what! He hadn't known what sort of reaction he would get, and he certainly hadn't expected this. It might take a little doing to disengage. "Here. This is a couple of years old. This was taken in Vancouver, Canada. The McGraths were nice enough to invite me up for Christmas that year." He extended the snapshot across the desk, and Tsung took it almost reverently.

"Beautiful," he breathed. "She is beautiful. But that wouldn't matter," he said again firmly.

"Uh, yes, she is quite attractive," Bruce said. "She's

going back to Vancouver at the end of summer to go to college, and we thought perhaps while she's here she might just—''

"College? Yes, of course. I'll pay for that. We must work out some details, Mr. Fenton.''

"No! She is adopted, Mr. Tsung. Her adoptive parents are willing…and quite able…to cover all her expenses.'' This was getting out of hand.

Tsung put the snapshot down on the desk and looked at Bruce. It was a long, measuring look.

"Does she need anything? Any money while she is here?'' he asked. His composure had returned.

"No. Nothing. She doesn't need a thing.'' Bruce spoke more firmly than he intended. "Actually, all she wanted was to just…uh…look you up, and perhaps stop in to meet you sometime before she goes back. If you have time.''

Tsung leaned back in his chair. "I have the time, Mr. Fenton.'' He smiled. "I have the time.'' He looked down at the picture on his desk. "May I keep this, please? When can she come? This afternoon? Tomorrow?''

"Why, I…tomorrow, I guess, would be best,'' Bruce said. "She's working, you know. She has a summer job with Fenton and Hunt.''

"Working, is she?'' Tsung laughed. "Imagine that. To-morrow will be fine. Yes?'' He glanced over Bruce's shoulder.

Bruce turned, and saw the elegant Miss Hu.

"I tried to ring in here but couldn't,'' she said in a faintly reproving tone. "I have Mrs. Tsung on line one.'' She walked to the desk and straightened the phone receiver Tsung had left crooked in its cradle.

"Thank you,'' Tsung said. "I'll take it in a moment.'' Then, turning back to Bruce, he said, "What time would you like to meet tomorrow? Shall we meet someplace else? Will you come here? How do you wish to handle it?''

"I thought that she and I would just stop in here, perhaps, if that's okay. We needn't stay too long."

"Fine. Can you come in the morning? Or would the afternoon be better?" He was looking down at the snapshot again. "I'm going to send this to my wife by courier. She'll want to see it."

"Afternoon, I think. I have to be in court in the morning, and Donna is a bit shy. I thought I'd come along, if you don't mind."

"Mind? Not at all." Tsung laughed. "Come at two, then. Okay?"

There was a gentle clearing of a throat behind them, and he raised his eyes. Miss Hu stood in the doorway.

"You have an appointment at two, Mr. Tsung," she murmured.

Still smiling benignly, Mr. Tsung said something in Chinese, which Bruce was positive meant, "Cancel it!" or, Mr. Tsung being Mr. Tsung, probably, "Cancel it, please." Bruce looked at his watch and rose from his chair.

"I'm afraid I've got to run," he said, extending his hand. He wanted out. He wanted to sort through his thoughts before he reported to Donna. Five minutes ago he had been ready to punch Tsung's nose if he rejected Donna, and now he wished the man had. It would have been much easier. This, he knew, wasn't going to be easy. Thank God he didn't have to talk to Donna until this evening, as he had outside appointments all afternoon. He'd have a little time to prepare.

As he went out the great doors of the Cathay Bank, he couldn't stop thinking about different ways of telling her. He must put it out of his mind. He had work to do. He must find a way to tell her that between them they had opened a kind of Pandora's box—and Raymond Tsung had popped out. And, somehow, he thought that Raymond Tsung wasn't going to pop back in again.

Plunging into the teeming mass of people along Grant Avenue, he phrased and rephrased what he could say. By the time he reached the corner he knew there would be no tactful way. It all came down to the same thing. In the course of a fifteen-minute interview with Raymond Tsung, he'd managed to get Donna another set of parents.

CHAPTER TWELVE

"I WON'T SEE HIM." Donna pushed Bruce away. "I can't. You've got to understand." She clutched the front of his shirt. "This is one of your not-very-funny jokes, Bruce, it has to be. Raymond Tsung doesn't really want to see me."

Her fingernails dug into his chest, but he let her hold onto him. She was desperate, and he didn't blame her. Neither of them could have expected the kind of reaction he'd received from Raymond Tsung.

"Calm down, Donna, love. It's not as bad as you think." Everything was exactly as bad as she thought, but saying so wouldn't help. "Sit down, please. Why don't we have a drink? Or wine? How about a glass of wine?"

"I don't want anything." Her eyes were dull now. She sat on the closest chair. "And I don't want Raymond Tsung and his lovely wife and their lovely sons."

"Your half brothers," Bruce reminded her gently.

"I don't want any half brothers," she said. "I've got one brother, Jim. I love him, and he's all I need."

"I know, Donna, I know. But you've got to face up to reality, sweetheart. We've got to face it. We've been over this moment a hundred times and decided exactly how we'd handle it—whichever way Tsung decided to jump."

"Bruce, you've got to help me."

Desperation overtook him. She needed him, and he wouldn't allow himself to fail her. "I'll help you," he said tightly, opening the French doors to the terrace. "It's just going to be a bit more difficult than we thought, that's all." Warm air rushed in with the scent of honeysuckle. "I've got to think, Donna. You've got to think, too, my girl. There's no magic wand in either of our cupboards."

He heard the click of her sandals on the brick behind him, but didn't look back. Instead, he stuffed his hands into his pockets and wandered down the steps beneath the massed wisteria vines climbing over the arbor.

From the end of the walk, at the top of the steps leading down to the garage at the back of his property, he could see over a patchwork quilt of roofs to a sparkling patch of San Francisco Bay. He sighed, and immediately stiffened at Donna's hesitant touch on his back. He was so aware of her, so intensely attuned to her moods. Lately, she was with him wherever he went, and the attraction intensified with every day, every hour. He held himself very still.

"I'm sorry for what I've done," she murmured, laying her cheek against his back. "I wish I was a kid again and someone would send me to my room. Then, when I came out, I'd be back in everybody's good graces and that would be that. Only it's not going to work that way this time, is it?" She slid her arms around his waist, and something inside him moved convulsively.

Bruce closed his eyes. Was it the honeysuckle he smelled now, or Donna? The scent was achingly sweet. "It can't work that way anymore, I'm afraid. And this is exactly what we were talking about—have been talking about for weeks. We've been talking about being adult and facing up to all that means. Adults can't expect someone else to make their troubles go away."

"I know—"

"No, I don't think you really do. And I'm partly to blame. I should have been able to help you more before we got to this stage."

"Help me now, Bruce. Tell me what I ought to know."
She was so vulnerable, but so was he.

"Growing up is the message. Kids can go spend a few
hours in a room, or a few minutes standing in a corner,
and the infraction is forgiven. But, Donna, you've done
something that affects many lives, and no adult is going
to come along to smack your wrist, then tell you to run
away and play. When you devised your plan you were
behaving like a child, convinced that what you wanted was
all that mattered."

She rubbed his ribs, and stroked his sides, his back; he
flexed his shoulders instinctively. "Maybe I started out
that way," she said, "but I sure don't think that's the way
it is anymore. And, Bruce, it isn't fair for you to keep
throwing that at me—the immature routine. I've already
admitted I've still got some growing up to do, and I intend
to do just that."

"Come here, runt." He reached back and pulled her
beside him. "You're right. That wasn't fair. And I'm not
trying to be tough on you. I'm worried, that's all. We both
need to step back and put things in perspective. Before
you know it, this episode will be resolved. And I honestly
don't expect the disaster you expect. I really anticipate
little more than a very charming meeting between you and
a very charming man. Donna, Ray Tsung is everything a
girl could want in a father—"

"I don't want another father," Donna said, stiffening.
"I've got a perfectly good father already. Bruce, what's
my dad going to say if he ever finds out what I've done?"

They were revolving in diminishing circles. Bruce tilted
Donna's face up to his. She was so lovely. He kissed her
lightly.

Her lashes fluttered shut, and she slipped her hands beneath the open neck of his shirt and around his neck. His

body wanted to give in to its responses, and his mind was rapidly following suit. When he crossed his arms over her back she felt small and insubstantial.

"Donna," he said against her lips. "I want you to go home." But even as he said the words, he was kissing her again.

She dropped her hands and rested her forehead on his chest. "You want me to go," she said flatly.

The floral air suddenly became cloying. "No, I don't want you to go. But you've got to, for both our sakes. Go home and think about meeting your Raymond Tsung. It could be far more special than you think if you let yourself relax."

Wordlessly, she led the way back into the house and out to the Lamborghini parked at the curb. When they arrived at Mark and Laura's, she gripped his hand on the steering wheel, and he sensed he should sit quietly until she'd said what was on her mind.

Donna looked at the purse in her lap, then at the curved steps to the Hunts' front door. Mark's Mercedes was parked beneath a tree in front of Bruce's car. "Bruce, this is serious. What if Raymond Tsung feels he should speak to my folks?"

"Why should he?"

"Who's burying his head in the sand now? I just said, what if? I don't know for sure why he would, but he could. Can you imagine their reaction if they get hit cold with what I've done? They'll think I don't love them."

"Donna—"

She'd stopped listening to him. Her door was already open.

Donna got out of the car without waiting to hear the rest of Bruce's reply. She'd tell Mark what had happened. The time for holding back was long past. From now on, she'd be honest with everyone. Mark was always so rational. He would know what to do next.

Bruce's door slammed a second after hers, and he rushed around to grab her arm as she started up the steps. "Please, Donna, slow down and think. You're panicking. I can feel it. All you have to do is—"

"I know. Keep calm and go through a civilized little meeting. But I don't think I can. I don't know how to cope anymore. Mark'll know what I should do. I'm going to ask him."

Bruce yanked her to a halt with enough force to make them both stumble. He held her arms. "I've told you what to do. And I'll be there with you all the way. Mark can't make this situation go away for you, any more than I can."

"He'll think of something, I tell you, I know he will."

"Dammit, Donna. You say you trust me, then you run to Mark. I don't want him brought into this."

"Why?"

"Because everything will come out. What's happened between you and me. The way I fell for your little hoax in the first place, everything—"

"And your pride won't take it." As soon as she closed her mouth she wished she'd never opened it. Bruce's warm blue eyes turned to pure ice. She bowed her head. "I didn't mean to sound like that. I didn't mean to say…"

He cut her off with a shake of his head. "That's exactly what you meant. And you're right. My pride doesn't like it one damn bit. But, just like you, sweetheart, I've still got some growing up to do. I've never quite gotten over Mark having to bail me out of scrapes years ago. Deep down inside Bruce Fenton, there's a nasty, snotty-nosed little kid who wants a chance to tell Mark Hunt he's not the in-control piece of perfection everyone says he is. I don't like that about myself, so maybe I'd better do something about it. Come on.''

Donna trailed Bruce miserably through the house. Laura sat at the kitchen table. The room was still and humid. The steady thud-thudding of the open window above the sink against the outside wall suggested a breeze, but Donna felt as if she were slowly suffocating.

''Hi, you two,'' Laura said, looking up from the book she was reading. Her smile faded instantly. ''What's happened? You both look miserable.''

Without preamble, Bruce announced, ''We want to discuss something with Mark. A lot's happened in a short space of time, and we seem to have gotten out of our depth. At least, Donna thinks we have, and she may be right.'' His mouth formed a grim line.

Donna twisted her hands together and sat on a stool by the counter. Was she being unfair to Bruce? She did trust him, but that didn't seem to be enough at this moment.

The kitchen door opened and Mark, in suit pants and white shirt, cuffs rolled back, collar open, strolled in. ''Hi,'' he said. ''What's up?''

Laura opened a cupboard and pulled out some glasses. ''It's stuffy in here. Let's have a cold drink and some snacks on the terrace.''

''Sounds great,'' Mark said, and Donna couldn't help noticing the look of longing in his eyes as he watched his wife. She wondered if Bruce had seen it, too, but couldn't bring herself to look at him to find out.

''We have to talk,'' Bruce said sharply. ''What has to be said may take some time, and you won't like what you're going to hear.''

''Bruce, do you have to come on like a Hummer?'' Laura asked crossly. ''Go outside and pull some chairs together while I finish this. Is sangria okay?''

"If there's something on your mind, Bruce, shoot," Mark said, as if he hadn't heard Laura. "What did you do this time?"

Bruce rocked backward on his heels, his lips drawn back in a mirthless smile. "What did I do this time? Always, what did I do, right, Mark? We must have had some of the same profs in law school. Attack, boy, attack. Never give the SOB a chance to find any dry powder. You've been attacking me as long as I can remember. What does it take to prove to you I'm not an irresponsible adolescent?"

"Stop it!" Laura ordered, and she stepped between Mark and Bruce. "Outside, Bruce. You too, Donna. Mark, would you please help me with the drinks?"

Mark stared at her, his lips parted as if he intended to refuse. Then his expression softened and he nodded, as he quickly gathered the lemons and oranges Laura had sliced and dropped them into a tall jug. Donna caught hold of Bruce's sleeve and pulled him outside, sliding the door shut behind them.

She dragged a white-painted metal chair forward and pointed silently at it. Bruce sat down and clamped his hands behind his neck. He glared up at her, his nostrils flaring.

Donna quickly assembled three more chairs in a circle around a low table. "Cool it, Bruce," she muttered. "You're using this as an excuse for some private war you've been itching to wage on Mark. Don't. If there's something you two need to get in the open, choose another subject to battle over."

He tipped his head all the way back so that she couldn't see his eyes. "Old habits die hard. I've always had to use whatever weapon came readily to hand with Mark. He puts me on the defensive."

"He likes you. You're the closest thing he has to a brother. Maybe he even loves you in a way, have you thought of that? Sometimes we're tough on the people we really care about."

Bruce sat up, his clear eyes speculative. "You could have something there. He's pretty special to me, too. I just wish he didn't seem to think of me as an incorrigible."

If there was one time in her life when Donna needed to keep calm, it was definitely now. "Give him a break for once, Bruce. He'll do what's right."

"Oh, hell..." Bruce sighed, his hands hanging between his knees. "You can't know how long I've listened to Mark being billed as a saint." Any antagonism he felt appeared to have drained from him.

The hand Donna passed over her brow came away sticky. She wasn't hot. So why was she sweating? Dumb question, she acknowledged instantly. Enough tension charged this small area to make an infantry platoon sweat. "Bruce," she said quietly, "you're as good as any man— better to me. I guess that's why I—"

"Drinks, folks," Mark announced, cutting off the rest of her sentence. He stepped onto the terrace carrying a brimming jug.

Donna swallowed. She looked at Bruce and he regarded her steadily, an oddly sweet smile on his lips. The smile, the softness in his eyes, told her he knew she'd been about to profess her love for him. Instead, she said, "I love sangria," and was certain she must sound as artificial as she felt.

"Me too," Bruce agreed, in a voice that suggested he felt as disconnected as she. Donna longed to hold his hand. How could she expect him to keep caring for her when she brought him nothing but trouble?

Laura brought glasses on a tray, and crackers and

cheese, and set them on the table. "Would you pour, please, Mark?" she asked and when Mark's eyes met his wife's, Donna felt the first spark of anything but misery she'd experienced for hours. In the adversity Mark and Laura must feel approaching, they were closing ranks.

As Mark passed Donna he squeezed her shoulder, and she smiled up at him.

When they sat, tall glasses held aloft, silence enveloped them again. Donna looked at each face. Bruce's expression was closed, Mark's enigmatic. Laura's marvelous blue eyes moved from one to the other, clearly nervous, until they connected with her husband's and he smiled. Laura smiled back, and Donna's coiled heart unfurled a little more in the reflection of the love that passed between the two.

Her relief was short-lived. "We've got a problem, Mark," Bruce announced, downing half his drink. "I don't think either of these lovely ladies in our lives has let you in on a little secret they've been harboring."

Donna's heart seemed to stop altogether. She met Laura's eyes and saw her own sick apprehension mirrored there. Bruce couldn't, wouldn't, tell Mark she'd thrown herself at him, proposed marriage.

"Mark," Donna said quickly. "Mark, I've done something awful. Not Laura, me. She told me I shouldn't, but I did it anyway. Now I've put everyone in a bind, at least Bruce and myself, and I may end up hurting Mom and Dad if…oh, Mark, don't get mad."

"Donna, let me explain," Bruce broke in. He took the glass from her shaking hand and set it on the table. "Don't get so upset. We all have to keep our heads."

"Bruce is right, Donna," Laura agreed.

"I did this," Donna said. "I'm the one who should do any explaining that has to be done."

Mark smacked his glass onto the table with enough force to spill the sangria. "That's it," he said. "I want to know what's going on here—now. Who tells me doesn't matter. Just get it out."

"Yes," Donna said, "I'll tell you, Mark. I got Bruce to look for my father."

She kept her eyes on Mark's face. He parted his lips a fraction, and stared back, frowning. "Your father?" he repeated finally. "I don't get it. I spoke to Evan earlier today. He calls almost every day about something or other."

"No. Not Daddy. My biological father. The man Prairie was living with. Raymond Tsung."

Donna saw understanding dawn in Mark's brown eyes. "You wanted to know about your real father, Donna?" he asked quietly. "And you thought I wouldn't understand that? Honey, I do. Seems like the most natural thing in the world to me."

Sure, Donna thought, *unless you use the search as a ploy to catch a man and then, when the hapless father in question has the gall to show up and be enthusiastic about you, you don't want to see him; unless you've sneaked around not telling your family what you intend to do.*

Donna felt sick. She'd behaved like a kid. It was time for a little plain honesty. She shivered, although it wasn't cold. The sun was sinking, but the breeze that moved the roses edging the terrace was warm. She concentrated on the peachy color of a single, heavy bloom until it blurred against the sky. Nobody had spoken for a long time. If only they could just stay like this.

Finally, Donna cleared her throat. "You see, Mark, there is more to the situation than that. The reason—the silly, juvenile, idiot reason I asked Bruce to hunt for Tsung was because I wanted Bruce's attention for the rest of the summer. I figured that the investigation would get it for me.'' The steadiness of her voice surprised her, but she could feel her face flaming with embarrassment. ''The reason I wanted his complete attention was...because I thought I could make him fall in love with me. I...I fell in love with Bruce when I was fifteen.''

''You what?'' He sounded very much like an attorney getting the facts straight.

Donna swallowed hard. ''You heard me, Mark. To you it may sound unbelievable. It sounded unbelievable to Bruce—''

Mark's head swiveled around. ''Bruce?'' There was an edge of anger in his tone.

''No,'' Donna interrupted him, reaching over and placing her hand on his arm. ''Don't shout at Bruce. He's the innocent bystander here—the one who gets hit by the iron safe falling from a window.''

''All the same, dammit, Bruce. You should have come to me immediately.''

''You heard the lady,'' Bruce said levelly. ''I'm out of it. I'm the guy the safe fell on.''

''Save your crummy jokes, Bruce. She's only nineteen! Nineteen years old, Bruce.''

Bruce's glass missed the table and crashed to the stone patio. ''Just a minute—''

''No, Bruce.'' Laura spoke for the first time. ''Stop it.'' She hit Mark's shoulder lightly. ''You have every right to yell at Bruce about work at the office if you want to. You have no right to say anything at all to him about his personal life.''

''His personal life! What about Donna's personal... Good Lord, Laura, she's just a kid—''

''I'm sure Bruce is as aware of Donna's age as we are,'' Laura said, speaking almost sharply. ''I'd stake my life on the certainty that he's been treating her like spun glass ever since she dropped her bombshell.''

''That's a good description of it,'' Donna said. ''I've been hanging onto his coattails, but I feel like there's an invisible ten-foot pole between us, and I'm the object he wouldn't touch with the end of it.'' She sounded so rueful that Mark gave her a halfhearted little grin and placed his hand over hers. There was a sudden bond between them. She sensed that he knew how much this was costing her.

''What your wife is saying, Mark,'' Bruce said lightly, ''is that the time is long past for you to stop telling me how to think. And what to do about what I think. I needed a guiding hand once, and you were there. You gave me more than I deserved, and no one could have done more for me or done it better. But you've got to let go, Mark. For God's sake, man, I'm your partner, not your son.''

''The thing is,'' Laura continued relentlessly. ''Whatever does, or does not, develop between them is just that, Mark, between them. And we should stay out of it. People—'' Her voice became slightly unsteady for just a moment. ''People should work out their own problems.''

''Thanks, Laura,'' Donna said softly. ''The point is, the point we're getting away from, is that Bruce found him, found Raymond Tsung.'' She felt very tired.

Laura's voice came from far away. ''Mark, dear,'' she said softly, ''I think Bruce and Donna need your help with this…this Mr. Tsung. I think things may have gone farther than either of them expected. You will help, won't you?''

Donna looked at Mark. He stared back. ''No kidding. You found him? I'm amazed. What do Evan and Sara say about it? They couldn't have expected anyone to have more luck finding your father than they did.''

''They don't know,'' Donna wailed. She poured out the rest of her story: how she'd planned her trip to San Francisco for almost two years, how she'd come up with the idea of trying to find her real father, the way Bruce had agreed to start a search, the mix-up over Raymond Tsung's name, the fact that the name hadn't mattered anyway because she'd never expected Tsung would be found. She poured out the details while her heart pounded faster and faster and Mark's expression changed steadily to that of a deeply troubled man.

"And now he wants to see me and have me meet this other family I'm a part of, and I'm sick, Mark, just sick about it. Mom and Dad will never understand, and they're almost bound to find out."

Mark had moved to the edge of his seat. "Did you realize Evan and Sara were in the dark about this?" he asked Bruce.

"No," Bruce said wearily. "But I didn't ask, and before you tell me I should have, Mark, I already know. The main thing is to get through this without too many scars—for anyone. Donna didn't mean to hurt anyone. She simply didn't think her way through all the possible consequences of what she'd decided to do."

"Don't blame Bruce," Donna interjected. "How was he supposed to guess what I planned to do. Having Prairie wander back in to my life every few years has been hard enough on them. They don't need this father I've produced, too. I certainly don't need him."

"You started something, then found you were out of your depth. It happens. But I wish you'd come to me earlier, Donna. We could have avoided the trouble we're probably going to be faced with." Mark turned to Bruce. "You used our names when you contacted the man?"

"He knows all about us. My appointment with him was made through the firm. And, Mark, this is the Raymond Tsung who's president of the Bank of Cathay."

Mark whistled through steepled fingers. "Then Donna has to finish what she's started. But Evan and Sara have to be told. I won't be a party to deceiving them any longer. If Donna were my child, I'd want to know."

He spoke as if she weren't there, Donna thought absently. When she checked each face at the table, all three seemed to have moved away from her; they all seemed to be deciding her fate while she just looked on.

Mark pushed his chair back and stood. "Laura, I know you're closest to Evan, but I think I can stay calmer. I'm going to call him now."

He went to the door and paused, turning. "Bruce?"

"Yes, Mark?" Resignation underlined the question.

"I was out of line a minute ago. My apologies. When the chips are down, your integrity is first-class, and in my saner moments I know it. I'm officially butting out. Okay?"

"Sure. Forget it." Bruce grinned, and gave a mock salute.

"And Donna... Look, honey, I'm only going to tell Evan about Tsung. I'll leave the business about your feelings for Bruce for you to tell him later. Whenever you decide the time is right. One thing at a time. No point in throwing everything at him at once. Right?"

She nodded, unable to speak.

SARAH MCGRATH CLOSED her son's bedroom door and stood in the hallway, listening for a few seconds. Jim murmured indistinctly, and she smiled through the tears that had welled in her eyes. Like a lot of young children without close siblings, five-year-old Jim talked a lot of his thoughts aloud when he was alone. When Donna was home, he chattered to her constantly. She was so good with him. Every few days since she'd been in California she'd sent Jim a card with a printed message. She'd always loved her brother, loved them all; Sara refused to believe Donna's feelings for her family had changed.

Her lower lip trembling, she climbed slowly down the spiral staircase to the main floor of the town house she and Evan owned. Evan hadn't turned on any lights in the huge living room. She saw him immediately, his back to her, his straight-backed, athletic body a dark outline against the wall of glass overlooking English Bay.

Her stockinged feet made no sound on the deep carpet, and Evan started when she slipped an arm through his. He lifted his chin slightly and continued to stare out at the evening sky. In the distance, to their left, the lights of Vancouver were coming on, a million glittering pinpricks against a lavender sky.

"You know what's so hard?" Evan asked. He covered his wife's hand. "No, don't think about it. I'll work everything out." His curly brown hair, still untouched by gray, stood on end in front, a signal that he'd pushed at it repeatedly, as he always did when he was troubled.

Sara massaged his arm. "Tell me, Evan. We've got to get through this."

He leaned to rest his forehead on the window. "Right now, I feel like I'm breaking up. Why didn't she feel she could tell us what she intended to do? What did I do wrong? I always thought she loved me. I sure love her, Sara. How I love her."

The tears that slid down Sara's cheeks were hot. Her throat ached. "Donna loves you," she managed to say. "Perhaps she was afraid you'd be hurt if you found out she wanted to know her…to know this other man."

He looked down at her, his own dark eyes glistening. She saw him grit his teeth before he pulled her into his arms. "She's hurt you too, Sara, and she should never have done that. Damn her, and damn Bruce. Wait till I get my hands on that—''

"Shhh," Sara whispered against his chest. "Shhh, sweetheart. From what Mark said, Bruce didn't have any idea Donna was acting without our approval. None of them did."

Evan smoothed back Sara's sleek dark hair, and moved her away until he could look into her gray-blue eyes. They'd been married six years, yet as always, he was struck afresh by the passion she aroused in him, as well as the desire to protect her. This debacle with Donna had to be his fault, and he'd iron it out. Sara had suffered enough over the years coping with Prairie Crawford. She'd coped very well, and he'd do as well with Raymond Tsung, but not without making sure Donna appreciated both what a wonderful mother she had, and the desperate unhappiness she'd caused through her own deceit.

"I'd better call back, darling," he said, his stomach clenched. "I couldn't go on talking before. Mark will be on pins and needles waiting, poor guy. I don't blame him, or Laura."

"Don't blame anyone, Evan. It won't help."

He kissed her, pressed his cheek to hers, and kissed her again before he went to a phone.

There were several rings before he heard Donna's voice. For a second his mind blanked, then he swallowed and held the receiver in both hands. "I'm glad you had the guts to at least speak to me yourself this time," he said.

"Dad—"

"Don't talk, Donna. I can't talk to you now. You can do your explaining in person. As soon as I clear the decks here, I'll be down. I'll let you know when I'm due in San Francisco. Goodbye."

Donna stood there, holding the phone in a cold hand,

until she heard the dial tone. Then she put it back in the cradle with a hurried gesture, as if she couldn't get rid of it fast enough. She crossed her arms, and stared at a painting of flowers on the wall until the colors blurred. Dad was coming.

"Well, what…what'd he say?" Bruce asked.

"That was quick," Mark murmured thoughtfully. "It was brave of you to answer, honey, but maybe you should have let me."

"What did Evan say?" Laura asked softly, getting up and moving to stand beside Donna.

They were in the spacious white-and-peach-colored front hallway, where Donna had darted to answer the phone on the first ring. She looked at the phone again now and had to try twice before she could speak.

"He's coming here. To San Francisco. As…as soon as he can. He'll let me know when his plane is due."

"He didn't give you any idea when?" Mark persisted.

Donna shook her head. "He just said as soon as he cleared the decks. I think that's what he said." Her voice sounded hollow.

"He's probably got some loose ends to tie up with the business," Bruce muttered. He went to her and put an arm around her shoulders. "I'll meet him when he comes, Donna. Don't worry about it."

"No, let me do it," Mark interposed.

"Thanks, Mark," Bruce said. He looked tired. "I know you'd go, and I know you'd say the right things. But this isn't your problem—it's mine. Evan will want to see me, anyway. All he knows about so far is Tsung. We all know he'll have to be told the whole story. The sooner the better, and—"

"No, Bruce," Laura interrupted. "I don't agree. He needs to see a neutral face first. I'd better do it." She turned to Donna. "I'm Evan's old buddy, don't forget. Your father and I go back a long way. He's making million-dollar deals now, but he and I share memories of one-dollar deals. We used to pick up money from the grass or the pavement when people tossed small bills or coins down after our clown act. We went through a lot together. If anyone can talk to your father, I can."

"No. It has to be me. I have to meet him." Donna kept her eyes wide, determined not to let the tears spill over. She reached out to touch Laura lightly. "Daddy and I go back a long way too, don't forget. And I'm the one who's…who's hurt him." How unbelievable to utter those words and know that they were true. "So I'll have to make it right somehow."

Make it right? How could she ever make it right?

CHAPTER THIRTEEN

THEY WALKED FROM Fenton and Hunt to the Bank of Cathay, allowing themselves plenty of time to arrive by two. Donna's earlier stage fright seemed to be gone, and she strode along confidently beside Bruce, her hand clasped in his.

She knew she looked all right. She and Laura had fussed for so long over what clothing she would wear today that she had almost been late for work. They had settled on her most sedate outfit, a plain gray suit she'd bought last year.

"I'll just be pleasant, but as firm as it takes," she said again. "He'll understand, I'm sure."

"Well, he was pretty thrilled at the idea of an unknown daughter, so don't expect this to be too easy. You should be prepared for a little resistance to your bowing out as soon as you bow in."

"I can handle it. Stop worrying, Bruce." There was an underlying tone of desperation in her voice now. "By the time Dad gets here from Vancouver, I'm going to be ready to tell him he can forget the whole thing. That I've seen Mr. Tsung, and said hello and goodbye, that's all."

Bruce squeezed her hand. "Okay, love, if you say so. But be aware. Your Mr. Tsung didn't get to be president of a bank by being unassertive. Here we are."

He pushed open the door of the bank. Donna stepped briskly inside with Bruce right behind her. "Straight back." He gestured ahead, and they went through the entry and past the desks and tellers' cages. They passed a line of people waiting behind the brass rail for teller service and reached the elevators.

On the executive floor, Bruce took Donna into Tsung's outer office. Miss Hu looked up from her typewriter and quickly rose to her feet. She bowed slightly in their direction, and smiled vividly.

"Mr. Tsung is waiting for you. Please go right in." The gateway slid back. She must have buzzed the inner office, for Mr. Tsung swung wide his door and stood back to let them enter his office.

"Mr. Tsung," Bruce said smoothly. "This is Donna. You said two. We walked, so I hope we're not late." He knew they weren't; he was just making conversation, Donna realized with gratitude.

Her mouth had gone totally dry because, before she was really ready for it, she was facing the man who had fathered her. The pleasant little speech she had rehearsed was gone. Her mind was blank.

"Donna," Tsung was saying softly. "Donna, what a lovely girl you are. Come over here." And somehow the hand she had held out was in his and he was pulling her toward the window. He looked at her keenly for a moment, then dropped her hand. "Ah, my dear, this is not a day for tears," he said in the same gentle tone, and Donna realized, as his image blurred, that her eyes had filled. She felt a tremulous sense of eagerness, of expectation, of uneasiness, all mingled together. She had not anticipated this, an emotional reaction to this stranger. She had expected anything but that. But he was not a stranger. He had the same opaque dark eyes she had, and they were set the same way hers were. And her teeth had been slightly crooked, the same way his still were, before her mom and dad had paid the earth to get them straightened.

What is it? she thought wildly for a moment. *What am I feeling?* Then she knew, without even first forming the thought coherently. *I am feeling kinship.* She wasn't the different one with this man, as she was different from her mother and father and brother. There was the same sense here of connectedness, of clannishness. It was like reaching out to like, and both of them were aware of the relatedness. She hadn't counted on that, and felt a flood of shame and guilt because of it, remembering her parents. It wasn't fair to them.

"Come, come, let's sit down over here. Miss Hu has made us some tea. We must get acquainted a bit. What a momentous day!" He led them to a grouping of soft gray easy chairs surrounding a heavy lacquered table on which sat an exquisite blue tea set. He seated her in one of the chairs, and he and Bruce took the other two.

"It's going to be almost sacrilegious, drinking out of these cups," Bruce said.

"Ah. You like them? Yes. They are very old." Tsung lifted one delicate azure porcelain cup between blunt fingers. "I'm trying to remember where I got these, and I can't. It must mean my wife put them here. She decorated my office when I was made president five years ago." He lifted the pot and began to pour out a thin stream of pale liquid into the cups.

"She did a lovely job," Bruce said, looking around and nodding.

"Yes, lovely," Donna echoed politely. Her poise was returning, but she still felt shaky, and she waited a moment before picking up her tiny tea cup.

"I talked to my wife yesterday afternoon after you left, Mr. Fenton, and she was very pleased. Very pleased."

Donna had the feeling that he would make conversation

until he was sure her composure had returned. She felt she should say something to let him know it had.

"Was she very surprised?" she asked.

"Surprised...and delighted." He coughed into a fist. "She called back twice last evening. Once to make sure I had sent out the picture by courier, and once so the boys could talk to me. Bruce, Mr. Fenton—"

"Bruce is fine," Bruce said easily.

"Bruce gave me a photo he had in his billfold." He smiled at Bruce. "You must call me Ray. All my friends do." He sipped his tea.

Donna wondered what he had told his wife. She must know, surely, that he had had some romantic involvements before his marriage. A relationship or two. She wondered, also, what he had told the boys, how he would explain her to strangers if they learned of her existence. The last question, at least, was answered for her when Miss Hu entered with a sheaf of documents.

"I am most terribly sorry, Mr. Tsung, but Mr. Wing says you want to sign this, and he has to take it to Chicago."

He rose. "Yes, yes, thank you, Miss Hu. I promised I would. Is he out there? Ask him in. But wait, I want you to meet my daughter, Donna, the girl I told you about, the daughter of my first marriage."

Miss Hu gave Donna her brilliant smile and bowed again. So he was passing off his relationship with poor little Prairie as an early marriage. Well, perhaps it was the kindest way; still, it seemed unlikely that the present Mrs. Tsung or any close relatives would actually accept the explanation.

She and Bruce both stood up to meet Mr. Wing, who was very old and looked as fragile as bone china. Tsung made the same introduction he'd made to Miss Hu, and the old man showed every evidence of delight.

"Will you take her around the office?" he asked Tsung. "The whole place is buzzing, you know."

Tsung laughed. "I don't know how it is at Fenton and Hunt, Bruce, but nothing beats the office grapevine here for getting news around."

Smiling graciously at the frail Mr. Wing, Donna thought, *I haven't given my little speech.* Almost as soon as Mr. Wing and Miss Hu were gone, she recited what she'd planned to say.

"I'm glad to come over and meet you today, sir. It didn't seem right to be in San Francisco and not at least say hello." That wasn't exactly right, she thought, but close enough.

"Of course. And you were correct. I can never tell you how happy it has made me. Are you up to meeting the others now? My staff will never forgive me if I don't take you around the office."

Donna wasn't sure she wanted a tour, but somehow they were in his outer office, with Miss Hu beaming at them, and she was meeting a Mrs. Taylor, and a Miss Woo, and two men named Wong, and then a young girl, Jenny, pushing a cart loaded with folders. She would never remember all their names. She was breathing a faint sigh of relief as they reached the end of the group, when Tsung said, "Okay. Now let's go down to the others."

"The others?" Donna echoed. And so began an hour and a half pilgrimage down through the bank building, to visit all the departments. She and Bruce met the vice-presidents and their secretaries, all the loan officers, all the people in first and second mortgages, personal loans, car loans and business loans. Next they met the people in accounting, and the people in collections, and the people in advertising. And Raymond Tsung knew everybody by name, and sometimes tossed in a little question or comment like, "And how is Johnny's leg?" or "Please tell your mother I asked about her." Donna's head was swimming by the time they finally reached the basement of the building, where they met the janitorial staff, who were just coming to work.

She had met all four of the janitors when the elevator doors opened and the beautiful Miss Hu stepped out.

"Mr. Tsung, the man from Gump's is here," she said, standing elegantly between two metal mop buckets.

"Ah! Gump's. Let's not keep him waiting," Tsung said. He hurried them into the elevator, which carried them swiftly and silently back up to the executive floor.

"I put him in your office," Miss Hu said.

"Thank you, thank you. I want to give you a small gift, Donna," he said as they went back into his office again.

She murmured, "Oh, no," but her words were lost amid introductions to the man from Gump's, whose name she did not catch. She was remembering how expensive a store Laura had said Gump's was.

All over Tsung's desk were arranged velvet jeweler's boxes.

"Pick out something you like, my dear. A keepsake to remember the day we first met." He turned to Bruce. "My wife went on and on about this last night. I was to select something highly suitable. Something girlish, but not too girlish for nineteen, and so on. I decided to let Donna choose her own gift. Don't you think that was wise?"

Bruce laughed. "Very. What do you think, Donna?" Bruce came to her side, and she felt the touch of his arm against hers. He was trying to reassure her silently.

She stood looking down at the display, dumbfounded. There were three golden chains with large diamond pendants. She hastily looked away from those. Too expensive, Donna thought. She mustn't take a valuable gift. She mustn't obligate herself to this man, for she knew how her parents would feel. There were four pearl necklaces. She placed a hesitant finger on a creamy strand with a rosy glow.

"That's lovely," she murmured uncertainly, and there was an eager intake of breath, it seemed, from all the men. They were looking at her, waiting. She began to feel terribly embarrassed.

"This is jade, isn't it?" she said, her hand hovering over one of several green jade necklaces.

"Yes. You like jade? Would you like to try one on?" Tsung asked.

"N…no." She hesitated. Maybe jade was too costly. Then she noticed a simple, plain necklace of perfectly round lavender beads. It looked like the least expensive of the lot.

"This is pretty," she said, picking it up carefully. She looked at the clasp. Metal. No diamonds or other precious stones. This was probably her best choice. "I…I would like this," she said diffidently. "And it will go nicely with my gray suit," she added inanely.

"Here. Let me." Tsung reached for the necklace, and she turned around to let him fasten the delicate strand around her neck. "Now, let us look. What do you think, Bruce? It suits her, don't you think?"

"Yes," Bruce said softly. "It does. Understated elegance, just the thing. Lavender jade."

"Jade?" Donna said in a strangled little voice, but it was too late; the necklace was already hers. The man from Gump's was shutting up his velvet boxes, preparing to leave.

"Thank you," she said. "Thank you very much. It's

just lovely. We really must…Bruce…what time is it?''
She was feeling desperate to leave.

Bruce laughed. ''It's after four. You can forget about
going back to work. Meetings like this aren't done in a
minute.''

''No,'' agreed Tsung. ''And I want a picture. My wife
said I had to bring the Polaroid to work today, and so I
did. Miss Hu, where did I…?''

''Here it is, Mr. Tsung,'' Miss Hu said, handing him
the camera.

''Thank you. Now, we'll get a little family portrait for
my wife. Bruce, could you do the honors?'' He extended
the camera toward Bruce.

''Sure. Why don't you stand in front of that screen? Or
do you think those light draperies would be better?''

The phrase ''family portrait'' nearly undid Donna. *No,*
she thought, *No. My family is in Vancouver. Oh, Mom.
Oh, Dad.* She wanted to cry. Instead, she pasted on a smile
and stood where they told her to. Before the screen. Before
the drapery. With Mr. Tsung. Without Mr. Tsung. She
seated herself in the chair, leaning back and smiling. Then
she posed holding a blue tea cup. She was surprised to find
the cup empty. And clean.

She wanted to go home!

And not back to Laura and Mark's.

Home to Vancouver. Home to her family.

But this was not yet to be. First, they must finish their
aborted tea party. Miraculously, the pot was full again with
scalding tea, courtesy of Miss Hu, she supposed. And after
the picture-taking, they had to sit and sip it.

I want to go home.

Her unspoken message must have reached Bruce, for he
started making leave-taking motions.

''I want you to come to dinner with me,'' Tsung said

at the doorway. "Please. You must. Soon. The day after tomorrow? Is that all right? Day after tomorrow?"

"Yes, yes," Donna said mechanically. "That would be nice. Don't you think that would be nice, Bruce?" She would promise anything to get away. Dimly, she heard Bruce agreeing that it would be nice, and then they were going through the bank again. Donna smiled brightly at all the employees, and soon they were walking on teeming Grant Avenue.

"Oh, Bruce," she said as she hurried along at his side. "What am I going to do?"

"Well, right now we're going to stop in at that little coffee shop near the office, and we'll just pause a minute and see where we stand."

"Oh, yes, yes," she said eagerly. "That sounds so good. We'll see where we stand." They walked rapidly toward the Fenton and Hunt building, dodging the swelling homeward-bound crowds.

"Actually, sweetheart, this does just sound good," Bruce said, pushing open the door of the restaurant when they'd arrived. Warmth, and the smell of freshly baked rolls greeted them. "Where we seem to be standing," he continued, "is on the edge of a precipice. Good, the place is practically empty." There was one long counter down the lefthand wall, with swivel stools in front of it. They sat on two stools at the end. Bruce picked up the menu and put it down again without reading a word. "They have old-fashioned ice-cream sodas here, if you'd like one. Would you?"

"Yes. Chocolate, please."

"Two chocolate sodas," he told the counterman, and they waited in tense silence until he brought their order.

"Pretty good," Bruce said, taking a sip through his straw.

Donna sucked her drink pensively for a moment. "What you mean by just *sounds* good," she said finally, pushing her glass away slightly, "is that Pandora's box is wide open and stuff is coming out."

"All sorts of stuff, I'm afraid."

"Like the revelation that Mr. Tsung isn't going to just quietly go away." She sounded thoughtful.

"No. Not immediately, anyhow. Now we've got this dinner date with him, which we didn't have this morning. I'd hoped we could get away with something less definite."

"Could I have gotten out of it, Bruce?"

"I truly don't see how. Not without bluntly hurting his feelings anyway."

"Oh, I couldn't have done that. I wouldn't intentionally, I mean." She moved the straw up and down in her soda.

"Do you know why?" Bruce asked softly.

She tilted her head to one side and considered his question for a moment. "I guess I know exactly why, don't I?"

"You bet you do. It's because he's such a damned nice guy. In a way, we kind of owe him. He didn't ask us to stroll in and turn his life upside down, but he's taking everything very well."

She bowed her head over her glass, and her hair fell forward to hide her face. Hiding was exactly what she felt like doing right now.

"You know I hadn't...I guess I really hadn't counted on that. On him being so...so like he is. What that means is that we, I mean I, will have to protect him as well as my parents. I mean from being hurt in the fallout from my little escapade."

"Do you want my recommendation on how we might do that?"

"At this point, I'll listen to anybody's recommendation."

Bruce took another noisy sip of his soda and pushed aside the glass. "This little dinner has to be *it*, Donna. This has to end it. The longer we let him hold the illusion that he's got a full-time daughter, the harder it's going to be for him. There can't be an after-the-dinner meeting. Do you understand?"

"Right! And this quiet little dinner should be the ideal occasion to set things straight."

"It should be. We'll simply lay the situation out for him, politely and kindly. I can't see how anything could go wrong."

"I can't either." She tried to sound confident. A small silence stretched between them.

"Donna?"

"Yes?"

"Do you have a funny feeling that it's not going to be that easy?"

"Oh, Bruce, I wish you hadn't said that." She stared at him with a worried frown, her soda forgotten. What was Raymond Tsung doing right now? she wondered.

CHAPTER FOURTEEN

DONNA STOOD ABOVE the ridge of froth veeing out from *Lake Lady*'s bow. The setting sun shot glowing spears of purple, lemon yellow and soft pink skyward from the horizon, tinting the smooth surface of the bay. Donna braced herself against the rail and lifted her face to a stiff breeze. Bruce had promised to put them under sail after they ate. She twisted to rest her chin on a raised shoulder, looking aft. She couldn't see Bruce.

While she didn't know enough to be of help, Donna thought she should at least offer. If she asked, maybe he'd teach her something about the boat. It was possible that he might even like her to show some interest. She walked toward the cockpit, staggering against each swell. Bruce had been a dear to suggest bringing her out on the bay instead of sentencing her to a long evening at the Hunts, where all she'd do was fret over Raymond Tsung and his dinner invitation.

The boat rolled, and she grabbed a taut line. She knew she'd worry about the dinner anyway.

On the top step of the companionway to the cockpit, Donna paused, looking down at Bruce. He sat on the jump seat behind the controls, a heel resting on each side of the wheel. He'd changed into shorts and a T-shirt, and the wind pressed the shirt to his lean body. His head was bowed, and she saw the slow, rhythmic tapping of a thumb knuckle against his chin. She wasn't the only one with a lot to think about after today's interview.

Holding a rail in each hand, she plastered a grin in place, lifted her feet and slid to the deck of the cockpit the way Bruce always did. She let out a hoot as she went—and a howl when she overbalanced and landed in a heap at the bottom of the steps.

"Hey, Donna, watch it, love." Bruce leaped from his seat to haul her up. "Where'd you hit? Did you hit one of those brass rims?"

She made a wry face and rubbed her bottom. "I guess I did, but at least I chose a padded spot to land on. That was supposed to be my seasoned nautical performance."

"A few more falls and you'll get it." Bruce grinned, then gave a low whistle. "How come that T-shirt never looked that good on me?"

"For a combination of reasons." Donna flung her arms wide and turned a complete circle for his inspection. "You have to have that certain something—you know, whatever it is that makes people say 'She'd look great in a sack.' It's probably the extravagant draping that appeals most, the way the garment accentuates my ample curves. Then, of course, the flapping, knee-length hemline does do something. I've always wondered what that meant—'do something'—when applied to clothing."

"Mmm." He continued to study her. "There's another point we're missing—probably the main one—the one that makes the biggest difference between Donna in shirt and Bruce in shirt."

"I've got it." Donna pointed her toes inward and stared at them. "The legs. If you shaved your hairy legs, you, too, could achieve this degree of loveliness."

Bruce laughed and put an arm around her. "You're a clown. Just be grateful that I had a spare shirt, or you'd be mincing around in that wonderful but stuffy suit you wore to your father's.''

The effect of his last comment on Donna was like a deluge of cold water. She lost the smile. Bruce let out a long breath and planted his hands on his hips. "I could have talked all night and not mentioned him, right?"

"Right," she agreed. "And, Bruce, could I ask you to do something for me?"

He arched one brow. "Here it comes. The last time you prefaced a request that way, I was told off for calling you a name I'd used since the day we met. What did I do wrong this time?"

"Nothing, really. Only Dad's—Evan that is—Dad's my father, and I don't want to even think of Raymond Tsung as my father. So could you not call him that, please?"

"Sorry." He grimaced. "What are you going to call him? Mr. Tsung was all right for this afternoon; expected even, but he's bound to want something a bit less formal."

"I'll figure it out later. Bruce, how am I going to face this dinner party?"

He shook her gently by the shoulder. "You will face it, love. I'll be with you all the way. We'll face it together."

"You're too good to me after what I've done to you." Donna laid her cheek on his outstretched arm. "I still have to find a way to back out gracefully. I'll do it after the dinner, of course, but I'm terrified I'll do everything wrong when I'm with him. From what I've read, the Chinese are so formal. I'd better get the chopsticks out again. If I splatter tablecloths in front of him, I think I'll die."

Bruce tucked her hair behind her ear and ran a thumb absently back and forth across her cheekbone. Donna closed her eyes. He couldn't know how his touch awakened her. Each time she was with him, alone, she wished they never had to go back to the rest of the world.

"We'll go over meal etiquette," Bruce said. "He'll probably want to make a fuss over you, and you must try to respond properly. Don't forget, even for a moment, that the Chinese don't like physical contact the same way we do. No hugging, cheek-kissing—"

Donna's laugh cut him off. "I'm not likely to start throwing my arms around Raymond Tsung, nice as he is. But so much for some people's theory of genetic influence on emotional makeup. I've been a hugger ever since Mom..." She stopped talking, as heat crept up her neck and over her face. "I'm just trying, in my usual diplomatic way, to say I'm very comfortable being demonstrative with people I care about. But I didn't have to tell you that. Shall I see what I can find in the galley? You must be starving." They'd had lunch at eleven, and the clock on the console read eight-thirty.

"Sounds good. You'll have to make do with canned stuff. I should have thought to stop and get fresh supplies."

"I'll manage," Donna assured him, already climbing back up the ladder.

The immaculate little galley lay beyond a functional, but attractively appointed, cabin. Softly cushioned couches lined the curved hull, fronted by low tables bolted to the carpeted deck. An extensive sound system was built in, as well as a bar. Batik hangings carried out a creamy white-and-gray color scheme. Donna thought, as she had so many times before, that Bruce had excellent taste. She glanced at the door leading to the master sleeping quarters. White had been used there too, and a darker gray, with the addition of black accent pieces and a lot of mirrors. There was also black in the compact bathroom. *Lake Lady* was one "toy" Donna could easily have gotten used to.

Half an hour later, she hailed Bruce, who helped carry

the feast she'd prepared to the shelter of the cockpit. "Sure you don't want to eat below?" he asked, when he'd set down a tray and taken one of her bare arms in his hands. "You've got goose bumps."

"I like it right where we are," she assured him. "The goose bumps are from coming through the wind up top. We're protected down here."

They ate rye crackers, slightly soggy, and cream cheese, slightly grainy from freezer burn followed by microwave thawing. Bruce devoured canned caviar; Donna took a tiny portion to be polite, and managed not to say what she usually said, that the disgusting stuff tasted like spoiled pickles to her. A tub of frozen raspberries disappeared with the remnants of a container of gourmet ice cream—thoroughly iced now and a little rancid, but delicious, Bruce assured Donna. Laughingly, she suggested the Chianti they were drinking had probably killed their taste buds. They'd grimaced with the first sip, and ended agreeing that it didn't taste so bad, after all.

"Good grief," Bruce moaned, spread-eagled in his deck chair. "That was awful, and wonderful. What a mixture. I can imagine what Irma would say about our menu."

"Why Irma?" Donna asked, licking salt from her fingers.

"Mark's mother is relaxed over everything but food. The lady is one hell of a cook, and she knows what's right, buddy."

Donna wrinkled her nose. "How much longer are you going to keep on thinking of me as your buddy, Bruce?"

He sat up and leaned close in the gloom. "You know that's not exactly the way I think of you anymore, don't you?"

She ignored the question. "You promised we'd put up the sails. There's enough wind, isn't there?"

He got up and flipped on the searchlights. "Sail it shall be, Donna, my friend."

There was no time for Donna to think of a snappy comeback. He sent her scurrying with orders to unsnap shrouds, coil lines and stand by winches. Since the sails could be raised mechanically, he could manage it all himself, he insisted, but he was sure she'd like to help.

A steely blue moon had risen by the time the black-rimmed mainsail and staysail had been raised and the jib billowed against a pearly sky. The balloon spinnaker, a fourth sail that filled eerily at the bow of the boat, seemed to capture the light and reflect it back across the decks. Leaning on the stern rail, Donna gazed upward, open-mouthed, at the spectacle of the joint power of man and elements in a night silent except for wind whining in canvas.

After a few minutes, Donna turned to watch their roiling wake. She couldn't forget her troubles for long. In Vancouver, right now, her father was making plans to confront her in San Francisco. Just being allowed to stay here for what little was left of the summer would take every shred of persuasiveness she possessed.

"Come and keep me company," Bruce called. "Come on, dreamer. You're the one who wanted to sail."

Donna went to his side, and he held her tightly with one arm while he kept a grip on the wheel with his right hand. "What's up? You were miles away back there."

"I was worrying about the famous dinner again." She turned her face to his chest. "Really, I was thinking about my folks, about Dad coming to San Francisco. He sounded so hurt and angry when I spoke to him."

"I'm sure he was hurt and angry. I feel guilty about that."

"It wasn't your fault."

"Mmm. I should have been smarter."

"Smarter than to be taken in by a no-good little schemer, you mean?"

Bruce leaned over to peer at the compass, checking their bearings; then he flipped a switch. "We'll hold course for a little while." He tightened his hold on her and tipped his head back to stare at the sky. "I should have been mature enough to save you from what you're going through. By that, I mean I should have seen through your initial plot, sweetheart."

"It would have made it a lot easier on you if you had."

"In some ways."

"How wouldn't it have been easier?"

"I think you've guessed that much by now. I'm not totally oblivious to you, Donna."

He was telling her, in his oblique way, that he cared for her, at least a little. "What do you think my dad will do?"

Bruce considered. "He'll ask why you didn't come clean with him. Then, after you've been together for a while, he'll be his rational old self and help you work through the rough spots. Don't worry so much. Fall will come, and school, and a new start."

Donna was suddenly cold, and her temperature had nothing to do with the night wind. "That's what you think? That I'll go away at the end of summer as if nothing different had happened in my life? I'll go home like a good little girl and start school, become a gym teacher and date a football coach...and...forget?" She heard the choking sound in her voice, and pressed her fingertips to her mouth.

"I...no, I don't mean that exactly," Bruce said, with more than a hint of desperation in his voice. "I just meant that everything passes. The bad times as well as the good, and this rough spot will pass for you too. The main thing is going to be getting your education so you're ready to cope with the world.''

Donna moved away. ''You've been talking to my folks. They put you up to persuading me not to make waves about school. That's it, isn't it? When did you call them? Or did they call you?''

''Okay, listen.'' Bruce backed her against the bulkhead. ''Before you even arrived, back in June, Evan told me he and Sara were concerned that you'd lost interest in school. They asked me to try to influence you in the right direction because they knew you and I had always had a rapport.''

''The right direction,'' Donna snapped. ''The right direction for whom? Isn't the right direction for me the one that'll make me happiest?''

''Not if it makes other people damned unhappy.''

''Like you, you mean?''

He raised his hands and opened his mouth. Seconds later, he clamped his teeth together and bowed his head so that she couldn't see his face. ''You don't make me unhappy, you little idiot. Confused as hell, but not unhappy.''

Donna kept very still. She could hear her heart beating. ''But you have spoken to my folks again about helping them do what's best.''

''No, I haven't.'' He shook his head slowly. ''Under the circumstances, Donna, I wouldn't know what to say to Evan and Sara. Surely you understand that.''

To her horror, Donna felt the tightening in her chest that meant tears. She opened her eyes and breathed through her mouth, but she was going to cry anyway.

''Raymond Tsung isn't going to be the only topic addressed when Evan arrives, is he?'' Bruce said.

She'd put this man she loved so desperately in an impossible position. ''It'll be all right,'' she said, choking. Then the tears started, and the sobs. ''I'll make sure Dad knows you had nothing to do with what I've done. I'll come right out and tell him I cooked the whole thing up and you've done nothing but try to make me see things…see things…''

''Don't. Don't,'' Bruce murmured, taking her in his arms and holding her with a fierce gentleness. ''Do you think I'd let you face the music alone? You aren't entirely to blame, Donna, no way. You did tell me how you felt, and I didn't exactly run away, did I?''

All she felt was Bruce. All she heard was his voice, although the words faded in and out as he spoke close to her ear. Driven by a force she couldn't control, she pushed her hands under his shirt and around his slim waist.

Bruce made a small noise, and pushed her head back with his mouth until he could kiss her, fully, deeply. And Donna kissed him back, parting her lips willingly, meeting his tongue.

''Have I told you I love the way you smell?'' Bruce whispered.

She shook her head and nipped a row of tiny kisses along his neck.

His broad hands slipped down her back and beneath her arms, until his thumbs rested against the sides of her breasts. ''Sometimes you smell exotic, like sandalwood or something. Sometimes it's a wildflower scent. I wake up thinking about it.''

Donna said, ''Mmm,'' but her thoughts were on the sensation of his thumbs moving back and forth on her breasts. An answering ache weighted her womb. Her legs were weak.

''Don't ever feel alone, Donna.'' He framed her face with his hands. ''If you're in any kind of trouble, I'm here for you. Remember that.''

She looked up into his face, a thought forming, a

thought she didn't want to consider. "The way you came over that night when I was so upset?"

"Like that night. But anytime. I'm your friend, love, and I want to look after you."

Look after me. His weight held her against the bulkhead, and she didn't need a medical degree to figure out that he was sexually aroused...but by what he saw as her need for his protection? He lowered his head to kiss her collarbone, and she looked blindly over his shoulder. Bruce was responding to her the way she'd longed for, the way she'd dreamed of his responding, but it wasn't right. It was his concept of her as a helpless female in need that turned him on.

"Stop it, Bruce." She forced her hands between them. "I don't want to be with you this way." She wanted him to love her the way a man was supposed to love a woman, or not at all.

Bruce felt the heels of her hands on his chest before he heard her words. He moved away instantly. "Oh, Donna, love. I'm sorry. Don't be frightened, I wouldn't hurt you." What the hell was he thinking of? She was inexperienced, and he had to go slowly with her. The thought excited and scared him—and surprised him. He'd fallen in love with her. Despite all of his resolutions, he'd passed over the fine line that separated a friend from a prospective lover.

"Of course you wouldn't hurt me," she said distinctly as she ducked away and walked to the opposite rail. "Buddies don't hurt each other."

He frowned. "I thought...I mean..." She was frightened, and reacting to protect herself. His timing was lousy. Damn, but he wanted her—now. "Sweetheart, I'll be the one to explain what's happened to Evan. He can take his anger about Raymond Tsung out on me. My shoulders are broad enough."

"Your shoulders are very broad, Bruce."

Her voice had changed. The softness was gone, the husky note of desire. Frustration gnawed at his belly, but he held on. He was a man, with a man's drive and expectations. Donna wasn't even twenty, and he suspected she was still a virgin; she was slowly melding the child with the woman in her, and he'd have to be patient.

He crossed the deck and stood behind her. When he put his hands on her shoulders, she stiffened. "What's wrong?" he asked, puzzled. Regardless of her reservations, a few minutes ago she'd come on to him without holding back—why the abrupt change?

"Nothing's wrong." She glanced up at him, a tight little smile on her lips. "We should probably get back. Mark and Laura will wonder where we are."

He smiled back and kissed her temple lightly. "You're right. Want to give me a hand?"

Donna followed his orders quickly while he lowered the sails. Returning to the yacht club under power would be simpler, and it would make getting ashore and home less complicated. He sensed that Donna needed some time alone. The sooner he got her to Mark and Laura's place, the better.

"Coil any loose lines, Donna," he called up to her.

"Aye aye, cap'n," came her light reply, and he smiled. Whatever opposition came their way, even Evan's being after his blood about Raymond Tsung, could be overcome. In time, when Donna was truly ready, would he pursue the kind of relationship she'd let him know she wanted? Letting Evan know that the plan was for his little girl to be initiated into womanhood by her supposed surrogate uncle was likely to produce a scene worthy of the silver screen. When Evan came out of shock, he was likely to consider murder. Bruce headed for the marina.

The boat bumped against the dock. Donna stood by while Bruce jumped ashore; then she tossed him a line. He ran along the wooden planking, his soft-soled shoes thudding, and tied *Lake Lady*, first fore, then aft.

A heaviness weighting her muscles, her bones, Donna stared at Bruce's bowed head, at the rapid working of his shoulders as he handled the lines. The spotlights glinted on his hair. Maybe she'd been all wrong from the start. Maybe he would never truly be hers.

CHAPTER FIFTEEN

"I LOVE THIS CAR."

"You already said that."

Donna tightened her grasp on the little purse Laura had lent her. "Did I? Well, I do. It's a beautiful car. Black's always been my favorite."

"Is that why you decided to wear black tonight?" Bruce came to a stop at the junction of Broadway and Battery and shaded his eyes against the glare of oncoming headlights.

"This was a bad choice, wasn't it?" Donna had a momentary impulse to open the door and leap out, to run away. "A black dress is all wrong, too sultry, or sophisticated, or—"

"Good Lord, no." In the light from the dashboard she could see his surprised glance. A horn blasted behind them and he stepped on the accelerator, swearing under his breath. "Everybody's in such a damned hurry. What was I saying? The black dress—you look terrific in it. It's wonderful; just right. The Chinese like subdued colors. They consider them tasteful. The worst thing you can do is turn up for a celebration in white—and a lot of westerners do it. White's their sign of mourning."

Donna didn't want another cultural lecture. "So the dress is okay? You like it?"

"I'm crazy about...the dress is lovely, Donna. But, as you once told me they say about women like you, you'd look fantastic in a sack. You *do something* to whatever you put on that sumptuous body of yours. And I'm glad you wore the jade necklace. That was sweet of you.''

She touched the lavender beads and stared straight ahead. He was only humoring her, loosening her up for the ordeal ahead, Donna reminded herself. But she reveled in every word he spoke. ''Bruce,'' she said in a small voice. ''Do we have to go through with this?''

''Mmm.'' He nodded. ''We have to go through with this. A quiet dinner, just the three of us, is the answer to a prayer, the ideal opportunity to iron things out. Let me know if you feel like bolting, and I'll handcuff you to me.''

Not such a bad idea, Donna decided. She said, ''As long as you're with me, I'll make it.''

''I'm with you to the bitter end. Let's hope it isn't too bitter.''

All too soon, they were crossing the marble floor in the reception area of the Harbor Village Restaurant on the lobby level of the Embarcadero Center. This was considered ''the'' place for Chinese food, Bruce had told her. Donna had driven past the beautiful high-rise building many times. She wished she were doing the same right now, driving past, and going on her way.

''The Tsung party?''

A hostess wearing an ice-blue *cheongsam*, her throat wrapped in a collar of white mink, inclined her head toward Bruce. The woman smiled, nodded, and motioned to a man in a tuxedo who glided toward them in improbable silence over the hard floors. Etched glass shot prisms of light reflected from crystal-festooned chandeliers. Antique Chinese art pieces were discreetly displayed: jade, ivory, glistening dark wood. The ambience flowed over Donna, and the muted noise of diners she couldn't see, and Bruce's voice—Bruce's voice!

"Donna?" He held her elbow. "You okay?"

"Yes!" She nodded emphatically. "Sorry. I was looking around. This is lovely."

"Thank you, madam," the man in the tuxedo said, smiling. "If you would follow me, please, Miss Tsung. Your father is already here. A wonderful occasion, the reunion of father and daughter."

Donna hesitated, her eyes meeting Bruce's and appealing to him. *Miss Tsung? Reunion?* Had Raymond's enthusiasm made him confide in the maître d', of all people?

Bruce's fingers tightened. "Hang in there, honey," he whispered. "Everything's going to be fine. Trust me."

"Our Marlin Room is considered beautiful. There's still a little light. You'll be able to see the fountains in the plaza."

She moved on numb legs, smoothing her hair automatically and trying to smile. Bruce would help her explain everything to Raymond. They'd have a polite little dinner in what she was sure was exactly the right atmosphere for logical discussion, and afterward, the problem would be resolved.

The maître d' entered a large room filled with round white linen-covered tables on which exquisite flowers nodded and crystal glittered. Donna hung back slightly, her hope for a small private dining room dashed. The maître d' turned and beckoned. Bruce gave her a firm little push. She went forward as Raymond rose from his table, a delighted smile on his face. There were other people around his table. Lots of people. All looking at her. All smiling. There must be four, five, six...

She forced a sickly smile in return, and managed to say, "Good evening." Her voice sounded squeaky to her, and she cleared her throat. "Good evening," she repeated. "I didn't...I thought..."

"Cool it," Bruce said, almost inaudibly, barely moving his lips. "Smile," he ordered. "Do it!"

She clutched his arm and smiled blankly as Raymond came toward her, holding out both hands. She extended her own and felt them clasped warmly in his. He pulled her forward to his table. Who *were* all these people? Maybe there were seven or eight. She couldn't seem to count. The men were all standing up, bowing slightly.

"Donna, Donna, my daughter, welcome to my family and my special friends. This is truly a great night for me." He began making introductions with joyful pride. "This is my sister, Lily Huang…" And in Raymond's happy flow of words, he was graciously including Bruce in the introductions.

Somehow Donna continued smiling and bowed to the pretty woman swathed in dusky pink silk, her hair drawn up into a shining chignon atop her small head.

"And this is her husband, my good friend and kinsman, Nicholas Huang." Donna looked at the surprisingly tall man who stood next to Lily Huang.

She kept smiling and going through the appropriate motions. There must be at least *ten* people here! She wasn't going to be able to end this charade tonight and bow out gracefully, as she'd planned.

"And this is Mike Woo, eldest son of one of our family's oldest and most respected friends—" Raymond was going on and on. The man, Mike Woo, bowed to her, smiling with something resembling amusement.

She would get them sorted out later, Donna thought desperately, edging toward the table. She wanted to sit down. But Raymond caught briefly at her elbow and made a sweeping gesture over the beautiful room.

"And these," he said, "are my very dear friends who have come to welcome you tonight." As he finished speaking, the people at all the surrounding tables started applauding. Donna was stunned. Frozen. Hypnotized. Slowly, like a wave breaking, they all began standing up until every person in the room was standing and clapping. The whole room!

Donna's mind went blank. She felt a flood of fiery color rush into her face.

"Smile," Bruce said next to her ear. "God, I didn't expect...you'll never trust me..." It was impossible to hear the rest of what he said.

She had to sit down. Now. Mercifully, Raymond pulled her chair out and she slid weakly into it. "You will meet them all later," he was saying. "We will form a line and they will all come by."

"Yes," she said numbly. "That's nice. Thank you. Thank you." She was aware that the others were subsiding into their chairs all around her. She was aware that she was still smiling, nodding, bowing to the other people at this table.

White-coated waiters were passing among the tables putting down trays laden with food.

"Let the feast begin," Bruce whispered in her ear as he sat down beside her.

"This is the Peacock Platter." Raymond was telling her about the first dish. "Here, my dear, take some of this..."

Still murmuring, "Thank you, thank you," Donna carefully selected a piece of food from what appeared to be a salad smothered with various meats. She had to collect her wits, somehow get her world back to normal. She had to do something ordinary. That was it. She would eat. She popped a piece of food into her mouth, grateful that Bruce had made her persevere with the chopsticks until she was fairly proficient.

Everything around her shone—translucent china, crystal, silver chopstick holders, the chandeliers overhead. A muted green-and-beige color scheme added serenity to opulence. She took another bit of food. Things were coming back into focus.

Ray leaned toward her. "Is it good?"

She chewed and swallowed. "Very good, thank you." There had been almost no taste. "What was it, please?"

"Jellyfish. Try some of the melon and a little duck with it." Ray waved his own chopsticks. "Marvelous. Will you have some wine?"

She drank several long gulps of her Chenin Blanc before she noticed that Bruce was frowning. She took another swallow, frowning back at him. If she was going to get through jellyfish and two hundred introductions, she'd need all the courage she could muster.

Courses were served and cleared away. Braised vegetables with conpoy—dried scallops, Ray explained. Sautéd prawns with Virginia smoked ham. Donna jumped when Ray came from his seat, carrying his own bowl, and ceremoniously placed a morsel of food in her bowl. He smiled, and the rest of the guests at the table murmured approvingly.

Bruce cleared his throat. "I've always admired your customs, Ray," he said, not meeting Donna's eyes. "I have many books on Chinese culture. The idea of a host giving a guest a particularly succulent piece of food from his own plate is charming."

"Mmm." Donna lowered her lashes, silently blessing Bruce for his resourcefulness. She ate Ray's offering and found it crunchy, but not unpleasant.

"Shark's fin is one of my favorites," Ray said, clearly pleased at her satisfied smile. "There will be abalone next, then garoupa fish, and squab, of course."

When Donna raised her eyes, closing out all thought of

shark's fin and the seemingly endless dishes to follow, she found Mike Woo regarding her steadily. He smiled quickly.

"Your father told us you were very beautiful," he said, no hint of sarcasm in his voice, "And you are."

"She certainly is, Michael." Mike's mother, a tiny woman in a plum-colored brocade *cheongsam*, agreed. She turned to her husband, an older version of Mike, the gray hair at his temples adding distinction to almost arrogantly handsome features. "Isn't Donna lovely, Hal?"

Hal Woo settled a speculative stare on Donna and kept it there until she squirmed slightly. "Your father is very proud of you," he said finally. "Rightly so. How old are you, my dear?"

"Uh, nineteen, almost twenty."

"Hmm." Wong's lids drooped as his son's had done earlier. "Michael," he said, looking at his son, "you must escort Donna to the theater, the symphony, perhaps some art exhibits." He bestowed a brilliant smile on Donna. "Michael will be good company, my dear. He knows everything going on in the City."

The joints in Bruce's jaw ached. This wasn't at all what he and Donna had planned. There would be no opportunity to set things straight with Raymond this evening. In fact, the situation could only become more difficult. And Raymond Tsung's primary goal of the moment was sickeningly clear. He intended to find a suitable husband for his newfound daughter. Even as Bruce watched and moved a piece of garoupa fish around his mouth, Raymond was introducing one young man after another to Donna.

Bruce felt a small rush of pride. Donna was doing great. Now that she'd gotten her bearings she was coping very well. Sensitive, innately kind, she was giving Raymond the performance he seemed to want. She was playing the

lovely, gracious daughter to his doting proud father. Tonight, before the relatives and friends, she would not falter
and embarrass him in any way. Smiling brilliantly, laughing, talking, she was terrific!

He gave Mike Woo a sidelong glance. The man was
handsome, and obviously Raymond's prime candidate for
the position of son-in-law. Mike must have felt Bruce's
stare. He met his eyes, raised one brow, but didn't smile.
Bruce's stomach made a slow revolution. The guy had to
be thirty-five—even older than he was. No way was Donna
equipped to deal with the kind of sophistication this privileged Chinese represented.

"Donna." He kept his tone light, laughing a little. "Did
you know each type of fowl has a meaning?" The tiny
roasted squab had been served.

She shook her head.

"Let me see," he went on. "Correct me if I'm wrong,
Ray. Duck is happiness and fidelity, right?"

"Absolutely." Ray's wonderful, crooked-toothed grin
split his round face. "You are an expert on these things."

Bruce gave a modest shrug while he willed Donna to
concentrate on him. "And squab is for filial concern and
longevity."

Beneath Donna's determined smile and laughter, Bruce
saw a momentary touch of sadness in her eyes. Moisture
sprang up along her lower lashes. He closed his own eyes
for an instant, wanting to kick himself.

Mike Woo's deep, pleasant voice interrupted him. "I
believe that's pigeon."

Donna dropped her chopsticks. "This is pigeon?"

"No, no." Mike reached out to cover her hand while
Lily Huang picked up the chopsticks and leaned them on
a silver holder. "I meant that the pigeon stands for filial

concern and longevity, not squab. Save room for the mango pudding, it's marvelous.''

Bruce settled a murderous look on Mike's hand, so firmly closed over Donna's on the stiffly starched white cloth. The man patted Donna's hand, once, twice.

''And you're a lawyer, I understand, Bruce,'' Mrs. Woo said.

He returned the woman's smile with difficulty. ''Yes, that's right.'' Mike's arm still extended across the table.

''I expect that's fascinating.''

''Fascinating,'' Bruce agreed. He would find a way to make sure Donna never saw Mike Woo again.

''I believe I met your sister once. Laura Fenton Hunt?''

The smile on his face hurt. ''My cousin.'' Donna was undoubtedly the most gorgeous woman he'd ever met, and she was perfect inside as well as out.

''Ah, I see. She does a lot of civic work for Mrs. Winthrop.'' Mrs. Woo was oblivious to his lack of concentration.

Mike Woo poured more wine for Donna, who was beginning to look dazed. This must be a hell of a strain for her. ''Have you ever been to a real Chinatown parade?'' Mike asked.

''No,'' Donna responded with polite interest.

''Then we must go. I'd love to take you.'' Woo and his father exchanged a glance in which Bruce read mutual understanding. The older man wanted his son married—to the right girl, from the right family—and he'd decided Donna was it.

''I think there'll be some sort of parade next week,'' Mike said to Donna. ''I'll call you and we'll go.''

Over my dead body, Bruce thought.

CHAPTER SIXTEEN

MIKE WOO HELD up his right hand, spread the fingers and mouthed the word, "Five."

Donna leaned closer to him and shouted against the blare of trombones, "So you're fifth-generation Chinese-American?"

A girls' band, their short red skirts flaring, the gold braid on their black jackets glinting, marched past, high-stepping in their white boots.

He watched the girls briefly and nodded. "So are you."

"Not exactly..." Donna began to explain, then yelped when a firecracker sizzled between her feet. Mike took her arm and guided her through straining crowds to a table in front of a café.

She was glad she'd accepted Mike's invitation to this parade—nervous, but glad, despite Bruce's opposition.

"Let's take a break from the din," Mike said, holding out a chair for her. After she was seated, he flopped down beside her and rested his chin atop folded arms on the table. "Can you believe this? I bet half these people don't know what they're celebrating."

"I don't either," Donna said. "What is it for?"

"It's..." Mike looked at her for a moment before amusement crinkled the corners of his fine eyes. His smile, and the light from the café, did wonderful things for an already unforgettable face. "You know," he said slowly,

"I'm damned if I know. My mother just said…" He stopped and gazed at the dark sky.

Yells, thrumming voices, the jumbled cacophony of the parade, swept around them, and seconds unreeled while Donna felt her muscles relax. He'd almost admitted his mother had put him up to this date. She grinned, a little at first, then more broadly, until tears stung her eyes and she laughed. She gripped his arm and laughed the tears free, and watched the gradual transformation of Mike's wry grimace into chuckles.

He shook his head and rubbed his face. "Smooth, huh? Look, I don't want you to think—"

"You don't have to explain." Donna sniffed, inhaled a whiff of acrid gunpowder smoke, and coughed. "Honestly you don't. I understand. Your mother put you up to taking me out to please Ray…uh…my father. They probably cooked the thing up together."

Mike held his lower lip between white teeth. He was, Donna decided, incredibly attractive. Fortunately, he was no more interested in her than she was in him.

"You're not offended?"

Impulsively, she reached over to hold his hand. "I'm relieved," she admitted, and they laughed again. "I guess we'd both take first prize in a How-to-Pay-Scintillating-Compliments contest."

He sobered. "You are a very beautiful woman, Donna. But I guess you know that."

She blushed, but said nothing.

Overhead, brilliant paper lanterns bobbled. A figure in a grotesque lion costume capered close, then backed away waggling a giant head.

"You are beautiful," Mike repeated. "Even more so when you're embarrassed. I wish we could be friends."

"And we can't?"

Mike's color heightened. "Of course, but you know what I mean. Any ongoing interest on my part, and our parents would be making wedding plans. Your father and mine are old friends, and they see a union between you and me as a blissful opportunity to join our families. Then, of course, a thirty-five-year-old son should be married and producing sons of his own."

"And you wouldn't want that?" Donna bit the inside of her cheek to keep a straight face.

"Well…I…that is…"

He was nice. And she was punishing him when she should be thanking him for putting an end to her misery. "Mike, Mike." She held his hand tighter. "Remember Bruce Fenton, the man who brought me to dinner at the Harbor Village?"

"Yes. Nice guy."

"The best guy, Mike. The very best."

His lips parted slightly, and he blinked several times. "You two have a thing for each other?"

"I have a thing for him. I think he's pretty interested in me, but he hides it well sometimes. Anyway, I want to marry him and, as you can imagine, that could raise a few problems in some areas."

"Like with Ray," he said thoughtfully.

A waiter forced his way toward them and took their order for iced tea. Donna waited until the man moved away. "You do know about my adoptive parents?"

Mike bowed his head, tapping his fingertips together. "Ray told my father. But your folks wouldn't have any objection to Fenton, surely."

Donna swallowed frustration. How would she ever make the factions in her life compatible? Everyone who had a stake in some part of her life thought their point of view was the only correct point of view. "I grew up with my adoptive parents. And, yes, frankly, I am concerned about their reaction to Bruce. They're already hurt that I hunted down Raymond Tsung.''

He thought for a long time, then said, ''Yes, I suppose they might be. I hadn't considered that. But why shouldn't they approve of Bruce?''

''They don't know about him. At least, they know him—very well in fact, but they don't know I'm in love with him. And he isn't helping me by dwelling on how shocked my parents would be if they found out there was something between us. He insists he's too old for me. Then, too, he's divorced, and he thinks that makes him a bad marriage prospect.'' She sighed. ''I know he feels the way I do, but he's so darned tied up with doing the right thing.'' Mike was easy to talk to. The realization surprised and pleased her. ''But I don't want to talk about Bruce. I was hoping you could help me figure out a way to handle Ray.''

''Handle?'' The iced tea was delivered, and Mike paid for it. He raised his glass and they drank. ''What do you mean, handle Ray?''

''Well,'' she said, then hesitated. ''Well, he wants to take me in. You see how quickly he's started thinking of getting me safely married into his circle and integrated into his world? He's ready for me to become a full-time daughter.''

Mike jiggled his glass on the white-painted tabletop. ''I got the impression you wanted that, too.'' He looked directly at her. ''Why did you look for him if you didn't want to find him?''

''It's…complicated.'' *And embarrassing,* Donna thought. She couldn't explain the whole situation to this man, nice as he was. ''Can we just say things have gotten out of hand, and leave it at that?''

He inclined his head toward her. "Whatever you say. But how can I help you? You do want some sort of help from me, don't you?"

Donna drank her iced tea too fast, caught a piece of ice that shot from the glass, and laughed nervously. She pressed a napkin to her lips. What had she hoped to get from Mike?

"Hey." He bowed his head close to hers. "We're soulmates, kid. Both fighting the old family-pressure routine. You'd help me, right? So I'll do the same for you if I can. Maybe I should tell you what I know about Ray."

"Yes, yes." Donna's spirits lifted. Any tiny lead she could get on dealing with this new and enthusiastic father of hers would be helpful.

"He's shrewd…in business, I mean," Mike started. He wrinkled his nose. "But you already know that. He's the kind of man who can listen. If you lay out whatever's troubling you, carefully, he'll try to understand your point of view."

Sure, Donna thought, if Ray would ever stop being enthusiastic for long enough for her to lay out anything.

"Don't you think he'll be receptive to your observations? Understand you'd like to go a little slower with the family involvement?"

"Mmm? Yes," Donna said quickly. "You're right, I'll do what you say. I'll explain exactly how I feel to him."

This discussion was useless. She might as well enjoy the wretched parade. Mike couldn't help her.

He grinned. "Good girl."

Ribbon streamers flew across the table, and more, and more, in myriad colors, curling around Donna's neck, over her head. "Help!" she cried, laughing. But Mike was busy tearing away his own paper bonds. He grabbed her hand,

and they dodged through clumps of people, heading for the mass of humanity at the curb.

"The dragon's coming," Mike shouted, ducking, working his way toward the street and pulling Donna with him. "See?" Miraculously, they were standing in the gutter with a clear view of dancing figures, clowns, and the last members of yet another marching band.

Donna clutched at Mike, and leaned out until she saw the fantastic head of the dragon advancing up Grant Avenue. "I see it." She hopped from one foot to the other, instantly feeling foolish, then realized she was one of thousands of hopping, shouting people, many old enough to be her grandparents.

"It's wonderful. Oh, Mike, it's wild." She craned her neck for a better view of the brilliant, twisting body winding through the night, smoke spurting from its scarlet-ringed nostrils. Lighted eyes flashed from jewel-studded sockets, a silver beard trailed from the snapping jaw, as striped horns of purple, turquoise and gold speared toward a moonless sky.

"I want to get closer," Donna urged. "Can we?"

Mike didn't answer. He'd become quite still. She glanced up at him and frowned. "What is it? What's the matter?"

He inhaled sharply and smiled. "I thought I saw your friend."

She followed the direction of his stare and narrowed her eyes to make out individuals in the shifting melee. "Who?"

"Fenton. Bruce Fenton."

"Bruce...but I told him...he knows I wanted to get away.... Damn him, now he's playing nervous father. As if I didn't have enough of those." Maybe Mike only thought he saw Bruce, she reasoned.

Mike was laughing suddenly, and Donna started to turn to him when she saw a familiar, tall, slender man shouldering a path purposefully through the crowd. *Bruce!* She'd told him she needed a complete change of pace, and a chance to talk to someone who might understand Raymond Tsung better than either of them did. And he'd still followed her.

"Why are you laughing?" she asked Mike without looking at him.

"Sorry. I was just thinking that I needn't have worried about my parents' matrimonial plans for me, or about Ray's. And I don't think you need to question Bruce Fenton's feelings for you. Whether he admits it or not, the guy's got a bad case. He must have been tailing us ever since I picked you up, otherwise he'd never have found us."

"Well, that's terrific, I guess." And it was, but Donna didn't want to confront Bruce now, here, where the meeting could only be awkward. "But I'd rather not talk to Bruce tonight."

The dragon's head drew level, then swept close to them. When Mike moved, Donna almost fell, and he half carried her forward, lifted the silken side of the make-believe beast and shoved her inside.

Donna opened her mouth, but no sound emerged. She tried to face Mike, but his hands at her waist propelled her forward, loping, tripping, gradually falling into step with the rest of the dragon's "legs."

Men shouted in Chinese, and Mike shouted back. Raucous laughter echoed deafeningly in the suffocating, smelly space.

"What are we doing?" Donna managed to ask between gasps. "They'll throw us out. We'll get into trouble."

"No way," Mike said. "You said you didn't want to talk to Bruce right now. This should lose him."

She had to grin. Wait till she told Bruce about her theatrical debut!

Bruce finally reached the curb. Damn it all, he'd lost sight of them. He should have stayed on the same side of the street, but when they'd left the café he'd been afraid they'd notice him.

The dragon passed, and he crossed over to where he'd seen them last. There was no sign of either of them. The crowd was closing in around the tail of the dragon, pursuing it up the avenue. He was carried along in the crush.

He shoved forward. Mike and Donna were probably following, too. He no longer cared what he'd say if they saw him. Donna didn't belong in this madness. She must go home. He'd find her and take her home.

Gradually, he broke out to the edge of the crowd again and ran on, searching, glad of his height. He reached the dragon's front end just as it wallowed out, cutting him off.

He stumbled and cursed under his breath, and at the same time looked down at the scuffling feet of the monster. His heart skipped a beat, then several beats, and Bruce wondered if he was going to have the cardiac arrest that crazy woman had been bound to cause him from the minute she'd arrived in San Francisco.

Among the dusty, trousered legs and tennis shoes ran one slender pair of feminine limbs moving as well as could be expected, perhaps better, in low-heeled but delicate fuchsia-colored sandals.

For an instant Bruce's mind went blank and the hubbub receded. He saw only those perfect, narrow, golden ankles turning this way and that, ankles he knew so well.

An elbow in his back sent him grabbing for support. He clutched at a luminous tassel. He regained his balance and jumped, caught the base of one improbable horn with both hands, planted his heels and jerked the glowing eyes toward him.

Enraged shouts bellowed through the dragon's mouth, all in Chinese; then Bruce heard a scream he recognized. Fury made him stronger than he'd ever been. He wrenched up silk by the handfuls until he was looking into Donna's flushed face. "Come out," he ordered. "You little idiot. What the hell do you think you're doing?"

She came out, or rather he dragged her out beside him. Mike Woo, his face impassive despite his ruffled appearance, joined them. "This is my fault," he interceded smoothly. "I thought Donna would get a kick out of seeing this—" he waved his arm at the dragon "—from the other side. She's fine. I wouldn't have let anything happen to her, Fenton."

Bruce absorbed Mike's words. He wanted to be somewhere else, now, with Donna. It was time they finally got a few issues settled.

Anxiously, Donna eyed first one and then the other man. Bruce was ignoring Mike while he concentrated on her. She didn't like the hard set of his mouth.

"You don't do that, man." The man who'd been operating the dragon's jaws rushed at Bruce, stopped short, but thumped his shoulder. "Who do you think you are, huh?"

"He's—" Donna began.

"Be quiet," Bruce snapped.

The man yanked Bruce's sleeve. "You don't mess with the dragon, man. What's your problem?"

"He was just—"

"Shut up, Donna," Bruce said. People pushed in on all sides. "Look, buddy. The lady got mixed up with your people in there, and I was—"

"Fred," Mike interrupted, clapping the man on the back. "Fred, it's me, Mike Woo. Where ya been? Haven't seen you in ages."

Fred turned bemused eyes on Mike. The dragon, its occupants yelling incoherently, was in danger of being crushed. "Mike? I'll be. What's new? I been…hey, I gotta get this thing moving. Call me, huh? I'd like to talk to you." He began sliding back into place. The instant before his face disappeared, he gave Bruce a parting glare and a warning: "You watch it, man. You better drop parades from your itinerary." Then the dragon moved on, and with it the crowd, a pall of smoky air hanging above their heads.

"I'm taking you home," Bruce announced.

She looked at her toes. "Mike will be taking me home, Bruce, when we're ready."

"Mike?" Bruce asked softly.

Donna glanced around. She and Bruce were alone. The hum of the parade swept steadily away, the bobbing tide of color leaving discarded food wrappers and paper cups in its wake. She pushed her hands into the pockets of her skirt. Mike had decided to take his cue and bow out.

"He was right to go," Bruce said, as if he'd read her thoughts. "You and I have some talking to do."

"Not tonight," Donna said. "Drop me off at home, if you don't mind. I don't need another lecture tonight."

Bruce's arm, wrapped firmly around her waist, surprised Donna. She tensed, but didn't pull away. He strode along, staring straight ahead, until they reached the same lot where Mike had parked. Mike's dark blue Aston Martin was gone.

Slipping rapidly past the glittering outlines of Chinatown's stores and restaurants in Bruce's car, Donna kept her head turned sharply away from Bruce. He made no attempt at conversation. His sleek car sped on, but instead of turning toward Mark and Laura's house, Bruce drove directly to his own place. Donna's heart raced until it thudded in her throat.

Bruce parked in the alley leading to his garage and got out of the car. Donna made no attempt to move. He opened the door and waited.

"I asked you to drop me off at home," she said at last.

"Get out...please," Bruce said.

"I'd rather go home."

"That would take longer than we've got tonight," Bruce said tonelessly.

Donna looked up sharply. His face was in shade. "I didn't mean I expected you to drive me to Vancouver," she said. "Laura and Mark's home is mine while I'm in San Francisco. I simply meant—"

"I know what you meant. I was just reminding you that you do have another home...a very permanent home."

"I'm not likely to forget. I don't want to."

"Watching you tonight, I wondered."

"Don't do this, Bruce. You're angry, and I don't know why. And I don't want to get into it tonight, or argue in the street."

"Then come in, because I'm not driving you anywhere until we talk."

"Fine." She slammed the car door. "I'll walk. It isn't so far."

He grabbed her before she'd taken two steps. "You little...you...Donna, Donna." The arms that held her were rigid, yet they trembled. Bruce averted his face, and she heard his hard breathing. The sensation inside her burned, throbbed. There was something different about him tonight. Vulnerability and violence, passion and fear, barely reined fury—she felt all these emotions in him, and more.

She twisted from his grasp and led the way to the house.

On the top step, she waited for him to unlock the door. Then she walked to his study without putting on any lights.

"You know this house as well as I do, don't you?" Light burst from corner sconces, and Bruce passed her to pull heavy velvet drapes over the French windows.

The room was warm, yet she shivered. She crossed her arms tightly. "You shouldn't have followed me."

Bruce came so close that she could see the pulse in his throat, the faint twitch at the corner of his mouth. "What do you want from me?" he asked.

"I've already made that very clear."

He tapped a fist quickly, agitatedly, against his chin. "You made it clear. And you want me to feel the same. But I'm not supposed to worry about you, is that it?"

"There wasn't anything to worry about tonight. I hoped Mike might be able to give me a different insight into Raymond, that's all. I haven't had much success dealing with him so far."

"You come from different cultures, that's all."

"Exactly. And I'm trying to understand those differences. I don't want to hurt anyone."

"Unless it's me."

She tried to turn away, but he wrenched her back. "Bruce, this is senseless. I didn't want you to follow me tonight. I was managing perfectly well on my own." Her throat ached unbearably.

"Ever since you got to San Francisco you've been asking me to help you, to stand by you. You've made sure you glued me to your side. Now, when I tell you I've been worried about you, you tell me to get lost."

"I haven't told you to get lost, damn it. I'd never tell you to get lost. I *love* you, Bruce. But I don't want another father figure. I don't want you treating me like a juvenile with a curfew."

His face contorted, and he gritted his teeth. "Decide, will you? Loving means commitment, caring, all the time. Don't you understand that? Grow up, Donna, grow up, will you?"

She tried to breathe, and couldn't. Tears, tears of pure rage sprang to her eyes. "You ever say that to me again and I'll..." Words failed her. She held his arms, drove her fingers into his biceps, tried to shake him. "I'm grown up, Bruce, very grown up."

"Are you?" He bowed his head, then looked into her eyes. "Are you grown up? You know something, ma'am, I love you, too. How does that grab you? You made it happen. I fell in love with you, God help us both. Can you cope with that?"

Donna opened her mouth to answer, and he immediately brought his lips down on hers, opened them wider, drove his tongue into her mouth. His arms went around her body, trapping her arms at her sides. Heat from his hands seared her flesh through her cotton blouse.

She couldn't move. Her eyes were wide open, watching his tightly closed lids, the flickering of his thick, bleached lashes. Finally he lifted his head, but he continued to hold her. She saw tears in his eyes, a bitter downward twist of his mouth. Now the sensation in her belly was recognizable—longing, and fear, and insecurity.

He kissed her again, and again, and she tried to respond. When he moved his hands over her back, her bottom, slid them up to massage the sides of her breasts, she tried not to think. *Feel,* she told herself, standing on tiptoe to clasp his neck, to stroke his ears with her thumbs. *Feel.*

He drew away abruptly, held her face against his chest. She felt the rapid beat of his heart and his quickened breathing. "Tell me to stop, Donna," he whispered. "Just say no, and I'll take you home."

"I don't want to go home," she said, and her voice sounded like a stranger's.

"You know what's going to happen if you don't?"

Fluttering nerves jumped around her ribs, shivered in her limbs. "I know. Will you let me stay?"

The noise he made was a muffled groan. "My love," he said, "my love. I'm the one who should be strong enough to stop this, but I'm not." He stroked back her hair, bit the lobe of her ear gently, and lifted her into his arms. At the foot of the stairs, he paused. "It'll never be the same, Donna." She sensed the sadness that wrestled with his ardor.

"I love you." There was nothing else to be said. She slipped a hand inside his shirt, over the hair-rough surface of his chest. "We can't go back, Bruce and it's already too late to try."

Beneath her fingers, his flat nipple tensed. A muscle in his jaw jerked, and he carried her upstairs. He kicked open the double doors to a large bedroom that was really two rooms, converted into a suite, a bedroom and a sitting room. A satin-shaded lamp glowed on a round table by one window. Blues, midnight, navy, dusky gray-blue, predominated. Piles of cushions littered a mahogany four-poster bed.

Bruce set her down on deep-piled carpet. He ran his palms up and down her arms, bent to kiss her neck, touched his tongue to the corner of her mouth. She stilled his head, held him away from her, and smiled gently.

While she felt him watch her every move, she closed the doors, then lowered the Austrian shades over the windows.

She kicked off her sandals and returned to stand in front of him. He shook his head. "You don't have to do this. I—"

She pressed her fingers to his mouth. With her other hand, she unbuttoned his shirt and pulled it free of his jeans. "Sometimes," she said as she reached to kiss him lightly, "you talk too much." She kissed him again while she pushed the shirt from his shoulders. "Have I ever told you that?" The shirt fell to the rug and she concentrated on his belt.

He stopped her.

Donna looked up into his face and pressed her lips together. His eyes were different, dark. He walked her backward until she sat on the edge of the bed. Slowly, he sank to his knees. When his face was on a level with hers, he kissed her, carefully at first, then so hard he forced her back on the bed and rose slightly to lean over her. His weight pleased her, and made it hard for her to breathe. His hands were in her hair, caressing her throat, smoothing her shoulders, moving to her waist, driving that new, burning sensation higher, making it sharper.

When he sat back on his heels, pulling her up, she felt disoriented. He looked at her face only once more before he unbuttoned her blouse, quickly, without fumbling, and parted the front. She wore no bra. Heat rushed over her skin. Her breasts were small. Would she please him?

"You are a lovely woman, Donna." His voice broke. He rubbed his fingers up and down her ribs, across her collarbones, circling her breasts slowly, coming close to her nipples but not quite touching them. She arched toward him slightly, confused. She wanted him to touch her there—everywhere. A little cry came unbidden from her throat.

"Do you know what you want me to do, Donna? Is it still all right? You don't want me to stop?"

She tried to speak. Only a moan was audible. She leaned forward and pulled his face to rest between her breasts, moved slowly until he gripped her, rubbed the slight roughness of his cheek over first one nipple, then the other, and followed with gently nipping, sucking kisses.

Breath rushed from her lungs, and strength from her body. She allowed her head to hang back. He stroked her thighs, slipped a hand upward to her groin, and the piercing heat in her breasts flared and the heaviness in her womb pulsed. The heel of his hand rotated against her pelvis, and she clutched his naked shoulders, shuddering. He pressed harder, repeatedly. Her skirt worked up over her hips. Bruce slipped off her panties, kissed her belly and down, down where his hand had started the raw, sweet pain. When the gnawing need came again, she knew she couldn't bear him to stop. She didn't understand, but she didn't care. This was Bruce and this was right. Then the pain she wanted to go on and on was gone and her body was a wonderful thing she'd never fully known before.

"Are you all right?" Bruce's voice was faint and far away.

"Yes," she whispered. "But...but..."

"Shhh. Come on, sweet." He took off her skirt, threw back the covers on the bed, and lifted her onto the sheets.

"Bruce. Don't go away." She held her arms toward him.

His laugh was mirthless. "I'm not going anywhere." He shed the rest of his clothes. She swallowed. He was a perfectly made man: very tall, broad-shouldered, narrow-hipped, well muscled but slim. His long legs, tanned from days on the boat, held her attention. They were good, strong legs, already showing the effects of running. His chest was tanned as well as his back, his arms, his whole body in fact, except the skin that had been covered by his shorts or his swimsuit. Donna glanced away. She had al-

ways wanted this moment of discovery to be with Bruce.
She had to be what he needed in a woman.

Bruce stretched out beside her and began a slow, rhythmic stroking of her body. Again he avoided her breasts
until she looked into his eyes and saw his intense concentration. He was preparing her—and himself. And he, too,
was a little afraid. She didn't want Bruce to worry about
her. She made herself lie very still.

When he kissed her, control fled. She strained against
him, turning sideways to meet his aroused body. They
kissed until they drew apart a few inches, gasping.

Gently, Bruce eased her onto her back and began a measured kissing campaign that covered her body. This time
he left no part untouched, and when she cried out, reaching
to hold his sweat-slick shoulders, he parted her legs with
a knee and eased himself over her.

In his face she saw passion mingle with struggle. He
entered her carefully, his weight still supported on his elbows, still watching her eyes. "Okay, sweetheart?" he
said very softly. "Okay?"

Donna turned her head away. She didn't want him to
treat her like porcelain. "Make love to me, Bruce," she
said, sobbing out her desire for him. "Please. I want you."

And he did make love to her, part wild love, part gentle,
hesitant love, and eventually love that couldn't be
stemmed by control. Donna smothered a cry at the one
small pain she felt, then met each thrust with the rise of
her hips. When Bruce rolled onto his back, taking her with
him, his legs clamping her body to his, she laughed, tipped
back her head and laughed, braced her hands on his chest
and bent to brush his face with her hair.

"Oh, you are something, my love. You are really something," Bruce said, and he cupped her breasts. "You are
probably addictive."

''I most certainly am,'' she assured him, shifting until he gritted his teeth and squeezed his eyes shut.

Then he was on top of her again, his eyes glazed, his body gleaming, and she couldn't talk anymore. A burst of energy drove her against him, and he met her again and again. Heat—intense, unbearable, essential, swept into her and came, sharper and sharper, and Bruce yelled, something she didn't hear clearly yet understood perfectly, and she answered in kind. He arched his spine once, twice, and fell over her, gathered her into his arms.

Later, she didn't know how much later, he pulled a sheet over them and they lay, facing each other, legs entwined, embracing tightly. Sleep came while she tasted the salt on his skin, felt the hair on his chest against her cheek.

Bruce drowsed. He didn't want to let her go, ever. Each time he opened his eyes, he peered down at her face, held his hand a scant distance above her face, her hair, longing to wake her but wanting her to sleep. She had given him all of herself. God, he hoped he'd done the right thing. He hoped he'd do what was right from here on, for both of them. He stroked her back lightly from her shoulder to the dip at her small waist, over her firm, rounded hip.

''I'm awake too.''

He'd turned off the light. Now he put a knuckle beneath her chin and tilted up her face. In the darkness, he saw the shine of her eyes, the vague glint of her teeth as she smiled at him.

They made love again. Afterward, Bruce lay on his back, Donna's diminutive body stretched on top of him, and passed a hand repeatedly over her hair, trying to formulate what to say next.

''I love you,'' Donna whispered, snuggling her face into the hollow of his shoulder.

''And I love you,'' he said, a hard little place forming

in the pit of his stomach. "Now." He said it, and felt her stiffen sharply.

When she didn't answer, he pressed on. "I can't imagine ever feeling different than I feel right now, but I want us to be sure. And I want you to be all you can be. Do you understand what I'm saying?"

"No," she said in a small voice, and jerked away from his arms and sat on the edge of the bed.

Bruce scooted behind her, put an arm around her waist and covered her breast. "We love each other now, Donna. I think marriage is probably where we're headed. But we can't risk a mistake."

"You sound so reasonable, and so cold."

He kissed her back and smiled wryly at the ripple that passed along her muscles. "I'm not either of those things just now. I'm holding on to logic by a hair. Donna. Sweetheart. Will you go back to Vancouver at the end of the summer and go to school like your folks want you to? And then, if we both feel the same after we've been apart a while, we'll know we belong together."

She began to cry softly. "I don't know if I can do it."

Swallowing caused a pain in his throat. He withdrew his arm and lay on his stomach. "Neither do I, darling. But I think we'd better give it a try if we hope to start off on the right foot. And I think your folks will find...us...us easier to accept if they see we aren't rushing into anything."

Donna was cold, so cold, and the tears she cried felt as if they were wrenched from deep inside her. "How long will it be before you...before we know if we can be together?"

"I don't know yet. We've got to give ourselves as long as it takes."

"What if…what if only one of us decides…" She couldn't go on.

"Don't, Donna, love. Please don't. Trust it'll all be all right. Sweetheart, sex that really works between two people is wonderful. And it sure works between us. But the couple that has it all is the couple that has love and sex and friendship in common. We need a little space and time to be sure we can have all those things. If what we feel now fades, then…well, will you do this my way? Donna, I've been around a while. I think I *know* how I feel about you, but—good God—you're only nineteen. I've got to give you a chance to…to… Please, Donna, will you go along with this?"

"You really mean," Donna said in a small voice, "that you want me to go back to Vancouver at the end of summer? But what on earth would I do in Vancouver?" Disbelief weighted her words, and tears continued to roll down her cheeks.

Bruce fumbled for the edge of the sheet and blotted at the tears. "School, Donna. You have to give it a chance. You—"

"Oh, Bruce, no," she moaned.

"Oh yes, my love. You've said, a number of times, that some day you'd work with young gymnasts. That will take formal training. You have to begin. And you'll be good at it, Donna. You have no idea how good you can be. You have a gift for it. Look, anybody who can get me out in the park in running shoes…" His words dwindled, and he hugged her close. "Please, Donna. Do it for me?" His voice was unsteady.

There was no choice, then, Donna thought helplessly. There was nothing she would not do for Bruce, for both of them.

"Okay," she said softly. "Okay."

"Good girl."

"Yes," she said, getting up and putting on the light. "I'll go to school and we'll see." The smile she tried to form didn't quite come off.

Bruce sat up and reached for her hand. He pulled her down beside him. "Can we make a promise to each other? Can we promise that if, by the end of your first quarter, we're both sure marriage is what we want, we'll get married and you'll finish school down here?" His blue eyes were almost navy in the half-light. His face was drawn. He did want the best for both of them, and he was hurting, too.

"I promise," she said, and pushed him against the pillows. She kissed him softly. "We'll wait and see. But, Bruce, while I'm still in San Francisco, we can see each other, can't we?"

He caught her hand and kissed each finger. "Try and keep me away," he said. "But we'd better avoid...well, I'm only human, and if I'm going to keep my head together I can't..."

She kissed him into silence. "Neither can I. So we'll go back to dinners at Fisherman's Wharf. Okay?"

He laughed, but stopped abruptly when the phone rang.

Donna glanced at the clock on his bedside table. "Oh, no, Bruce. Look at the time. It's one in the morning. You don't suppose that's Laura looking for me?"

"I hope to hell not." Bruce lifted the receiver. "Fenton."

Donna watched while he listened. Three times he said yes, nothing more, then replaced the phone.

"Well?" she said, as he stared broodingly into space.

"Mark's out of town, thank God."

"Yes."

"That was Laura."

Donna blushed fiercely. "She asked if I was here and you said yes?"

"I make it a point not to lie. I'd better get you back."

"Bruce, Laura knows how I feel about you. She isn't going to judge us."

"You'd better hope everyone else is just as reasonable."

He stood up and started dressing.

"What does that mean? I thought we had everything settled for now."

"Yeah. I hope we do. I guess I'd allowed myself to forget some of the possible ramifications of letting myself have you." The sadness in his face hurt her.

"You're sorry about tonight."

"Not sorry. Never sorry. Just worried, suddenly."

"Why?"

He stood still, his shirt trailing from one hand. "I guess I don't like thinking of what you may have to face in the next few days. Laura's worried, too. That's why she was looking for you. She wanted to tell you that nothing's cooled off in Vancouver. Evan arrives on Friday—and Sara's coming with him."

CHAPTER SEVENTEEN

DONNA HURRIED HOME from the office after work on Friday. The feeling of dread had been building all afternoon, but dread or not, she was determined to go to the airport herself to meet her parents. Mark had offered to do it for her. Donna felt a sting of gratitude in her eyes as she thought about his kindness.

"No," she had said. "This is my responsibility. I don't mind, really. It's something I have to get through."

Mark grinned. "You mind like hell, honey. Irate parents can be pretty daunting. I have to be at the office late tonight, but I could leave in time to pick them up, buy them a drink and bring them home. It might cool them off a bit, take the edge off, kind of. Okay?"

She'd shaken her head. These were her people, irate or not. All her life with them she had been willing to take the good things they had given. Now there was a rough spot—of her own making—and she had to weather it herself.

"All right," Mark had said. "When you stop by the house before you go, will you tell Laura I'll be late? I'm expecting a call from Brussels. It won't come through till about seven our time."

Now, on her return, Donna couldn't find Laura, and E.J. was no help.

"Well, she's around," he responded vaguely in response to Donna's question about his mother's whereabouts. He was absorbed in TV cartoons.

"But around where, E.J.?"

"Well, she didn't go any place. That means she's around, doesn't it?" he asked, turning back to the set. "You didn't notice I'm dressed up. I'm wearing my best suit. I'm going out to eat with Grandma. And I'm going to stay at her house for a few days."

"Oh, great. That's great, E.J."

Donna gave up looking for Laura temporarily and dashed up to her room to change. She was about to snatch up a pair of jeans, but then she paused. No. She couldn't wear jeans. Her parents had seen her in jeans for too many years, and would associate them with her childhood—the little girl in jeans. She carefully selected a beige skirt and blouse, then added a white sweater looped about her shoulders in case it got cool later. She'd make one last attempt to find Laura, who hadn't been downstairs or in the garden. She rapped at the closed door of the Hunts' room, and there were some muffled words from inside.

She opened the door a crack. "Laura? You in there?"

"Ah. Yes. Come in, Donna. Don't turn on the light. I've...ah...got a headache."

"Oh. I'm so sorry." Donna crept in and stood at the foot of the bed on which Laura lay huddled. The room was dark with all the draperies drawn. There was a shaky sigh from the bed.

"That's not true, really," Laura said in a small voice. "I'm sorry. Friends ought not to lie to each other. I'm having a bad day, and I guess I just gave up and had myself a good cry. Open the draperies will you, love? I've got to get presentable before Mark gets home."

Donna went to the window. She made much of opening the drapes, explaining that Mark would be late and giving

Laura time to get up and into the bathroom. Laura crying! Something was wrong. It made her feel shaken. The Hunts' marriage had always seemed so solid. Good old Rock-of-Gibraltar Hunts. Now this!

Laura came back into the room and sat in front of her dressing table, her face shining, but her eyes red and puffy. She reached for a jar of cream.

"How come you're dressed up? Oh, yes, you're going to meet Sara and Evan." She looked at Donna, her eyes wide. "It'll be okay. Evan is making heavy father noises, but...well, you know him, he's a pussycat. I mean, don't worry about it. What time does their plane come in?"

"Nine-ten. Laura, at the moment my main worry is you. What's the matter? And please don't tell me nothing is, because you don't usually spend your afternoon in your bed crying your heart out." Donna went to Laura and sank to her knees on the floor beside the dressing table.

"Play it by ear about when to bring your folks home. Their room is ready—as it always is." Laura reached out and pushed back Donna's hair in a tender gesture. "I'm not avoiding your question, Donna. I'm just trying to figure out a way to answer it that doesn't make me seem a jerk."

"As if you could."

"Mark and I are...having a...some difficulty at the moment."

"I had kind of gathered that from before," Donna said softly. "Is there anything I can do? Anything, Laura! Walk on my knees across Golden Gate Bridge? Climb the outside of the Coit Tower—"

Laura laughed shakily. "No. But be prepared. One of these days Mark Hunt is going to explode and take the roof off. Just don't get hurt in the fallout, that's all."

"Why, Laura? Why would he?"

"Listen, love, if you're going to be there waving as your folks come off the plane, you'd better scoot."

Donna clasped Laura's hands. "Laura, why?"

"Because I...I've lied to him. And one of these days... one of these days...maybe even tonight—"

"Lied. You!"

"Well, not exactly. But I've kind of...lived a lie. You knew we lost a baby, didn't you? Our second little boy?" Her voice was unsteady.

"Yes," Donna said softly. "I knew that."

"Well, I was pretty sick, too. And Mark exaggerated how bad it was for me. He was frantic. I admit my condition wasn't too great, but it wasn't as bad as he's let himself believe. And now we're bringing up E.J. alone, and it's all wrong. I want another child—children. I was a lonely child, and I want my son to..." Her voice trailed off, and her huge blue eyes looked into the distance.

"Have you talked to him, really talked, laid it on the line, and..."

Laura laughed faintly. "A dozen times. We've had more fights over that one question than over everything else in our marriage combined. Trying to get Mark on the subject is like batting my head against—against solid iron. So I took things into my own hands."

"You what?"

"I'm pregnant, Donna. And he doesn't know."

"Laura!" Donna sat back on her heels and stared at her friend. "But when he finds out..." She breathed deeply.

Laura laughed again. "Yes. Like I said. Whoosh. There goes the roof. And what's more, I feel so damned guilty about it. Mark and I have always been so open, so honest with each other, and I...I'm the one who broke the trust. Oh, Donna! Look at the time! Forget about me, darling. You've got to get to the airport. And please, don't worry your head about my problems. I'll cope with them. Listen. What I meant to say about Sara and Evan.'' She was rising from the bench and pulling Donna up from the floor. ''Play it by ear with them. Bring them home immediately or not, however it works out. If all conversation fails, you can always bring them back here and Mrs. Cooper can provide a good late dinner. Or—''

''No. I think I won't,'' Donna said slowly. ''Don't plan on seeing them until tomorrow. I mean to talk to them, just the three of us. And then, however it works out, I'll take them someplace to eat. Don't wait up for us. It may take a while. Oh, Laura, I'm so…'' She put out her hand, and the other woman clasped it.

''Forget me, Donna. Concentrate on making things right with your parents. My troubles will wait. You can solve them tomorrow.'' The laughter they shared was closer to tears than mirth.

Donna arrived at San Francisco Airport a good fifteen minutes early, so she scouted out a place to talk privately with her parents. At one end of the baggage claim area a carrousel was out of order. Several seats lined a wall. That would do. She went back to wait for her parents' flight. Despite her dread of the coming scene, she felt close to tears with the sheer joy of seeing them again. She had missed them.

When they came down the escalator in the straggling line of people, she felt a rush of mingled love and pride. Mom was absolutely beautiful, and Dad was the best-looking man in the airport. Nobody, nobody in the world had parents like them. But there were people, people everywhere, pushing her, getting in her way. Finally she found a space and wiggled through, flinging herself at them, trying to circle them both with her arms and not making it. They could all get on with the quarrel later.

Right now she had to kiss them. Mom was clutching at her, saying, "Baby, baby." Dad's arm went around her and lifted her clear of the floor. She shouted, "I love you. I love you."

"Come over here," she said, breathless from the hugging. "I've staked out a place where we can talk. We'll pick up your bags in a bit."

"Here in the airport?" Evan said. "It's not the most private place, but if you say so." His voice was tight. The quarrel was coming. *Oh, please God, don't let it damage our relationship,* Donna prayed. She looked keenly at their faces for an instant before she led the way to the empty waiting area. They looked tired. No, not tired. They looked sick. They were dreading this as much as she was. She must somehow make this as easy on them as possible.

Then, the very moment they were seated, Evan asked, "Why did you do it, Donna? Why did you need to find him?"

"I didn't need to, Dad. I didn't even want to." She could feel embarrassed color flooding into her neck and face as she told them of her childish plot to capture Bruce's attention for the summer. Her father was a moment slower to understand her meaning than her mother was.

"You're kidding," Sara said with mingled scorn and exasperation. "You mean you've got a crush on Bruce? Bruce, of all people!"

"No," her father interposed. "She can't mean that. She means…" He looked at her searchingly. "She does mean it! Oh, I can't believe this." He got up and paced to the end of the row of empty seats and came back. "Donna, for Pete's sake, you're nineteen years old. I'd have thought surely by now that you'd have more sense. What did Bruce say to this idiotic idea when you sprung it on him?"

"You have told him, haven't you?" Sara asked, looking worried.

"Yes. Bruce knows." Donna passed her tongue over her lips. "He was…well, at first he was a little appalled."

"Ha! I don't wonder," Evan said. "At least he's got some sense. What'd he say? Did he burst out laughing?"

"Bruce didn't laugh," Donna said in a small voice.

"In the first place," Evan continued, keeping his voice down with an effort, "you haven't even started college, Donna. What about that? That's the reason you've been stalling about college plans, isn't it? You had this in mind all along. You—"

"Evan, wait a minute. Donna, what *did* Bruce say when you told him?"

"He…" She swallowed hard. "Don't laugh. Please don't laugh at me. But to be flat-out honest, the first few minutes I thought he was going to turn and run screaming out of the house."

"Good. I should think so," Evan said bitterly. "Of all the devious…and to dig up that Tsung character as an excuse, just an excuse, mind you. Donna, that was sneaky. That was underhanded. I never thought, I never thought you would ever—"

"Dad, it wasn't devious. I mean, it wasn't intended to be. It was just…just…"

Sara reached over and touched Donna to get her attention. "Wait a minute. Let's go back a minute. What does Bruce say now, Donna?"

"Just a sec, Mom. Daddy, Raymond Tsung isn't a character. He's your Mr. Solid Citizen. He's a bank president. You can't get much more solid than that. And he's nice, he's…" She stopped herself as both her parents seemed suddenly to freeze over at her defense of Raymond. "Now, about Bruce's feelings," she went on hastily. "He's beginning to see it my way now. He's—"

"He's what!" Evan shouted. "Now just a goddamn minute!" Heads swiveled as the streams of people passed them. Some of the strangers paused. Sara caught Evan's arm and squeezed it. He cleared his throat and lifted his head, looking at Donna levelly, his eyes like agates. "I see why you wanted to have this little meeting in the midst of a million people. So we can't actually speak our minds."

"Evan, wait a minute," Sara interjected again, rubbing her hand back and forth on his arm. "We have to figure out what we're going to do—"

"I know what we're going to do," Evan said grimly. "We will pay our respects to the Hunts and then get the first plane back to Vancouver—with our daughter. And at home, in the privacy of our living room, I'm going to talk some sense into that sneaky little mind of hers—"

"Now, Evan, that's not fair," Sara said, her own voice rising slightly. "She's been trying to explain. Let her, for heaven's sake."

"She's been explaining for ten minutes," Evan said, standing up, "and so far she hasn't made any sense that I can see."

"Daddy, please. Sit down, please. Just listen. Bruce and I have talked it all over—"

"Oh good. That solves everything, doesn't it? You and Bruce have talked it over. Fine." He walked to the end of the row of seats and back again, his hands in his pockets, jingling coins and keys. "And what have you and Bruce decided, may I ask? I say 'may I' since I am only a parent, and of course, I have no rights here at all."

"Oh, Daddy," she said miserably. She swallowed tears and forced herself to continue. "We know I'm young. We know that Bruce has some things to work out for himself. We are willing to wait a while." Her tone was pleading.

"Donna," Evan said, holding back his rage, "you are nineteen years old. Nine years ago you were a child of ten. You are not adult enough to make a decision that—"

"Now hold it, Evan," Sara said. "She's not rushing into anything. She just said—"

"Make up your mind, Daddy," Donna said, speaking sharply for the first time, then quickly modifying her tone. "A minute ago you said at nineteen I should have some sense. Now at nineteen I'm still a child. Which is it?"

He sat down, leaned forward, and reached out to her for the first time. It almost broke her heart. She took his hand and clasped it. "You see, honey," he said desperately. "You are just too *young*. Marriage, even the promise of marriage, is such a commitment. It may be the biggest commitment that a man and woman can ever make. You don't want to…to…blow it because of being too hasty, too impatient. Give yourself some time, just a little time, that's all." He lifted her hand absentmindedly to his lips and kissed it, the way he had a thousand times before. The gesture nearly undid Donna, but she held on to her control.

"And then, too," he continued pleadingly, a sheen of tears in his own eyes for the first time. "There is the… uh…personal side of it, you see. A girl like you, having had a pretty sheltered life and all. Well, I mean, to be blunt, honey, there could be some sexual adjustment between you that you haven't counted on. You see?"

"There won't be any sexual adjustment, Daddy," she said quietly.

"But how can you know that, baby? How can—"

"Wait, Evan," Sara, still holding Evan's arm, slid her hand down and clasped his fingers in hers in an old familiar gesture. "What are you saying, Donna?" Her voice was tight with anxiety.

"I'm saying there won't be any sexual adjustment, Mom. That's all okay."

"Donna, you don't mean…you don't mean…" Sara stammered.

"She doesn't mean what? What doesn't she mean?" Evan asked, glancing from one to the other of his women. Then a dull red rose had mottled his face. He stood up and walked over to the plate-glass window looking out on the end of the landing field. A plane's lights revolved as it taxied by. A truck loomed, then passed going in the opposite direction. White uniforms stood out in the gloom as workers crossed the tarmac. Inside the airport, endless feet clacked across the tile floor, the metallic voice from the public-address system spattered words, and TV monitors constantly rolled over more lists of flights coming and going.

Finally he came back. There were pinched white lines around his nostrils, and he was muttering softly, "That bastard, that bastard," as he sat down.

Donna felt tears slipping from her eyes for the first time.

"You are coming home, Donna. Now. We will skip going to the Hunts. They'll understand. I'll get us a flight." He didn't move from his chair.

"I'm not going back, Daddy," Donna said gently. "Not until it's time for the fall quarter. This is it, Daddy. Please. Try to understand."

He looked at her dully for a long moment, and Donna's heart ached. It was the first time she had ever defied him. Oh, loving was a costly, costly thing. For a moment, she wasn't sure she could pay the price.

"Evan," Sara said. Her voice was gentle, and she gripped his hands again, her fingers entwined in his. "Just maybe Donna's right. Maybe, when we weren't looking, she grew up. I'm not asking you to face it just yet, but maybe you should think about it, consider it.''

"Well, don't ask me not to talk to Fenton," Evan said, his voice hard. "Because I intend to."

"I'm not asking you anything, love," Sara replied.

"And not only that," he said with a rasping laugh. "I'm even asked to share my only daughter with her other father. What about him?"

"We'll cope with it," Sara said with determination. "We'll deal with Tsung. Tsung's no problem."

Donna made a small sound.

"What? What did you say?" Evan asked.

"Nothing, Dad. Oh well, I was just going to mention that…uh…Raymond Tsung, that is, Mr. Tsung is someone I rather think you'd like. I mean if the situation weren't…ah…if it weren't this situation.''

"But it *is* 'this situation,' as you put it, so I rather think I won't exactly enjoy meeting him. I…'' He stopped almost in mid-word, his eyes following a young pregnant woman who was walking by with the passing crowd. She was pushing a stroller with a sleeping toddler in it. She looked exhausted.

Evan turned stiffly to Donna. "You aren't…you aren't…''

"Aren't what, Daddy?" she asked blankly.

"Uh…'' He gestured vaguely toward the receding back of the pregnant woman. "Pregnant?" he asked faintly.

He looked so horror-struck that Donna flung back her head and her laughter pealed out. "Oh, Daddy, no." She put her arms around his neck. "Whatever gave you that idea?"

Sara was trying to hold back a smile.

Evan took Donna's arms down. "What do you mean?"

he asked, sounding like a testy old man, "whatever gave me that idea? Sudden decisions to marry have been made for that reason."

She clung to his hand. "But, Dad, it isn't a sudden decision—I've been working on it since I came down from Vancouver."

"Do you have to put it like that?" Evan hunched his shoulders and shuddered slightly. "You sound so...so..."

"And it's not going to be a sudden marriage, Evan," Sara interposed as if he hadn't spoken. "Donna has said they'd wait. Didn't you say that, Donna?"

"Yes, Bruce and I have definitely—"

"Donna, nothing is definite," Evan snapped, "if you and I mean the same thing by the word. Nothing will be definite one way or the other until I have talked with Fenton tomorrow. Is that clear?"

Donna sank back into her chair and looked at her father.

"I wish you wouldn't call Bruce 'Fenton,'" she said in a small voice. "And you say it so...so meanly."

"I feel mean, Donna. Can't you understand that? How would you feel if you were in my place?"

Her eyes filled up with tears again. "Mean, I guess," she admitted, swallowing hard.

"Look, we're just going in circles," Sara said, sounding unhappy and exasperated at the same time. "Let's leave it until tomorrow. Until we talk with Bruce. Come on, let's go on out to the Hunts'."

"Oh, God, do we have to?" Evan slid down in his chair.

"Evan, what on earth do you mean? They're our best friends! Of course we have to. We want to."

"It's just that they'll want to talk about this mess and, oh hell—"

"That's all right, Daddy," Donna said, suddenly remembering her conversation with Laura. "I told Laura I was taking you out to eat, and then we'd be over later. They don't expect to see you till tomorrow. And I mean I'll take you out. I'm picking up the tab with money I earned myself.''

"We accept," Sara said. "Don't we accept, Evan?"

"Yes." He gave Donna a smile. "The only thing is I'm afraid I can't do your offer justice. I'm not exactly hungry at the moment."

"Mom?" Donna asked anxiously.

"We could have something light, Evan." There was a pleading note in her voice.

"Crepes?" Donna said with sudden inspiration. "I'll take you to the Crepe Vine and we'll have crepes—any kind you want. And I can afford the Crepe Vine without too much sweat."

Evan stood up. "Okay," he said, his lips twisting slightly. "Let's all go push crepes around on our plates. It's better than going out to the Hunts' this early and trying to avoid talking about subject A. Okay, I'm sorry I said that." He reached over to touch Donna's face. "Don't look so crestfallen. We'll work it out somehow. I think."

CHAPTER EIGHTEEN

LAURA HEARD THE BEDROOM door open, then Mark's deliberate cough, but she didn't turn around.

The door closed.

He was late. Hours late. Outside, the tree that almost touched the window reached its limbs like black arms into the moonlit sky. She huddled into a tighter ball on the window seat, folded her robe around her legs and rested her cheek on her knees.

"Sweetheart, you okay?" Mark spoke in a low voice as if he was afraid of startling her. "You're ready for bed. Don't you feel good?"

Poor Mark. He'd made his mistakes, but then, so had she. And she hadn't been fair to him. A breeze slithered through the partly open window, and she shivered. She had to find the words to tell him her news, to make right what had gone so terribly wrong between them.

His hand, placed tentatively on her back, made her jump. "Laura, honey, we've got to talk. We can't go on like this."

"No."

"Will you discuss it with me? Please don't keep shutting me out. I stayed at the office trying to decide what to do, then I drove around. But all I wanted was to be with you. You and I can work it out, I know we can—if we just stop avoiding it."

She glanced up at him, and her stomach contracted. He

looked so tired. How long had he looked that way, drawn, dark shadows under the soft brown eyes she loved, eyes she could see whether he was with her or not?

"I don't want to avoid it anymore either, Mark. I've been thinking the same things as you all day." Sometimes she took him for granted, this arresting man with an aura that usually suggested total control. Mark was her rock, her best friend—and he had also been the most exciting lover a woman could dream of—until she'd drawn away from him.

He took off his suit jacket, pulled his unknotted tie from beneath his collar, and sat close to her feet on the dark green velvet seat. He bowed his head, holding the coat and tie on his knees, waiting.

"E.J.'s spending the night at your mother's. She's going to have him for a few days. I've got to tell you something, Mark."

"Why did Irma decide to…what, Laura? What do you have to tell me?"

She tried to return her cheek to her knees, but he dropped the coat and slipped his hands quickly around her neck, held up her chin with his thumbs. "Something's wrong. You're sick! I knew—"

"I'm not sick." Laura closed her eyes. "I'm just a little tired, that's all. I was going to go to bed early. I'm very healthy." Whatever she said, she knew he would still be angry and frightened when she told him her news, the way he had been whenever she'd tried to suggest having another baby.

He parted his lips, the expression in his eyes slowly changing. He released her and got up. "You don't like me near you anymore, do you?" he said, and walked to the foot of their great, pillow-strewn bed. "We only make love when…when…don't you want to be married to me any longer? Is that what you're trying to tell me?''

In an instant, Laura was off the window seat and at Mark's side. She grasped his tense biceps and urged him to face her. When he did, she reached up and kissed him swiftly and fully on the mouth. ''I want to be married to you forever, Mark. You know that. I love you more than anything, more than my life. Irma's taken E.J. because I asked her to, so that you and I can say what has to be said.''

He smiled, a small, tight smile that let her know he was still wary.

''Promise me…'' Laura inhaled deeply, smoothing her palms over his chest. ''Promise me you'll hear me out and think before you say anything.''

His smile disappeared. He held her wrists. ''Tell me.''

''And you'll hear me out before you say anything?''

''*Tell me.*'' He pushed her down gently on the edge of the bed and stood over her.

''First…'' She lifted her chin and tried hard to swallow. ''First, I saw the doctor again today, and he says I'm absolutely fine. There's nothing to worry about, and no reason to believe that there will be. Do you understand?''

He sat down beside her with a thud, as if his legs wouldn't support him. ''You said you weren't ill.'' He held her hands so tightly that they hurt.

''I'm not, Mark. I'm well, and I feel great, physically.''

He frowned. ''You didn't go to a psychiatrist?''

''I went to an obstetrician.''

She held her breath and watched the slow dawn of understanding. His fingers dug even deeper into her flesh. ''No, Laura. No! You aren't pregnant.''

''Almost four months, Mark. The baby will be born early in January. I wasn't sure—''

"No!" He'd stopped listening. "They said you shouldn't have another baby. They said we were lucky with E.J., and then..." He stood up and strode back and forth in front of her, slamming a fist into his palm. "Then—the little boy. Our other little boy. They told me you almost died. You agreed we wouldn't have any more children. Oh, Laura, I couldn't stand it if you died."

Tears ran from his staring eyes. She felt sick, desperately, mortally sick and for a moment, helpless.

"Mark," she said and repeated, "Mark," louder, and stood to stop him when he passed in front of her again. "I never agreed not to have more children. You decided for both of us. Sit down and listen."

He only took her in his arms and held her in a viselike grip, murmuring incoherently into her hair. She circled his waist and hugged him back, crooning as she would to a child, willing him to be calm.

"You can't have it," he said abruptly. When she tried to tighten her grip, he held her away with one hand and smoothed back her hair with the other. "Now, listen," he continued. "I understand how much you want another child. I do too. And when this is all over, we'll look into adoption. Evan and Sara have Donna, and they all love each other."

She tried to speak, but he shook his head vigorously. "Don't say anything," he said. "You're so sweet, the sweetest. You've got so much love to give. I should have done something about this earlier, then it wouldn't have come to this."

Laura's own knees wobbled. He hadn't accused her of deliberately becoming pregnant. He didn't have to, but he knew that was exactly what she'd done, and now she must make him listen and accept the truth.

"We'll go and see this doctor together." Mark spoke

faster and faster. "Tomorrow, we'll go. He'll understand once he knows the whole story. Evan and Sara will be here, but they'll be occupied dealing with Donna. They'll probably be glad if we aren't around for the day."

Laura lifted her chin and looked directly into his eyes. "Stop it."

"It'll be all right once the doctor knows—"

"He knows. Sit down."

He rubbed a hand over his eyes. "He can't know."

"He does, and he says everything's going to be fine. When…when our other baby died, there was a lot of over-reaction, Mark. Understandable. It was horrible. But Dr. Perris isn't the kind who panics, or makes rash judgments. I was wrong to stop the pills without telling you. I'm sorry I did that. But I'm not sorry I'm pregnant."

A film of sweat had broken out on Mark's face. "I want you, Laura." His voice broke. "We have E.J., and I couldn't love a child more. I wish our other boy had lived. Sometimes I think about him just as I know you do. But I won't give you up for another child. I won't, I tell you. I can't…"

"Okay, Mark. Now you're going to listen. Sit." He reluctantly let her guide him back to the edge of the bed. She was tired, very tired, but she knew she must finish this discussion. "I've told you the obstetrician is confident. He wouldn't put his reputation on the line by saying he was if he wasn't."

"You should have told me." He turned his back and hunched forward, hugging his chest. "You should have asked me, Laura. This wasn't just your decision to make."

She massaged his neck, and pressed her cheek against the smooth fabric of his white shirt. "Sweetheart. Your mind was made up four years ago. I have asked you—again and again. You wouldn't discuss it. You wouldn't

even talk about it. I know that isn't a good enough excuse
for what I did. All I can do is say I love you and I want
us to have another child so badly I don't think about anything else anymore.''

Mark was still, silent.

''Dr. Perris will talk to you, Mark. He'll talk to both of
us, and then I'm sure you'll stop worrying.''

''I'm scared.''

She had to take away the fear somehow. ''Remember
how it was when…when…what happened the last time?''

''Don't! I don't want to remember.''

She twisted him around. ''And that's the main problem.
You won't face exactly what happened and try to analyze
it. You're a logical man. When you're in court you won't
allow people to evade issues.''

''We aren't in court, and I'm not on the witness stand.
There's only one issue here—whether or not I'm prepared
to risk losing my wife in order to gain another child. The
answer is no. No, Laura.''

She inhaled slowly. ''Wrong, Mark. That isn't the issue.
And even if it were, I'd still have this baby. I'm sorry if
that hurts you, but this isn't a decision you can make for
both of us. A long time ago, you and I promised each other
honesty, and I've been doing a lousy job lately. From here
on there won't be any more deception. This baby—our
baby—is a part of us now, and he—or she—is alive inside
my body. I want this child. And you will, too, if you'll
only relax and let yourself.''

He raked at his hair. ''Where's Donna? And Evan and
Sara?''

''Not back yet,'' she said impatiently, recognizing his
clumsy attempt to buy time to think. ''Evan and Sara's
flight wasn't due in till nine. In case you've forgotten,

they'll have a lot to talk about. I told Donna to make her folks comfortable, and we'd see them in the morning.''

"We can't do that. They'll think something's wrong."

"Something is wrong. Damn it, Mark, will you stop slipping away from me?''

He stared at her for an instant before kicking off his shoes and stretching out on the bed, his hands behind his head.

"Something went wrong with my last delivery."

He turned his face away.

"Dr. Perris went over the records with me. I shouldn't have been allowed to continue in labor so long, Mark. The baby was presenting by the shoulder. He couldn't be born vaginally.''

"The doctor said the baby wasn't vertex, or head down...I don't understand these things. He said he couldn't get him turned properly.'' Mark sounded remote now, factual.

"But the records show it was more complicated than that. A cesarean should have been performed.''

"It was.''

"But too late, Mark. Too late. The doctor waited too long, and that's what probably killed the baby and almost killed me. There's no absolute proof to substantiate a thing like that, but it seems logical, even to me.''

"What's going to stop the same thing from happening again?''

Laura sat beside him and smoothed the backs of her fingers lightly over his jaw. "This time the cesarean will be scheduled. We'll set a date and go get our baby. Mark, darling, this time there won't be any problems—just another wonderful baby coming home afterward. And in the meantime I'm going to take the best care of myself. And I'm going to be happy, sweetheart—and I'm going to make sure you are too. That will be all I need to do a perfect job for you this time.''

He sat up and held her arms, then shook her. ''The other time wasn't your fault. And you aren't on some sort of trial to do any kind of job for me. This is our baby. We'll do a perfect job.''

Laura couldn't help smiling. Through a swimming film of tears, she smiled into Mark's serious face. ''We sure will.''

He swept the tears from her cheeks with his fingertips. ''You're devious, but I adore you, Laura Hunt. And you think I'm going to be a pussycat to deal with from here on out, but you're wrong. I'm going to have more questions for your Dr. Perris than any doctor ever fielded. He's going to feel as if he's on the stand.''

''I'm not worried.'' She laughed and sniffed. ''He'll tell you what he's told me. I shouldn't have waited so long to say all this.''

Mark looked at her critically. ''You haven't put on any weight.'' He spread one broad hand over her stomach and raised his brows, then smiled. ''Well, a little, I guess. Why didn't I notice?''

''I've been sucking my stomach in.'' She let out a noisy breath and pretended to slump. ''What a relief. Roll out the muumuus.''

''I want you to knock off the volunteer work. And I don't want to see you pulling and pushing in the garden. We'll get some more help for the house—''

''Shhh,'' Laura started to laugh and cry again. ''I'm not planning on living like an invalid for months. I'll do everything I normally do, only now I'll do it better.''

''Better?''

''Because you're with me again, Mark, really with me. You are, aren't you? And it's okay…about the baby?''

Mark felt tears in his own eyes. He touched her cheek. She'd never lost that ethereal quality he'd seen and been captured by years ago. How many years? It didn't matter. The incorrigible girl smiling up at him from a blanket in a childhood garden—the garden outside their window now—the lovely young woman's face emerging from clown makeup in a Seattle dressing room. In those moments and in so many more, he'd been captivated by Laura's blue, blue eyes, the mass of shining dark hair, her soft, ready smile. His throat constricted. He couldn't live without her, but he couldn't deny her plea that he be with her, body and soul, in the months to come. He'd trust that the pregnancy would go smoothly, and above all, he'd make her happy for as much time as they were given together. He prayed silently for a long, long life with this lady.

"Mark, is it all right?" Her voice hadn't changed either. It was still slightly husky and low, with a heart-stopping hesitancy. And he loved her.

"It's all right, my love." He kissed her forehead, her brows, tilted up her chin and brushed his mouth across hers. "But I do think you ought to have that early night you talked about. I think you're tired out. That's my fault. I'm sorry. Give me a little time to get used to what's happened, okay?"

She pushed him back against the pillows and leaned over him. "I might forgive you," she said. Her hair slipped across his jaw and neck, and she kissed him. "If you're very, very good from now on."

Something stirred in his belly. Her breasts were firm on his chest. "All you have to do is tell me what to do, ma'am, and I'll try to straighten up and fly right," he said against her slowly moving lips.

She kissed him fully, and sat up to take off her robe and

to pull her nightgown over her head. "Sir, I think you just handed down your own sentence."

He watched her. Her stomach was slightly rounded, her breasts fuller. She was a lovely woman, ever lovelier to him—especially carrying their child. The excitement came, wild, surging, and he laughed. "Okay, Your Honor, let me have it. What do I get for my sins?" He spanned her ribs, stroked her body, and shifted slightly at the urgency of his erection.

Laura's pupils dilated. She unbuttoned his shirt. "An early night for you, my man. Disrobe."

CHAPTER NINETEEN

LAURA ALWAYS GAVE Sara and Evan the same guest room, a large L-shaped room with a sitting-room arrangement in one end and a king-size bed in the other. The "bed-sitter," she called it.

Sara nestled herself against Evan in the big bed, and felt his body curve around hers in their customary manner. She smiled into the darkness at the small sound of contentment he always made.

"Do you want to talk?" she asked softly.

"You mean about Subject A, I guess," he muttered into her hair.

"Not necessarily, darling. We can do the San Francisco fog bit, or, now, those crepes were really good, weren't they? We did all right for two people who had lost their appetites." She felt him laugh silently against her.

"Kidding aside, Sara. Can a nineteen-year-old girl really be in love?"

"Certainly," she answered briskly. "I believe Juliet was only fourteen—"

"Be serious," he interrupted. "I'm talking about Donna. What happens if Donna, who believes she loves this jerk—"

"Now, Evan—"

"*Jerk*, I repeat...what if she really isn't in love, and gets over it after they've been together six months? Then what happens if by that time she is pregnant?"

Sara moved out of his arms to reach over and turn on the bedside lamp. They faced each other.

"That's a lot of ifs, Evan."

"Life is full of ifs, love. We should know, we've both encountered a few. And I've got a funny sickness in my gut about this."

"Well, for that matter, so have I," Sara agreed. "True, I hadn't thought to call it a funny-sickness-in-the-gut, but the description does fit. What do you have in mind, Evan?"

"What do you mean?"

"You've said half a dozen times that you're going to talk to 'Fenton.' I'm with Donna there, by the way. You're going to have to stop calling him that. You keep saying you're going to talk to him, but talk to him how? What do you intend to say to him? Walking in with your trusty hunting rifle is a little out-of-date."

"I don't own a trusty hunting rifle. You know that. I've never hunted. If the animals don't shoot at me, I won't shoot at them. I was thinking more, I suppose, of a clout in the kisser."

"Oh, that would be just great. That would be one terrific way to solve the problem. Thank God you're only kidding." But she looked at him sharply, not really sure he wasn't serious.

"Clouts are out, huh?"

"Absolutely out, Evan. Bruce is very smooth—"

"You can say that again."

"Don't be nasty, Evan. You didn't let me finish. He's very smooth and sophisticated. I won't have you going in there and looking like a fool coming on as the heavy father."

"Okay, let's review the ground rules." Evan twisted around, punching up his pillow so he was sitting up, braced against the headboard. "I can't call him Fenton. I can't clout him. I can't look like a fool. I can't come on like a heavy father. Do you have anything that I can do?"

"I would suggest we listen to him and Donna first," she said softly, rubbing her hand gently back and forth over his muscular shoulder.

"Well, I may have it all backward, but I kind of think it is their place to listen to us, dammit. A few months ago at home in Vancouver, we could have won first prize in any perfect-family contest, and now, a matter of weeks later, all our plans for Donna are knocked into a cocked hat and she's completely out of control. And it's all that jerk's fault. And I'm supposed to listen?" Evan was outraged. He punched the pillow again, savagely.

"Ssshhh. Keep your voice down. Think about it a minute. Has Donna ever been 'out of control'—and that's your phrase, not mine—before?"

"No. Of course not."

"In fact, back a few years you were grousing because she was too self-contained, too controlled. You said you didn't want her to turn into a tight-mouthed, little old woman, didn't you?"

"Yeah, I suppose that sounds familiar."

"Then my thinking is that she wouldn't be 'out of control'—"

"I know, and that's my phrase not yours," he said, mimicking his wife.

"This business of breaking out of our customary guidelines, of resorting to subterfuge, which she did, is totally unlike Donna. So something made her do it. Something cataclysmic has occurred somehow to change her."

"Cataclysmic? What do you mean by that in this context?" Evan's voice sounded tentative, and all his attention was on her.

"I mean," Sara said patiently, "it makes me think that this is far, far more important to her than perhaps anything else in her life has ever been. Suppose Bruce really is the big love of her life, Evan, and it just happened a little early? Don't you see that if we handle the situation incorrectly, it could be very damaging? To all of us?"

Evan was quiet, staring at the ceiling.

"Do you see, Evan?"

"The big love, when it hits," he murmured, "can be pretty cataclysmic. You think that step one is just to listen to what they have to say, then?"

"I do, lover. Regardless of the funny feeling in your gut, regardless of your anger—and it is justifiable anger—first, we just listen to what they have to say. Okay?" Sara waited a moment and then repeated, "Okay?"

He regarded at her for several seconds before he leaned over to kiss her. "Okay," he said against her mouth, and then bent slowly to kiss her neck and her shoulder. "Anything you say, wise one. I may get an ulcer out of this, but I'll try to keep my cool."

"HE'S HOME, BECAUSE there's his car," Donna said as she pulled Laura's small car to the curb behind Bruce's. "Now, Dad, you're going to keep cool. Remember, you promised."

"Oh, I'm cool, all right," Evan said somberly. "That's why I waited until today to speak to him. If we'd come over last night..." He left the sentence unfinished and opened the car door to get out, turning to help Sara.

Evan had spent part of the day at the office with Mark, since Fenton and Hunt handled his legal affairs in the States. Sara and Laura had talked together for hours. The announcement of Laura's pregnancy had done a lot to ease the tension, somehow. Evan and Laura were old, old friends and, once assured that the pregnancy was probably a safe one, Evan had been pleased. He would have been more pleased if his mind hadn't been taken up with Donna, Bruce, and the Tsung matter.

Bruce had apparently been watching for them, and he came out onto the porch to greet them. He held open the double doors to let them pass through.

"Hello, Bruce. It's nice to see you again," Sara said graciously, leaning over to kiss him on the cheek the way she always did. Bruce gave her a tentative smile and held out his hand to Evan, which Evan either didn't see or deliberately ignored. Donna cast Bruce a pleading look as she followed her parents inside.

She glanced quickly at the antique clock on the mantel. It was not quite three. They would never get through this afternoon.

"Please, make yourselves comfortable," Bruce said with an expansive gesture. "Is it too early to offer you a drink?"

"Too early for me. Anyhow," Evan said curtly, "this isn't a social call."

"No, of course not," Bruce said quickly.

"I've always loved this old place," Sara interjected, trying to smooth the waters, and Donna gave her mother a grateful look. They had both insisted on coming along.

"It was nice of you to arrange to come home early for this, Bruce. You probably had plenty to do downtown," Sara went on, evidently determined to set a peaceful tone.

"Better here than the office," Bruce grinned, "in case Evan has decided to punch my face in."

Evan glanced at him sharply. "Don't think I haven't thought of it, Fenton."

"I'm sure you have," Bruce said quietly. "And I can't say I wouldn't feel the same way in your place."

Evan made a little wordless grunt, and Donna murmured a placating, "Now, Dad." Then she added quickly, to change the subject, "Bruce, is that new? The chess set?" She got out of her chair and went to lean over and look at it more closely. The set was spread on its black-and-white board on a small table beneath a window. The afternoon light came through the curtain and shone through the delicately carved almost translucent, white pieces.

"It's new to me," Bruce said, "but actually pretty old, I'd say. Couple of hundred years."

"What's it made of? Alabaster?"

"Jade. Black and white jade."

Sara had walked over to it. "It's lovely, Bruce. Where did you get it?"

"I got it by messenger last evening. It's from Raymond Tsung. Just a little token of his appreciation, his note said, for introducing him to Donna."

"He didn't!" Donna said, almost laughing. She had showed her parents the jade necklace the previous evening. They had admired it, but their dismay had been evident. She had put it sadly back into its velvet box. The gift had, more than anything, made Raymond Tsung real to them. Now she wished that, somehow, she'd been able to refuse the necklace.

"That's another little loose end we've got to tie up today," Evan said. "We're going over there to see him at four. We'll tell him thanks for his interest and so on, but Donna has a complete set of parents with whom she's satisfied—at least, I'm assuming she is—and she doesn't need any more. Goodbye, etcetera."

"Good luck." Bruce smiled. "He's hard to put off."

"I think I'll manage," Evan answered grimly. "And shall we get to the point here?"

"Yes, of course," Bruce agreed, straightening up. He

had been leaning against the mantel. Donna couldn't take her eyes off him. He hadn't changed from his business suit, and he seemed formal and, in a way, remote. He half-bowed to Evan and waited. She saw—watched—felt—all of him, the lean form, the loose fair hair, the worried, guarded look on his face. Never, never had she loved him so much.

Evan stood up, one fist inside the other palm. He kept beating them together. There was a brief, almost ugly silence, and there was the tense sensation of the two men circling one another. It passed in a moment. Then, invisibly, control of the meeting shifted from Evan, who was angry, hurt, and frustrated, to Bruce. He had taken charge.

"First, I will say…to you both…to all three of you… that I am sorry," he said gently. "I will be sorry all of my life. I was way out of line. I didn't handle this right at all. When Donna first broached the subject, I should have picked up the phone and called Vancouver. I didn't. And Evan, if you want to take a poke at me, man, you're entitled. Go ahead."

"I'll pass," Evan muttered. Then he exploded. "But God damn it, did you have to—" He choked on his words.

"No, I didn't, Evan. If she was in love with me, and— after a while—I knew I loved her, I should have left it there."

"Well, what's done is done," Sara murmured. "It isn't the end of the world, you know. As I recall, Evan, we didn't exactly wait until after the ceremony ourselves."

"You weren't a teenager," Evan snapped, turning his eyes back to Bruce. "I'm listening."

"You know how it started, with that cooked-up story about locating her original father, Donna being sure he wasn't around to locate. Almost as soon as I found him,

Donna began to have second thoughts about it and leveled with me."

"And the soup hit the fan," Evan said glumly.

"No, Dad, the soup didn't hit the fan until I told Bruce I was in love with him. Then it did," Donna said with a look of chagrin. "I see Bruce is going to be all gentlemanly and skip that part. He shouldn't. I threw myself at him, is the basic fact of the matter."

Evan turned a brooding look in her direction. "Don't interrupt, Donna."

"One more thing," she persisted, "then I'll shut up. I had to do something, Dad. To Bruce's mind I was still a thirteen-year-old. I had to jolt him out of that notion."

"And did she?" Evan asked, his eyes on Bruce.

A reluctant grin tugged at Bruce's lips. "I would say so," he said mildly. "It set me thinking. 'Out of the mouths of babes' and so on. I don't remember really just when I realized she was right. I love Donna. I did not know how deeply I could love until I loved Donna." He made another little bow, this time in her direction. It was a private tribute, brief and delicate, just between the two of them, and she cherished it.

Evan cleared his throat. "So that leaves us where? You love my daughter. She loves you. She is still only nineteen years old and hasn't even started college yet."

"I'll tell you what we've worked out between us," Bruce continued, "and see what you and Sara think about it. Right now, Donna likes to think that being my wife is all the existence she wants. 'The world well lost for love' and all that. I know better. We'll have had a good summer. Both of us have made discoveries—too many to take without thought and consideration—kind of a waiting interval. We have tentatively planned that she go to school in Vancouver for the fall quarter." He paused.

"So far, so good," Evan said grudgingly.

"At the end of the quarter, if we still feel the same way, we'll be married and Donna will transfer down here to complete her college—and graduate work, if she decides to go on with some special training."

Evan uttered another of his little wordless grunts.

"During the interval," Bruce went on, "we will not be in touch at all. By that I mean we will not see each other, we will not talk or write to each other. It will be a time of being absolutely apart."

Donna swallowed hard and kept her eyes as wide open as she could. She *must* hold onto her composure, but it sounded like a death knell. The idea of being completely apart from Bruce, even for a few months, seemed unbearable at the moment. But she must bear it.

Evan turned to her. "Donna?" His voice was gentle. "You go along with this? With what Bruce is promising?"

"Yes," she said clearly, "this is what we've decided." And she took pride in sounding controlled.

"Well," Sara said, "we certainly can't ask for anything fairer than that, Evan."

"I...guess I must agree, certainly," Evan said after a moment. A near-smile touched his lips. "Bruce talks about a jolt. I guess the biggest jolt I've had is that Donna—"

"Grew up?" Sara asked softly.

"Yeah, I guess." A look of sadness and confusion, mingled with just a touch of pride, came and went on Evan's face. His expression made them laugh, and he joined in.

The tension which had filled the room melted away. Evan held out his hand to Bruce.

"Okay," Sara said briskly. "Next stop, Mr. Tsung, I suppose." She made leave-taking motions. Donna knew it was actually too early for her parents to leave in order to reach Tsung's office by four, but by tacit agreement they all accepted the small breathing space Sara offered. Her mother and father needed some time together, and so did she and Bruce. They would meet again later, when all were gathered at the Hunts' house for dinner.

AT TEN MINUTES past six, Donna watched her parents come into the Hunts' living room with slightly bemused expressions on their faces. They had visited Raymond Tsung. She exchanged a quick glance with Bruce.

"Welcome. Just in time," Mark said, getting up from the couch, where he had been sitting close to Laura. "What would you like? We've started the unwinding hour."

"I don't know if we need to unwind or not," Evan said, as he put a bulky package he'd been carrying on the table. "I feel a bit unwound already. Just Scotch on the rocks, Mark."

"Same for me," Sara said, "but add a splash of water, will you?" She, too, was carrying a package, which she still held when she sat down.

"Were you shopping, Mother?" Donna asked, grinning maliciously.

"You know we were not," Sara said, returning the grin.

"Wow," Evan exclaimed. "That Raymond Tsung is quite a guy, I must say."

"Quite," Bruce agreed, holding up his glass for Mark to refill. "I take it you came away carrying gifts. Are you going to show us what he gave you?"

"All in good time," Evan said, accepting his drink from Mark. "I've got it figured out, though."

"Terrific," Bruce laughed. "Tell the rest of us. Each time Donna and I see him, it's for the specific purpose of saying goodbye forever, but somehow or other it just doesn't happen."

"It's simple," Evan said, smiling. "It's two things, actually. One, he is such a damned nice guy. Two, you can't help liking him. It's tough, under the circumstances, to say, 'Hi, Raymond. Goodbye forever.'"

"So it's Raymond now, is it?" Laura said from the couch, her eyes dancing with mirth.

"Well, what did he give you?" Bruce asked, and Sara started unwrapping her gift.

"This is embroidered silk. It's a very old art in China. See?" She held up a small screen of white silk held taut in a delicate enameled frame. It was embroidered with nearly invisible stitches, and bore the image of an ancient Chinese lady with a high black headdress. "Now look. Magic," Sara laughed and reversed the screen. The other side was embroidered too, with a young girl who had flowers in her hair. Each stitched portrait was embroidered on the back of the other in exactly the same shape. The taut silk background was so thin that the light shone through, and a wrong stitch would have been clearly evident.

"Isn't anybody going to ask what I got?" Evan asked, amid much crackling of paper as he unwrapped his gift. "I think I won on points, though. I've persuaded him that it's not necessary for him to reopen his house here for Donna to live in."

"What?" Donna gasped.

"Oh, yes," Sara said. "While his family is in Hong Kong he's living with his sister's family, and his house is closed. He was all for opening it and installing himself and Donna there for as long as she wants to stay in San Francisco."

"Oh, no!" Donna buried her face in her hands. "He's so...so..."

"Nice," her father said. "Now look here." He held up his gift. It was a black enameled jewel chest for a man, touched with gold. Though it was small, the lines were massive and masculine. "For my watch and my old school ring," Evan explained, grinning. "Poor guy did pretty well, considering he'd have had no way of knowing I almost never wear jewelry since I work with tools so much. But it was a nice try."

"There is kind of a problem, though," Sara said pensively, sipping her drink. "As Evan says, he's so blamed nice, so kind, and he...he means so well. Despite all our kidding, he wishes Donna could be a permanent part of his life. I read that between the lines."

"Oh, no," Donna breathed. "Surely not."

"Mark, is there any way you can help them out with this?" Laura asked, trying unconsciously to suppress a smile. Mark frowned, and shook his head slightly.

"How about that?" Evan turned to him. "You are sort of once-removed family, as it were. Why don't you see him, Mark? I let him know that Donna is coming back to Vancouver for the fall quarter, but that's about as far as I got."

Mark gave a gutsy sigh and grinned sheepishly. "Well, since my loyal little wife has blown the whistle on me, I'll confess it. I've already been over to see Raymond."

"What? You did? What did he say?" They all spoke at once.

"Let me put it this way," Mark said, getting up from the couch and placing his drink carefully on the coffee table. "I'll just go get my present and show it to you."

CHAPTER TWENTY

THEY MADE SOME JOKES during dinner about what time it was in Hong Kong or Dresden or Cairo, because Mark had put his gift on the dining-room buffet temporarily. It was a world clock made of heavy glass, mounted in polished brass, which showed the time anywhere in the world at any given moment.

"That goes on my office desk," Mark said. "From somewhere Raymond must have found out we have some multinational business clients. He put some thought into these things, as well as a real bundle of money."

"Laura, what plans have you made for the evening?" Donna asked as they left the table and headed toward the living room. Mrs. Cooper had just set out the coffee tray. "Are we going to play cards or something?"

"Nothing! We're going to talk," Laura said positively. "We've got a lot to catch up on. It's been months since your folks have been down here."

"In that case, I think I'll skip coffee, if nobody minds. I've been carrying a real load of guilt most of the summer. It's time I did something about it. I'm going to talk to Raymond Tsung myself. Just me."

There were several demurs from the group.

"I mean it," she said. "Nobody's been able to get past Raymond Tsung's personality to tell him that I made a mistake—a rather bad one, really. So, since it's my mistake, it's up to me to correct it."

They were all looking at her.

"I think Donna is right," Sara said finally.

"Well," Evan said hesitantly, "if you think so, but—" He cleared his throat. "You won't be... You won't say anything to...uh...hurt his feelings, will you? He's really such a decent guy."

"Oh, I'll be careful, Daddy."

"If I promise to keep my mouth shut," Bruce said, "can I tag along?"

She looked at him thoughtfully for a moment. "On that condition," she said at last. "It's my problem. I'll do the talking."

Bruce gave an exaggerated imitation of zipping his lips together.

Donna telephoned Tsung at his sister's home. She thought she'd better be frank. "I need to talk with you," she said candidly. "It needs to be as private a conversation as we can have." As she said the words, Bruce winced and covered his face, so she knew she was making a faux pas. She knew from Bruce's tutelage in Chinese customs that any matter with Raymond Tsung would be a family matter, and that if he followed his own inclinations, he would have the meeting in the midst of his sister's whole clan.

There was a very short silence at the other end of the line before he said smoothly, "Of course you need to talk, my dear. I know just the place. Meet me in front of my sister's house. Do you have the address?"

"Yes. I have it from the phone book," she answered.

"Bruce will know where it is," he said easily, letting her know that though she required privacy of him, it was all right for her to bring Bruce if she wanted to.

"Yes. I know the neighborhood," Bruce said after

Donna hung up. "It's out in the Richmond, almost within sight of the park."

The house, they observed when they reached it, was a two-storied rosy stucco too big for its long narrow lot. Slanting rays from the setting sun glittered on the windows. Raymond Tsung was walking up and down in front of the house, as if he were taking an evening stroll, dressed in jeans and an open-necked plaid shirt. At first glance, neither of them recognized that this was the same man as the bank president in his elegant office. He saw them immediately and waved them to the curb, smiling broadly.

"Right around here," he said as they got out of the car. "There's a tiny garden back here, and it's a fine warm evening. My brother-in-law is the family's best gardener. He fixed a small place back here where we sometimes eat." He opened a high gate and led them along a skinny strip of cement walk, past the long house to the very back.

"Here we are," he said, opening another gate and letting them into a tiny private garden arranged mostly with planter boxes holding a wild array of blossoms. There was a white umbrella table and chairs. "It will soon be time to take this stuff in, I guess," he said. "Summer can't last forever." He pulled out a chair, and Donna seated herself.

On the table were a blue pitcher and glasses. "I thought you might not want tea, so I took some of my sister's fruit drink. She makes this with chopped citrus fruit and pineapple, and who knows what else. Refreshing." He poured three glassfuls and very carefully passed them around. Seated at the round table, they all sipped appreciatively while a little silence fell.

Donna looked at him. He seemed broader-chested in the sport shirt, and she noticed the light dusting of gray at his temples. He had helped them get settled with courteous small talk. Now it was up to her. She put her glass down.

"I've come to make a confession. And to apologize," she said.

He said nothing, and there was no change in his expression.

"At the beginning of summer I was a silly adolescent. I hope that by the end of it, I will have passed that phase," she added wryly. His sudden smile gave her keen pleasure.

"I had really fallen in love with Bruce. Poor Bruce." She reached over and patted his hand briefly. "And in order to hold his attention as fully as I could, I pretended I was looking for my biological father."

"Pretended," Raymond murmured without inflection.

"Yes. There's no other way to say it. I really hadn't wanted any parents but Mom and Dad. Even Prairie, my original mother, I only think of as a vague kind of relative whenever I see her, never as a real mother, I'm afraid. I thought my father would never be found, couldn't be found." She paused.

"And Bruce, clever Bruce, found me. He pulled the rabbit out of the hat." Raymond smiled, but with a tinge of sadness.

"Something like that. I didn't know what to do then, so I just sort of went along with it. But now that my parents are here, and Dad was a little upset—" She took a sip of her drink.

"I talked with your parents today. I saw that he was upset," Raymond said. "I believe he is less upset now."

"Yes." Donna smiled. "You must have said the right things."

"I did my best. It was the least I could do for those good people. I should let you know that, as fathers go, I'm a very hard-core father. I care a great deal for my children. If I'd known I had a child out in the world, outside my care, I would have moved heaven and earth trying to find him or her. So you can understand what a shock it was to me to learn that I did indeed have a child, and a daughter, more vulnerable than a boy. You can understand then how profoundly relieved I was when I learned someone else had found you, taken care of you, loved you, shaped you into a self-sufficient young woman. I owe your parents a debt I can never repay.''

"I'm…sure they don't see it that way," Donna said, an odd ache in her throat.

"I'm sure they don't," he agreed. "But I please myself by sending little gifts to the people who care about you."

"After I met you," Donna went on, "I began to feel ashamed and sorry. I guess this is time for my apology. I used you. And it's unforgivable for one person to use another. I apologize."

He gave just the briefest nod. Donna wasn't sure whether that meant that he agreed with what she'd said, or that he accepted her apology.

"I think I have a small confession and apology to make, too," he said after a long pause. "My wife is ecstatic about the discovery of a daughter. My interval as a wannabe artist has long been a source of family amusement. She told me on the phone this afternoon that she wished all my past indiscretions could have this happy an ending. So, to my small confession." He took a sip from his glass.

"I have always remembered my days with Prairie with some embarrassment, possibly, at times, even shame. It was actually rather a bad time for me, full of rebellion, of mistakes, misconceptions and cheap phoniness which I thought was reality. Yet when you walked through my office doorway, Donna, the whole shabby, shoddy incident was suddenly given value, great worth. Something very fine had come out of something I had thought of as a worthless time. So tonight I make my small apology to

Prairie." He sighed. "I'm sure that there is some excellent old Chinese proverb that would say all this better than I can, but I can't think of one."

"You did okay," Bruce said gruffly, clearing his throat.

Donna reached over without a word and clasped Raymond's blunt hands; she looked into his round face, with its opaque dark eyes the same shade as hers. She felt their kinship intensely, and she knew he felt it too. There was a sense of timelessness in the lengthening shadow from the umbrella, but she felt no hurry. There was all the time in the world.

"Now," he continued. "We come to the matter which troubles you. I value you more because of your loyalty to your parents—and I say 'parents' advisedly. Prairie and I are not your real parents, Donna. We were the heedless, headstrong young couple who precipitated your birth. Only that. Your parents are the people who loved you through the years, took care of you, put up with your nonsense, wiped your nose, worried about you when you got sick—and were proud when you did something good. Those people are your parents. I could use another one of those fine Chinese proverbs here, and don't have one."

He lifted his glass and took a swallow.

"Oh, when you first appeared, I don't deny the thought of having a full-time daughter enchanted me. I was besotted with the idea—until I met your parents this afternoon. Then I realized I can't be your father, Donna. I missed the first nineteen years of your life, so I lost out." She could feel him giving up, letting go. They looked at each other for a long time. It was as if she was memorizing his features, his eyes which held so much kindness and understanding, and ten thousand years of gentle wisdom.

Donna leaned forward. "But," she said very softly, "you can be my friend, can't you? You can be my friend."

"I would love to be your friend," he said simply.

She saw Bruce look at his watch and knew that it was time to go, but she could not leave Raymond Tsung yet, not just yet. But they had said it all, had they not? And the dusk was gathering. Already the colors in the planter boxes had faded into the approaching evening so that she could discern little of hues that had been so vivid earlier.

She began to talk, not knowing exactly why, not hurrying, just saying whatever came to mind.

"I didn't tell you, but I've been into gymnastics all my life. Not meaning to boast, but I've become pretty good at it. I have my little collection of blue ribbons. I'm hoping to work with young gymnasts. That's what I'm going to aim at when I start college.

"My dad, Evan, that is, got me started on my thirteenth birthday. That was the first day I met him. He came—you knew he used to be a clown with Laura Hunt, when they were much younger—well, he came and showed me tricks, and he knew right then that I should do something with gymnastics."

"Ah, of course," he said softly. "That explains the grace in your posture and the spring in your walk. I did wonder." A pause lengthened between them. She was glad she'd told him something he wanted to know. "Have you been long at the bank?" she asked.

"All my working life," he answered easily. "I had to start at the very bottom. True, my uncle was then president, but I had to earn my promotions every step of the way. I always had to prove myself, you see, because I was the only nephew who had strayed. Ah, well, I don't complain. It was good for me."

"But you made it," Donna said, with a great sense of satisfaction that he had, and a trace of anger that he had had to prove himself while the others had not.

He spoke again. "And besides the gymnastics, how are your grades, and what will your major in college be?"

She told him, and then asked him a question about his sons, her unknown half brothers. Why was she doing this? And why did it feel so right, so comfortable, so precious? She and Raymond continued to talk in the thickening darkness. Little fragments of conversations, with pauses between them. Bruce said nothing now, remaining completely silent in his place at the table. Nor did he look at his watch again. She realized, with a sense of gratitude, that he understood what was happening and knew its importance to her. She and Raymond were acquainting themselves with each other as best they could in the time allowed them, trading small bits and pieces of their lives back and forth, so that later, little pseudo-memories could be built upon them.

In this way, at some time, Raymond would remember her blue ribbons and she would remember his starting at the very bottom of the Bank of Cathay.

Finally she faced the fact that the time to leave had long passed, but she gave up their meeting sadly.

"And some time, when I come back to San Francisco, I...maybe I could meet your wife, and your boys?"

"Oh, they would like that. They would really like that."

"I'm going to be in Vancouver soon, after the summer is over," she said slowly. "I don't expect to be very happy there for a while. Do you suppose that, sometimes, we might talk on the phone?"

"You don't think your parents would mind?" He put his glass down. The daylight was almost gone, and the blue pitcher was now more gray than blue.

"No," she said, secure in her knowledge of them. "They won't mind."

She and Bruce left shortly afterward, walking down the

narrow ribbon of walkway beside Raymond's sister's house to the street.

Donna felt smaller to him, almost as small as when they'd first met. Bruce took her hand and remembered how he'd held it when she was thirteen, and scared, and they'd been walking along Grant Avenue.

He glanced down at her face, not wanting her to know how protective he felt toward her, how proud, how desperately, overpoweringly in love he was. But she sensed his feelings, and her lovely dark eyes stared seriously up at him.

The wind sent dust eddies along the avenue, and whipped color into the faces of some children playing in the street, and tossed her hair across her face. She pushed it back, and he reached to pull free a last strand caught against her lips.

"You were wonderful," he said. "He loves you, and between you, you two found a way not to spoil that love."

Donna shivered. "I think I love *him*. He's a special man. I'm lucky to have so many special people in my life."

He smiled, at a loss for words.

"It's getting colder," she said, huddling a little closer to him.

He put an arm around her shoulders. "Yup. I even smell a good old fog coming in."

"Know something?"

He knew. Oh, he knew, but he let her say it. "What, Donna?"

"Summer's over."

CHAPTER TWENTY-ONE

"WHAT'S A CONTRACT?"

"Something you agree to do for someone."

"Who are you gonna do all that for?"

"Me, Jim."

"That's nutty, Donna. Why d'you have to write down what you're gonna do for you?"

She sighed, and dropped her pen on the desk. "Because it makes me feel organized. I agree to get through so many projects, spend so much time on each one, and then I can check them off when I do."

Jim sniffed. "Kinda like Mom's shopping lists and stuff. She puts things on there she's already done, y'know, just so's she can cross some off before she does anything else."

Donna laughed and ruffled her small brother's dark, curly hair. Every day he looked more like their father, only with their mother's blue eyes. "Mom's got a good trick there. But you're a little pest, James McGrath. And you aren't helping me get my studying done. Scat and let me work."

He planted his feet wide apart and locked his sturdy knees. "I heard something."

Donna ignored him and took up the pen again.

"Don't you want to know what I heard?"

"I want you to get out of my bedroom and let me work."

"What is it you're waiting for all the time?"

She gripped the pen tightly, but kept her head down. "Okay, Jim. What did you hear?"

"Will you play ball with me if I tell?"

"You little crook." She darted from her chair, going down on her knees in front of him and grabbing his shoulders. "Five years old and already into organized crime."

"What's that?"

She sighed, bowing her head. "In this case, blackmail."

"What's—"

"Jimmy," she warned, "spill it."

He tried to whistle, but gave up and grinned instead. "Nothing, I guess, except I heard Mom say it was hard on you waiting. She said…she said she could feel you waiting." His brow furrowed. "What?" he began to ask, then changed his mind.

She sat back on her heels. "Leave me alone for a couple of hours, and I'll kick a ball around with you in the park, okay?"

When the door finally closed behind him, she went back to her desk and opened a drawer. Carefully, she removed one pin from a row of pins jammed in a crack in the bottom. She counted the ones still standing, and the ones dropped in an old pill bottle. Days, days, days. So many gone by since San Francisco, so many to go until… She shut the drawer and leaned over to peer down into the street. Seven weeks. Forty-nine days since she'd seen Bruce. She'd kept her promise not to write or call—and so had he. Her mother felt the waiting, too. Donna smiled. Mom had always understood.

FALL BOWED BENEATH a furious winter. Donna plodded on—school, home, study, run, more school. And she joked and laughed and drew even closer to her family. Their

lives, their happiness, chipped little pieces from the cold
shell that threatened to choke her heart. Her parents, their
faces pink from walks in Stanley Park, sitting close together in front of the fire, holding hands, planning, sharing,
were handsome and vibrant and obviously in love. Jim
bounced through his world, a ball or a bat and at least one
bloody knee seeming to be permanent parts of his strong
body. And Donna drew strength and hope from all of them.

Routine saved her from giving in and calling Bruce, or
writing, or catching a plane to San Francisco—or going
mad. School was a challenge she enjoyed. She made one
or two friends, but steadfastly turned down dates until even
the most persistent candidates stopped asking her out.

A heavy snow, unusual for Vancouver, came early, before Thanksgiving, and stayed on the ground. Straggling
along the treacherous sidewalk outside the townhouse each
day, Donna would kick at lumps of ice, pull her woolen
cap more firmly over her ears, and wonder what Bruce
was doing. She caught the bus to and from school. If she'd
driven herself, there'd have been no chance to use the
travel time for study. The bus allowed her to read—and
wonder what Bruce was doing.

Three weeks before winter break, twenty-one days, she
sat in her philosophy class, staring at the back of a man's
head. His hair was sort of blond, light brown with those
sun-bleached streaks. Bruce's hair was like that. She
closed her eyes and concentrated on seeing his face. In her
mind he sprawled on his back in Golden Gate Park,
groaning with pretended pain, then laughing. Then he took
her in his arms and she felt his warmth.

"Ms. McGrath, are you still with us?"

She jumped, and blood rushed to her face. The professor
must have asked her something. "Ah, yes, yes," she replied.

He tapped his chalk on the board. "Is this argument satisfiable?"

The words blurred together. She couldn't think. "Ah, yes."

A titter rippled across the room. The professor was young, and enjoyed his job and his own sense of humor. He tossed the chalk in the air and caught it behind his back. "You haven't been listening for a long time, I'm afraid. Contradictions are always…" he paused, palms up, inviting a response.

"Unsatisfiable," she responded in a small voice. "Sorry about that."

More days crawled by. Donna checked every mail delivery, tried not to leap for the phone when it rang, tried not to strain to hear if she would be called to answer. And when the call was for her, she walked with deliberate steps, and managed an expressionless face or a benign smile when, as was always the case, she heard her friend Amy's voice who kept in touch from her college in Alberta, or from one of the other students from her own school. Twice she spoke to Raymond Tsung. Hearing his voice only deepened her sadness, somehow.

And then it came, the last day of the fall quarter. Donna fumbled through her classes, trembling inside, watching the clock.

"Going home for the vacation?"

She almost slopped the coffee she was putting on her tray in the cafeteria. "Home?" She looked over her shoulder at the man who had spoken. He was the one who sat in front of her in Philosophy. She pulled a paper napkin from the holder.

"You going home for the holidays?" he said, smiling. A nice smile. They'd never spoken before.

"This is home," she said. "I live in Vancouver. How about you?"

"Seattle's home for me, and that's where I'm headed." He smiled again and she saw he was excited. She liked him for it. He was young, maybe still eighteen, and he wanted to go home and share with his family the experiences of his first months in school.

They sat at the same table, and he talked. Donna felt old and anxious. She checked her watch and tried to listen, and returned his thumbs-up sign when he got up to leave.

He hesitated by the table.

"Bye," she said. "Have a great time."

"Yeah, thanks." He didn't go. "See you next year, huh?"

Donna looked up at him, puzzled; then she managed to laugh. "I...here's to next year," she replied, raising her empty coffee cup.

When she emerged from her final class, snow instantly settled on her hair and dusted her lashes. She walked slowly to the bus stop, her bag heavy on her shoulder. At the curb she searched the street in both directions, squinting against the snow to peer at every figure.

Her throat tightened until it hurt. The bus came and she climbed aboard, squeezed past bodies and umbrellas and bags spilling into the aisle until she found a seat amid the moist warmth and the smell of wet wool.

The vehicle jolted forward. She rubbed a smeary patch on the steamed-up window. Had she expected him to be waiting outside the school for her? She leaned her forehead against the clammy glass. Yes, she had expected that or, at least, she'd hoped.

"EVAN, YOU'RE A show-off," Sara yelled, lunging for, and missing, the tennis ball he shot across the net. "And if you don't start hitting some *to* me, I'm going to quit.'' She glanced at Donna. "We're going to quit, aren't we?''

Donna did a jig and planted her feet in time to return her father's next serve with a lob that sent him dashing for, then crashing into, the corner of the bubble.

"You missed!'' Sara chortled, mimicking Donna's jig. "Sure you shouldn't be the one over here with me and put Donna over there on her own?''

"Donna,'' he called, ignoring Sara. "This is Australian tennis, remember? I get to use the alleys, you two don't.''

Donna put her hands on her hips. "That shot wasn't anywhere near the alley.''

"Come on. It was alley. Look, here's the mark.'' He jabbed his racket at one of a thousand ball scuffs on the court.

Sara started to laugh. "The old man's tired, Donna. I knew it. Now he's grasping at straws.''

Donna joined the laughter and changed places with her father. As she passed the window to the lobby she hesitated, and watched a man straighten from the reception desk. For an instant her blood seemed to stop, only to pound through her veins again when she saw him turn. He was much shorter than Bruce, and darker. She pressed a fist into her stomach.

"You okay, honey?'' Her father had turned back and come to her side, bending over her. He looked into the lobby, then down into her face and grimaced. "Is every guy you see Bruce, Donna? Is that it?''

She nodded.

"I thought the tennis was a good idea to take your mind off things. It's not working, huh?''

"I guess not.'' Her voice was lost in the great canvas bubble.

Sara came to them silently and slipped her arm through Donna's. "You having another sad spell?"

Had she been so bad at covering her feelings? Had they known all along that she felt time was running out and now she'd been out of school a week and Bruce hadn't contacted her, that she was starting to give up?

"You know," she said levelly. "I think I'd like to go home and light a fire. We could pick up the Christmas tree on the way and decorate tonight."

"Great idea, don't you think so, Sara?" her father said, too heartily.

"Terrific," her mother agreed, with a smile that only intensified the worry in her eyes.

They went through the motions of being cheerful, picking up Jim from the sitter, making much of selecting just the right tree, laughing at Evan as he struggled to straighten it in its stand.

They were laughing when the phone rang.

Evan picked it up. "McGraths'," he said, a little out of breath. He bent over until Donna couldn't see his face. "Hi…thanks. Happy holidays to you, too…fine, how are all of you? Yes, of course, she's right here. Donna?"

She jerked the tinsel garland she held through her fingers, and felt the cord cut her thumb.

"Donna, it's…uh…Ray. He wants to wish you a happy holiday."

For a moment, she couldn't move. When she did, it was with a sensation of unreality. Why couldn't it have been Bruce who'd called? As soon as she formed the thought, she hated herself for it.

Raymond Tsung answered her soft "hello" eagerly, and she heard anxiety in his deliberately light comments. How was she? How was school? He and his family had sent her a little gift which should arrive soon. And as they talked she warmed slightly, then warmed more, until she could feel again the kinship she'd felt with him the last time they'd met.

"I guess I should let you get back to your family," he said, after a pause had lasted too long.

"We're decorating the Christmas tree," she replied lamely.

"Enjoy, my dear," Raymond said. "Are you...are you happy?"

What could she say, either answer would be...her philosophy prof would have laughed. Neither answer would be satisfactory. She turned her back to the room and evaded the question. "Have you...seen..."

"We had lunch. Several weeks ago. All he wanted to talk about was you, Donna. But I guess that was easy for both of us." He laughed, and she liked him even more.

A minute later, she hung up and stood bracing her weight on the table. All Bruce could do a few weeks ago was talk about her. What had happened to make him stop caring?

"Come on, Donna," Jim said impatiently. "Help with the tree."

DONNA'S FEET CRUNCHED into frozen grass, thudded on ice-dead earth. Mist-veiled shafts of white light sprayed skyward from the morning horizon. Donna ran on, listening to her footfalls, her breathing, watching the vapor clouds her breath made, and the awakening of another winter day. The last day of the year.

It was all over. The packages, the ribbons and bows, the great meals she'd helped her mother and Aunt Christine prepare, the treks to Christine and Ben's wonderful, confused house that was truly a home. The holidays were over.

And Bruce hadn't come, or called, or written, except for a Christmas card sending them all his "love."

Blessing her luck at living so near Stanley Park, she veered back toward the path, deliberately cutting this way and that through slender, leafless trees. *I'm practicing for ski season,* she told herself, knowing her friends had been skiing Whistler and Grouse Mountain for weeks and she'd steadfastly refused to go.

She reached the winding pathway again and headed deeper into the park, past the cricket oval. Then she opened up, and sprinted. *I mustn't think. I mustn't think.* But she was breathing through her mouth, and she began to feel in her throat the ache that was almost never gone now. Her nose ran, and she sniffed.

A little while longer and she'd be back in school. Donna heard a noise and instantly realized it had been her own cry raked past an indrawn breath.

Another runner was behind her now. She remembered being afraid of strangers in the park when she was alone. She wasn't this morning. She felt strong, and angry, and…immune.

The other runner's shoes made a different noise from hers. They cracked sharply on the concrete. Cracked. Like street shoes, a man's dress shoes. Her stomach dropped, and she ran faster and could tell she was pulling away.

At the next bend, she turned and ran backward. And stopped.

The man who loped toward her looked like a parody of Sherlock Holmes, a tall, contemporary version. His long camel's-hair coat flapped. A paisley scarf had come loose, streaming under his arms, and he wore a shapeless tweed hat jammed on his head.

"Donna!" Her name came to her on a pant. "Wait, will you?"

She couldn't speak. Someone had snatched all the air from the world. Her blood trembled in her veins.

A few yards away from her he slowed, then walked until he stopped, too far away to touch, close enough to see...so clearly.

"You never called," Bruce said, "or wrote."

"Neither did...did you."

He pressed a hand to his side. "I know. I promised I wouldn't."

"So did I."

"I know, but I hoped...I mean... Oh, Donna, this has been the longest winter of my life."

"Mine too." Why couldn't she move?

"I almost persuaded myself I should stay out of your life. Give you a chance to get further into school, but—"

"Is that why you waited so long to come?"

He nodded, still holding his side.

"What's the matter?" Donna asked. "Do you hurt?"

He pulled off the hat and stuffed it into his pocket. "A stitch, that's all. I could be just a tiny bit out of shape."

She covered her mouth.

"Don't laugh," he threatened. "You wouldn't have wanted me running alone in Golden Gate Park."

Then she did laugh...until she realized she was laughing alone.

"Donna," he said, "have you had enough time to decide? Would you still be happy somewhere warmer than this? San Francisco, say? Married to a grumpy lawyer who loves you more than he knows how to say?"

She opened her mouth, but no sound came.

Bruce took another step and held out his arms. "Say yes, sweetheart. Please say yes."

Finally she could move, she could cannon forward full tilt until she barreled into his chest and wrapped her arms around him. He reeled slightly, then framed her face with his hands. She looked up into his anxious blue eyes, glanced at his hair, awry and spiky, and back at his eyes.

"Say something, Donna."

"Yes." She buried her face in his shoulder and felt herself lifted from the ground and whirled around.

"Thank God," he yelled, and he set her down, still holding her close. "But remember, my love. Yes is forever."

"Yes," Donna said. "Yes, yes."

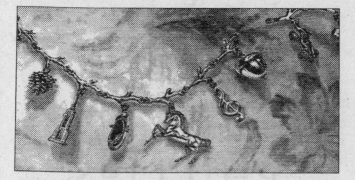